*Angie,*
*Hope you enjoy!*
*Danette Majette*
*8/29/09*

# GOOD
## *Girl*
### *Gone* BAD

*By* Danette Majette

Essence Magazine Bestselling Author of Deep

Life Changing Books in conjunction with Power Play Media
Published by Life Changing Books
P.O. Box 423 Brandywine, MD 20613

Library of Congress Cataloging-in-Publication Data;

www.lifechangingbooks.net

ISBN- (10) 1-934230669  (13) 978-1934230664

# Dedication

In Loving Memory
Of
Marquan Andrews

On July 9, 2008 you were taken from me. It still, until this day, doesn't seem real. It feels like you're away at college (where you would be if you were here), but you're not. For months all I felt was anger and pain, but you've helped me let go of the anger and embrace the fact that you are safe with God, laughing at every silly thing I do like you've done so many times before. There isn't a day that goes by that I don't think about you and wish you were still here. The small things I took for granted like you calling to check up on me or coming over just to tell me something crazy are the things I wish I could have right now. The last time we talked you called like you always do to see when we were coming back home from N.C. You must've told me you missed me and KeKe a dozen times before I finally said, "Marquan, we've only been gone a couple of days. I'll be home soon!" We ended the call after telling one another, "I love you." Had I known that would be the last time I would hear your voice, I would've never hung up. You're gone but not forgotten because I find myself trying to live my life the way you did. Always there for others and always giving even if it meant giving your last and doing without yourself. You were definitely an angel on earth. I miss and love you so much!

Until we meet again,
Love Ma

Please…please support your local chapter of MADD (Mothers Against Drunk Drivers). They are fighting to keep our children safe from careless people who choose to drink and drive.

# Acknowledgements

I know this is such a cliché', but Father I never would've made it without you. This year has been filled with so much sorrow for me, but you helped me through every minute of it. Just when I think you have forgotten me you always show up in the nick of time and I thank you for it.

Nellie Best, once again you've stood by me and been there for me when I needed you the most. You have been my rock and I hope that I have been yours. I'm so blessed to have a mother who sacrificed the way you did and still do. Love you to pieces!

My dad Melvin Hester, we tried this father-daughter thing and it didn't seem like it was working for a while, but I'm so glad we are finally getting it right. Don't think for a second that I don't need you because I'm grown now. I'm spoiled so I still want to be daddy's little girl. LOL!

To my wonderful kids Bryan Majette and Marketa Salley (author in the Teenage Bluez Series), when God was handing out good kids he blessed me twice! I love you and remember… PLEASE DON'T PUT ME IN A HOME WHEN I GET OLD!!! LMAO

My brothers Ronald and Melvin Williams and sister in law Keisha, having you and my nieces and nephews in my life now is such a joy for me. It's gonna be a pain for you because I plan on spoiling them rotten then giving them back to you to deal with. My brother Kevin Levy, OMG after ten long years you're finally going to be home!!! I've missed you so much and I can't wait to give you a big hug.

To the woman who stayed on me and helped me so much with this book, Shelly Majette Carrington. I truly don't know what I would've done without all of your help. My guess is I wouldn't be sitting here writing acknowledgements. You are a gem!! Shawn, Pud and Jabria are so lucky to have you and so am I.

My God Father Earl (The Pearl) Taylor, here we go again. You're still hanging in there with me. I am so lucky to have you in my life.

To my ex-husband Marc Salley, thanks for being such a great baby daddy! LOL. Just think, in a couple of months we'll be sending our baby off to college. I don't know about you but I'm going to be in one of her suitcases.

Harold (Smax) Morning, for nine long years we drove each other crazy and even though we've gone our separate ways you still support any project I'm working on, even the crazy ones I come up with. So, for that I thank you. And I know I don't act like it sometimes but I do still love you in my own little way. I'm guessing a part of me always will. OMG! Did I just say that??????

I would also like to thank my family: the Majette's in Norfolk, VA, the Hester's in Long Branch, NJ, Betty Hamilton of Jacksonville, FL, Martin and Devon Salley of Newark, NJ., Tamika Gordon, Colleen and Nicole Jennings. And a special shout out to my cousin Allen Bailey.

To my girls Michelle Butler, Pamela Young, Kimberly and Dominique Brunson, I am going to miss us getting kicked out of games and putting the ref's on blast. I'm sitting here laughing so hard right now. They have no idea we will put those college degrees on the shelf and get it in when it comes to our babies. If they didn't, they know now!! AND TO THE CENTRAL LADY FALCONS: Marketa Salley, Andrea Thomas, Tiarra Moore, Alexis Brunson, Danielle Burrell, Regina Williams, Shauntese Cowan, Tyree Joseph, Tionna Jacobs, Alexus Davis, and coaches Renee Jamison and Billy Laporte'! You guys had an amazing year and you should be proud of all of your accomplishments.

To all of my God children, D'miyah Butler, D'metrius Smith, Demetrius Davis, Elrico Collins, Alphonzo Johnson, Danielle Joseph, Amber Owens, and Andre' Tibbs, I love all of you. Now can someone…anyone go get me a sweet tea from McDonalds? LOL!

Tonya Ridley (Author of The Takeover and Talk of The Town) you are the craziest person I know. You also have the biggest heart of anyone I know. You helped me get through one of the roughest times in my life by calling me and just listening. You were honest and told me it was going to take some time, but none the less it would get better. When I didn't want to get out of bed, you made me and I can't thank you enough for that. They say you'll know who your real friends are when you're going through stuff and hands down you have been a true friend to me. I can't wait to move down to Raleigh so I come over and borrow sugar from you. LOL!

Laron Profit, dude you are the best! Whenever I'm having a bad day I just call you, because I know that if anyone can make me feel better you can…first with your compassion then second with your humor. Now let's get started on that book, the rest of the world needs to hear what you have to say.

To my girls Anita Belachew and Tiffany Adkins, thanks for hanging in there with me again. I know we don't get to kick it like we used to because of our busy schedules, but we will always be friends for life.

Joe Collick (from Off the Rack in Baltimore) and Larry (from Patapsco), you guys are the best. I've had so much fun hanging out with you and that's the thing I'm gonna miss the most when I leave MD.

Well Tressa, LCB is still going strong even though we didn't get any of that bailout money. LOL! Once again, I'm so blessed and thankful to you for all you've done for me not only as an author…but as a friend. You are one in a million! Thanks for putting out Good Girl Gone Bad.

To Leslie Allen, just know that none of us would be where we are right now had it not been for your hard work and dedication. I watch you sometimes and wonder how you managed to do all the stuff you do. If it were me, I would be in the psych ward. I thank you from the bottom of my heart for everything you've done and continue to do to make my books a success.

Natasha Simpson, even though you kick me out of the warehouse sometimes, I still want to let you know how much I appreciated your help with this book.

To all of the editors and test readers who worked on GGGB, thanks so much.

To my fellow LCB authors and Ms. Nakea Murry, we made it through another year, but there's still work to be done. Let's go get'em!

To Kevin Carr of New Media Dezign, thanks for the hot cover. It's my best one yet!

Ms. Ann Joyner of Norfolk, VA, you've been such a great supporter of my work and I can't thank you enough for spreading the word about not only my books but every book that comes out from LCB!

To my friends in the DMV: Polo (TCB Band) Big L (Big L Entertainment), Kurt Bone (All Daz Clothing), DJ Kid Kannon (Crank Muzik Go-Go Magazine), Alana Beard (Washington Mystics), Cheryl Bruce, David Wilkerson, Teresa Davis, Elliott Benton, Jeffery Smith, Kisha Poole, Lisa Owens, The Andrews family, Kelly Fox, Terrence McKinley, Terron Hampton, Chiquita Reid, Wanda Lewis, and Ebony Kiser, for supporting me through this journey.

To all of my friends down in Raleigh, N.C., Peter (Lee's Kitchen), Karen, Charletta, Danny, Carla, Jackie Davis, Sherry, Robbie aka Apples, Big Mike, Pooh J, Chris, Kim, Ms. Lena Ridley, Ms. Debra, MiMi, Annetha, and the ladies at Talk of the Town Hair Salon, thank you for embracing me and making me feel like family. I would also like to thank Mr. Ronnie Enoch at Johnson C. Smith University in Charlotte, N.C.

I would also like to thank authors KiKi Swinson, Wahida Clark, Trey Chaney (The Wire) and Deshawn Taylor for always…always showing me love.

Thanks again to all of the bookstores, vendors, my friends at Black and Nobel, Afrikan World Books, and all the other distributors that push my books and support LCB.

Last but not least, to all the readers who have supported me since day one, I thank you so…so very much. I hope you enjoy the book and please check out our website for all of the hot new releases from LCB! And as always I would love to hear from you: www.myspace.com/danettemajette, or you can write me at P.O. Box 471396 District Heights, MD 20753

P.S. I know some of you are probably saying "Damn, she sure used LOL a lot." Well, I'll tell you why. We're in the middle of a freakin' recession, and my daughter is about to go to college so I'm experiencing the early stages of empty nest syndrome. I need to laugh to keep from crying…so please indulge me!

*Danette Majette*

# Chapter One

Tired from arguing with her husband all night, Jazmine slipped out of bed and tip toed over to their oak wood dresser. Quietly opening up the top drawer, she was careful not to make too much noise because the last thing she wanted was to wake her husband, Vince. Hell, it had only been two hours since their yelling match ended, and she wasn't ready for another episode. Pulling out an oversized t-shirt and a pair of Aeropostale sweat pants, Jazmine quickly put on the unattractive outfit after glancing at the clock on the nightstand. Obviously forgetting to turn on the alarm, she'd overslept for the third time this week and only had twenty minutes to get their son, Omari to school.

Slipping on a pair of flip flops, Jazmine was just about to snatch the flower printed scarf off her head, when Omari burst through the door. Her eyes widened immediately then darted in the direction of Vince, who suddenly began to move.

"Ma, I…" Omari attempted to say.

"Sshhh, oh my God why did you do that?" Jazmine whispered. "Omari, you know you're supposed to knock when the door is closed."

She quickly motioned for him to leave the room, but it was too late. Vince was now wide awake. He shot straight up in the bed and gave both of them an evil glare, then started yelling. Something he did on a regular.

"Why are you talkin' so fuckin' loud, Omari? Don't your dumb-ass see I'm tryin' to sleep?" he yelled. "You always doin' some stupid shit! You know Jazmine, you might wanna get that boy checked out 'cause his ass might be autistic."

"Vince, please don't start. He was probably just coming to wake me up. I overslept. You know he doesn't like to be late for school," Jazmine replied in her son's defense.

"I don't give a fuck what he thought. He knows better than that!"

Jazmine tried her best to ignore Vince to avoid yet another argument. She looked down at her son's poor choice of clothing. "Omari, why do you have on that thick sweater? It's gonna be seventy-three degrees today. You can't wear that over your uniform. Go take it off, honey."

"Ahh, Ma, I like this sweater. Can I just wear it this one time?"

Even though he was only in the second grade, Omari was really into dressing himself whenever he got the chance. "No, that's not a good choice. Go in your room and change. I'll be there in a minute."

"Noooo. I want to wear it. Please," Omari pleaded.

"What the fuck did I tell you about that whinin'? That shit is for girls!" Vince belted. He held up his fist and started beating on his chest. "We men up in this bitch! Soldiers! Do you understand me?" When Omari didn't answer Vince asked him again. "Do you understand me?"

Tears welled up in Omari's eyes as he shook his head and finally headed out the room.

"Now, go take the damn sweater off. It's fuckin' spring outside!" Vince called out. He looked over at his wife. "I'm tellin' you, that boy might be special."

It crushed Jazmine to see Omari's feelings hurt over something so minor, but at the same time she knew exactly what he was going through. She'd been up until 3:00 a.m. the night before arguing about why she decided to cook steak versus chicken. It was stupid to be fighting about something so petty, but Vince was known to go off about the craziest things lately. As a matter of fact, he'd been a ticking time bomb waiting to explode over the past year, and until Jazmine could find out the reason why, she just tried to keep Omari and herself out of his way. It was a miserable way to live.

Trying to rush at this point, Jazmine went into the bathroom and brushed her teeth, washed her face, then pulled her long jet black hair up into a ponytail. When she walked back into the bedroom, she noticed that Vince had gotten out of bed and was already sitting at his weight bench pumping iron. Lifting weights was something Vince did constantly, and he'd turned their bedroom into a miniature Golds Gym, without Jazmine's consent, of course. Her thoughts and opinions about anything Vince did were no longer accepted. A bicep arm curler, an abdominal board, and a two-tier dumbbell rack had all been crammed into the 280 square foot room. Even their comfortable king sized bed had been downsized to a tiny full size just to accommodate his obsession.

Jazmine watched as Vince lifted the 250 pound iron weights like they were plastic. He constantly worked on his rock hard biceps and abs while Jazmine did just the opposite. She'd let herself go and had gone down from a size eight to barely a four. Keeping up her appearance up was no longer a priority, however keeping her sanity was.

Grabbing her purse, Jazmine was just about to walk out of the room when Vince placed the chrome weight bar back on the rack and sat up. "You got twenty minutes to have your ass back in this house."

"What?" Jazmine asked.

She wasn't surprised that Vince had placed a time limit on her outing because that's what he did whenever she left the house. But he'd never pulled his normal deranged rank when it came to taking Omari to school.

"You heard me. It only takes sixteen minutes to get to that school and back, so don't get cute. Shit, I even threw in an extra four minutes just in case you drive under the speed limit."

Jazmine wanted to scream. She was tired of living like a prisoner in her own home. Always having to check in, always having to abide by his rules and time constraints. She wasn't even allowed to have a job anymore.

"But I don't have time to cook Omari breakfast. I need to try and swing by McDonalds and get him something."

"If you can do all that in twenty minutes then fine. If not, then that lil' nigga will just have to starve until lunch. Stop treatin' him like a baby anyway. I don't want no fuckin' mama's boy for a son."

Jazmine wanted to respond about his own parenting skills so badly, but knew it wouldn't have worked in her favor. Besides, it would've only added fuel to an already blazing fire. Instead, she turned around and headed towards her son's room.

Five minutes later, she and Omari left their East Orange, N.J. home, and headed toward the school. Jazmine managed to grab a cinnamon roll on her way out the door and handed it to Omari, who'd talked her into letting him sit in the front seat. It wasn't her ideal version of a good breakfast, but it would just have to do.

"Ma, why does daddy yell so much?" Omari asked licking his fingers.

Jazmine was caught off guard by his question. Clearing her throat she answered, "Well sweetie...when your dad is under a lot of stress at work, he sometimes forgets to leave it at work and we end up getting the brunt of it."

"Then why doesn't he quit?"

"Well, it's not that simple, but I promise you things are gonna get better."

"I hope so. I get scared when he yells at us. Sometimes he acts like he's gonna hurt us."

She grabbed Omari's hand. "Hey, I promise you your dad would never hurt you. He loves you. Now stop worrying so much." Jazmine knew she was taking a gamble by making that type of promise to her son because at this point, she wasn't sure what Vince was capable of.

When Jazmine pulled up to the front of Langston Hughes Elementary she placed the car in park, then glanced at the clock. She only had thirteen minutes left, so their goodbyes had to be brief.

"Okay, honey. I'll see you when school is out. Have a good day."

"You too, Ma."

Omari took off his seat belt and grabbed his belongings before exiting his mother's raggedy 1994 Nissan Maxima. It was sad how Vince drove around in his brand new Yukon Denali, while

4

Jazmine had to cross her fingers every time she started hers.

"Hey, wait. I don't get a kiss?"

"Ma," Omari whined. "Not in front of my school."

Jazmine laughed but she was a little sad that her son was growing up so fast. Even though he was seven years old, he would always be her baby.

"Hey, Ms. Jenkins," Omari said, as he jumped out of the car. He waved his tiny hand back and forth.

"What up," Ms. Jenkins replied.

The sight of the ghetto teacher's aide who always sported a platinum blonde weave and long red fingernails made Jazmine's skin crawl. She hated her ass and often wondered how she even got a job in the first place. The elementary school, was only two years old, and technically hadn't gotten hood yet, so Ms. Jenkins just made the place look bad. She needed to be around inmates, not children.

She rolled down the window and yelled to her son, "Have a good day. Mommy will see you after school."

Jazmine wanted desperately to put Omari in a private school, but Vince refused to pay the tuition. His philosophy was why pay for school when it was free. As she drove off, thoughts of Vince's other crazy ways of thinking when it came to their son began to dance around in her head. Like the fact that he never re-warded Omari for behaving good in school or bought him gifts on his birthday. He even went as far as not allowing Omari to open the refrigerator without permission whenever he was home. Jazmine hated the fact that she allowed her husband to control every aspect of their lives, but she didn't know what else to do.

Turning on Roosevelt Avenue, she looked at the clock again, then pressed the gas pedal a little harder. Jazmine hoped like hell that she didn't get behind any old-ass drivers. The minutes were now down to nine. Driving over the speed limit by this point, she began to shake her head back and forth.

"I can't believe I'm willing to kill myself in an accident as long as I make it back on time." Jazmine wondered how her life had changed so dramatically, and if it would ever return back to normal. If things didn't change, she wasn't sure how much her sanity could take.

With exactly four minutes to spare, Jazmine was back at home. Once inside, she laid her keys on the counter and went upstairs. When she got to the top of the staircase, she noticed the door to their bedroom was closed.

*I know he don't call himself locking me out of our room,* she thought. She rushed the door.

"I gotta go. I'll call you back later," Vince said, hanging up his cell phone in a hurry. Already showered and in his police uniform, he snatched his Glock off the night stand and placed it in his holster.

Jazmine knew better than to ask a whole bunch of questions, but couldn't hide her curiosity. "Who was that?"

"Nobody."

"So, you had to close the door and hang up the phone on nobody 'cuz I walked in?"

Vince's blood began to boil and he leaped off the bed, "What is this, a fuckin' interrogation? Don't ask me shit else!" he yelled, towering over her. Jazmine was five foot four. Vince, on the other hand looked like a football linebacker. He stood six foot five and weighed two hundred and eighty pounds.

"I'm just trying to figure out why you're so secretive. I mean you've been acting really strange lately. Is there someone else? Is there something I should know?"

"Are you hard of fuckin' hearin'? Are you stupid like that son of ours? I just said, don't ask me nothin' else. Contrary to popular belief, I run shit up in this bitch," he said, smacking her with an open hand.

Jazmine grabbed the side of her face. She couldn't move. *Here we go again. Does this nigga ever get tired of making me his punching bag?*

She immediately began to think about the promise she made to Omari in the car. Sure she'd promised that Vince would never hurt him, but she couldn't speak for herself. The violence started with a few shoves here and a few pushes there, but now it was actual slaps and punches. Not one part of her body was exempt. Not even her stomach. The stomach that carried their second child two months ago. Jazmine miscarried shortly after she found out she was pregnant.

Still holding her face, Jazmine looked at Vince. "Don't ever hit me again, or I swear I will take Omari and leave!"

Vince laughed. "And go where? When I met you…you were flippin' burgers at Wendy's and livin' in a fuckin' public housing apartment with your mother. I doubt very seriously you want to go back there."

"My mother told me not to marry you. I should've listened."

"Your mother…please. How is that bitch gonna give somebody some marital advice? Didn't your pops leave her for your aunt?" Vince asked with a slight chuckle. "Picture that...a preacher leavin' his wife for his sister-in-law. What kind of shit is that?"

Even though the things Vince said were true, Jazmine hated when he talked about her family. "Don't put my family is this. They don't have anything to do with the type of man you are. If you were a better husband, you wouldn't be so defensive."

Vince acted like he was about to leave, but came hard with a blow that sent Jazmine flying onto the bed. Not finished with her yet, he grabbed her feet and began pulling her down onto the floor. Jazmine kicked and screamed but she was no match for Vince. He leaped on top of her and started hitting her hard across the face. She tried hard to block his blows, but her attempts were useless.

"What did I tell you about disrespectin' me, bitch?"

"Stop…please!" she yelled in pain.

"Shut the fuck up! You wanted a fight, so I'm gonna give you one."

Vince punched and punched until his hands got tired. Standing up, he gave her a few hard kicks. After one last kick in the stomach, he grabbed his keys and wallet. Wiping the sweat from his forehead, he looked down at Jazmine and shook his head.

"You ungrateful bitch! I work my ass off night and day so you can live in this nice home and not have to work and you got the nerve to disrespect me. You wouldn't have none of this shit if it weren't for me!" he yelled. "You ain't goin' no fuckin' where!"

Vince continued to look at her for a few seconds before

continuing. "I'll be home early tonight, so have my dinner ready. I want spaghetti." He turned around to leave the room then looked back. "You're only to leave here today when you go get Omari. Other than that, your ass better be in the house."

Once Jazmine heard the front door close and the base in Vince's truck get further and further away, she finally felt a sense of relief. Aching and in pain, she managed to pull herself up on the bed. After she wiped the tears from her face, she looked down and noticed her hand was covered in blood. She ran to the bathroom and looked at herself in the mirror.

Motionless, she was shocked when she saw how bad her mouth and nose were bleeding. She quickly grabbed a wash cloth and wet it. When she wiped the blood from her face and saw that she was completely black and blue, she began to cry. Her first thought was to call Roslynn or Alyse, but she was just too ashamed. After all this time, she still hadn't found the courage to let them in on what was going on. In her mind, this was something she might have to take to her grave and she feared if she stayed with Vince that's exactly where she would end up.

Jazmine was still in a daze as she undressed and took a shower. The feel of the hot water soothed her aching body. However, it didn't do much for her aching heart. She just couldn't believe that the man she married and shared a child with would hurt her so badly with no regard.

Minutes later, she turned the water off and stepped out. Walking up to the counter, all the makeup and concealer that almost covered every square inch was a constant reminder of how bad things had gotten. Unfortunately, there wasn't enough makeup in the world to help her bruised heart. Eventually things would have to change before Vince ended up killing her or even worse, before she ended up killing herself.

# Chapter Two

As soon as Alyse walked through the sliding glass doors at the shabby Howard Johnson Hotel in Newark, she ran right into her boss, Jackie. The last person she wanted to confront at the moment. It was the second time that week she'd been late and she knew Jackie wasn't going to be happy about it.

"I know what you 'bout to say," Alyse said out of breath.

"Oh, really," Jackie replied, placing her hand on her wide hips.

"Look, I have a good reason for bein' late 'dis time. I was havin' trouble gettin' my car to start 'dis mornin'."

"Alyse, if I had a fucking dollar for every time I heard one of your excuses I would be rich." Jackie looked at her watch, then turned around and walked toward her office near the break room. "You betta straighten up girlie or you're gonna have to find somewhere else to work. I'm not gonna put up with your mess much longer."

Alyse didn't even bother responding because she knew Jackie would eventually get the last word. Instead, she walked into the break room, opened her locker and placed her purse inside. After changing into a comfortable and faithful pair of Reebok Classics, she watched as Jackie walked up to her with a huge smile. A smile that looked more devious than friendly.

"Here are your room assignments. You're on the third floor today," Jackie informed.

When Alyse looked down at her room numbers, she instantly became upset. "Hold up. I got fifteen rooms to clean. I normally only do ten."

"Well, you got fifteen today. That's what happens when you're over an hour late. You were supposed to be here at ten. It's 11:15," Jackie responded. "Oh, and before I forget. There's vomit in room 306." Displaying the same devious grin as before, Jackie stood there and waited for Alyse's response. Taunting was her specialty.

The two women were known for never liking each other, and it took all she had for Alyse not to throw the paper back in Jackie's pale face. She wanted badly to tell Jackie to clean the rooms herself, but instead Alyse simply sighed in disgust. She was lousy at pasting on a smile, pretending to care, but she had to do it. She needed her job.

"I'll get right on it," Alyse responded with a fake smile. She grabbed a cart and some special solution for the vomit, and got right to work.

However, as she pushed the cart to the elevator, Alyse tried her best not to think about how much she hated her job. In fact, to her she was only working for a paycheck, which made the job even more difficult at times. Awful was too weak of a word to use when describing how much she despised cleaning up after people. She often wished she had money like Roslynn and her husband, Adrian, and envied her friend for marrying such a paid dude. Alyse and her husband, Lance, weren't financially stable enough for her to be a stay at home wife, so she had to work. Even though she only made twelve dollars an hour, it helped with the small bills around the house.

After reaching the third floor, Alyse didn't waste any time knocking on her first room door even though she wanted to say fuck it, and push the cleaning car down a flight of stairs.

"Housekeepin'!" When there was no answer, she knocked again. "Housekeepin'!"

"Come back later!" a man yelled.

"Shit. He needs to get his ass up. I don't wanna be here all fuckin' day," Alyse mumbled to herself. "Sir, just a reminder 'dat check out is at noon."

Not waiting for a response, Alyse went to the room next door and knocked. Again, when no one answered after the second housekeeping call she stuck her master key in the door and opened it. She was stunned to see a man standing there ass naked and pulling on his dick.

"Come on in pretty lady," the guy said with a sick grin on his face.

"Fuck you!" Alyse yelled before slamming the door behind her. "Crazy muthafucka. I'm so sick of doin' 'dis shit!" she yelled, then headed to the next room on her list.

This was a typical day at the hotel. Some guests were cool, but the others were mostly nut cases. She finally found a room that was a check out. She started with the bathroom first. It was the part of the room she hated cleaning the most because it was so disgusting. She picked up all the wet towels and threw them in her cart then she proceeded to clean the tub.

Unlike some of her co-workers and despite the fact that it was just a job, Alyse made sure to do a first-rate job when cleaning. Most of the other housekeepers could care less how well the room was sanitized. They barely vacuumed the carpet, ignored the mold around the tub and only changed the sheets whenever they saw blood or some other type of fluid.

As Alyse's mind kept wondering, she didn't understand how she'd ended up cleaning hotel rooms for a living, especially since she was a straight A student and had been offered scholarships to several accredited universities. Scholarships that she regrettably didn't take advantage of. Instead, she managed to tell herself that people from the hood didn't go to college and decided to run the streets with Roslynn and Jazmine instead.

That is until she met Lance. From that point, she got married at the young age of twenty and had a baby. Every time Alyse stepped foot in her dead end job or thought about the stack of bills on her kitchen counter, it reminded her of the once in a lifetime opportunity that she'd passed up.

As Alyse sprayed more cleaning solution around the soap holder, she also thought about how her third generation welfare recipient mother, hadn't convinced her to go either. Talk about a bad influence, Alyse often blamed her mother for her lack of nurturing and horrible parenting skills. When Alyse was growing up, she longed for the day when her mother would be boasting her accomplishments to neighbors with a wide cheesy grin. Instead, the only praise she ever got was when she came back from the store with her mother's Marlboro Lights and forty ounce of Colt 45. To Alyse, her mother had failed as a parent, and even though she'd taken the wrong road to life herself back in the day, she was determined not to make the same mistakes with her own daughter.

When Alyse finally made her way over to the sink area, her cell phone began to ring.

"Damn, I thought I had it on vibrate," she said, dropping the rag. She looked toward the door to make sure Jackie's nosy-ass wasn't around before she answered it. Cell phones weren't allowed once their shift started, but nobody really abided by the rule anyway.

"Hello," Alyse answered.

"Hello. Mrs. Greffen, this is Amy. I'm the nurse at Ivy Hill Elementary. Your daughter, Brie is feeling a little under the weather. I don't think it's anything serious, but…"

"Well, I'm at work right now. I can't come get her," Alyse said cutting her off.

"That's understandable, but I'm sure you know our policy. If a child is sick, it's better for parents to come and get them so they don't pass the illness on to other students. We especially use this policy for our pre-K students. Their little immune systems can't fight off germs like the older kids. It's better safe than sorry."

*Shit*, Alyse thought. "I just started my shift, and can't leave right now. What's wrong wit' her?"

"She says her body hurts. I checked her temperature and she does have a slight fever, so it's possible that she could be coming down with something."

Brie had been sick off and on for the past month, and always complained about her body aching, but Alyse had held off from taking her to the doctor. Lance's lousy new HMO insurance plan required a $2,000 deductible, which they obviously couldn't afford. They didn't have any other options. The hotel where Alyse worked could only give her thirty-two hours a week now, which wasn't considered full time, so she didn't even have benefits at her job.

"Maybe I'll have my husband come," Alyse mentioned.

"If it helps, I can keep Brie here in the nurse's office until he gets here. She's asleep anyway."

"Okay, thank you."

After hanging up, Alyse thought about what she'd just said and tapped her fingers against the counter. *Actually I don't wanna bother Lance at his job.* "Fuck it. I'll just have to go get her."

Alyse knew Jackie was going to be pissed, especially since she'd just gotten there, but going to get her sick daughter wasn't an option. Grabbing the dirty rag, Alyse quickly walked out of the room, then threw the rag on top of her cart. After shutting the door, she made her way back toward the elevator, ready to face whatever Jackie was going to say.

As Alyse raced past the first room she'd tried to clean, a man with long dreads stuck his head out the door.

"Miss. Excuse me, Miss!" he yelled.

Alyse stopped and turned around. "Yes."

"Is it possible to get a late check out?"

"Sir, I don't handle 'dat. You need to call the front desk." She turned back around, but he continued to talk.

"Well, can I at least get some extra towels?" he asked. "Oh, and some extra soap."

Sucking her teeth, Alyse grabbed her cart and pulled it back toward the door just in case his ass asked for something else.

"Honey, hurry up. I want you to dry me off," a masculine voice said from inside.

Alyse's eyes widened a bit as she spotted another man coming out of the bathroom naked. Water dripped down his back as he walked over to the nightstand and picked up a condom. He never turned around. At that point she wondered which one of the gay men had told her to come back later. Trying not to stare, she quickly turned her head.

"Towels, please," the man with dreads said in a very low tone. He then closed the door a little bit more.

"Umm…yes towels," Alyse replied, as she reached under her cart.

"Thank you." He didn't waste anytime shutting the door in her face.

"Don't get mad at me cause you doing that nasty shit,"

Alyse said walking away. She got about a foot away from the door before she turned around.

"Hold up. I know 'dat voice from somewhere," she said to herself thinking about the guy with the condoms. She looked around to make sure no one was in the hallway before sticking her ear up against the door.

Unfortunately, her investigation didn't last long. When she heard the elevator door open, she nervously walked away with her mind wondering about who the mystery man was. However, if this was their secret hideaway, then hopefully she would soon find out.

✻✻✻

Lance's head began to throb as he sat at his computer. He'd been staying up at night worrying about how he was going to tell his wife that they were in once again in financial trouble. He hoped things would get better before she noticed, but it was clear that they weren't. He was thinking so hard he almost didn't hear the house phone ring. When he looked at the caller ID and saw it was their bank, he let out a huge sigh. He'd been ignoring their constant calls all day but finally decided to answer.

"Hello," he said with an instant attitude.

"Is this Mr. Greffen?"

"Yeah."

"Mr. Greffen, this is Barbara from American General. I'm calling about your February and March auto payments. We haven't received them as of yet and we were calling to see if you could possibly make the payment today."

"No, I've had some trouble and I won't be able to make them until next week," he said, trying to get them off his back.

"Well, it's April the 20th, what day should I expect your payment?" the assertive woman asked.

"I can make it on the 27th." When Lance heard the door open he quickly cut the lady off. "I have to call you back." He hung up and quickly exited out of the Monster.com website.

When Alyse and Brie walked into their apartment, she was surprised to see Lance dressed in jeans, a dingy white t-shirt, and

14

some slippers. It was one-thirty in the afternoon and he was supposed to be at work.

Alyse walked straight over to the couch. "What you doin' home so early?" she asked, giving him a quick peck on his lips. "Why didn't you call me? You could'a picked up Brie from school. She was sick. You know how Jackie is."

"I'm sorry, babe. What did Jackie say about you leaving?"

"She wrote my ass up, 'dats what," Alyse said slamming Brie's backpack on the coffee table. "Why you home?"

"It was so slow at the store this morning, they told me to go home. You're right. I should've called."

"Hi, daddy," Brie spoke in a weak tone.

"Hey, princess." Lance smiled showing his deep dimples. He wasn't exactly Alyse's type with his dark complexion and short 5'7 stature, but his great personality and profound love for his family outweighed the flaws.

"So, you didn't sell anythin' today?" Alyse inquired. By Lance working on commission, their high stack of bills relied on how much furniture he sold.

"Just an ultra suede couch," Lance informed. "So, what's wrong with my baby?" he asked, trying to change the subject.

"Like I said, she's sick," Alyse answered.

Lance looked at his beautiful daughter, then stood up. She'd inherited Alyse's good grade of curly hair, and what he called a 'white person's' nose. Brie's complexion was also very light, so she could've jumped into the portrait of a white family and fit right in. "Oh, baby. You're not feeling good again. What's wrong?"

"My body hurts, daddy," Brie replied.

Picking her up, he'd noticed how tired she'd been lately and the lack of energy she had. He felt her forehead. "Well, you don't have a fever."

"Give her some Children's Tylenol, Lance. Maybe that'll help," Alyse suggested.

"Maybe we should take her to the doctor. We can't always think Tylenol will do the trick."

Alyse gave him an evil glare. "Do you have the $2000 de-

**15**

ductible for the insurance?" When Lance didn't answer she continued. "I didn't think so. The Tylenol is in her room."

"Come on, pumpkin. Let me give you some medicine, and
then you can lay down for a while."

Under normal circumstances, little four year old Brie
would've put up a fight about taking medicine or laying down, but
this time she just shook her head. As Lance walked into Brie's
room, Alyse went into the kitchen and pulled out a pack of chicken
wings from the freezer. Besides ice cream sandwiches, frozen waffles and a box of hot pockets, the chicken was the only decent
thing left to cook.

"Where's yo' car?" she yelled.

Lance was caught off guard by Alyse's question. "Umm."
He thought for a moment. "I had to take it to the shop. I heard a
funny noise so I had it checked out," he called out from Brie's
room.

"How long is it gonna be in the shop? Don't forget 'dat my
shit has been actin' up too."

"Yeah, I know. I need to get yours fixed. I'm not sure when
mine will be ready," he replied.

The truth was, he was almost three months behind in his
truck payments so he'd hidden his truck at a co-workers house so
the finance company couldn't repossess it. Lance couldn't believe
how he'd just lied to his wife of four and a half years for the second time without even blinking, but he felt he had no choice. The
truth would've been too humiliating. He was afraid of what she
might think of him. He'd always been brought up that a man was
supposed to support his family, but so far that was a hard task to
complete. Ever since he'd met Alyse, he'd encountered an endless
series of dead end jobs, and could barely keep his families head
above water most of the time. Jobs that had condemned him and
his family to a life in the roach infested Columbia Avenue apartments near downtown Newark.

From cashiering at Boston Market to squirting Armor All at
the Gotham Wash & Detail Center, he'd done it all. Now, his latest
employment was a struggling commissioned salesman at Parkview
Furniture and Appliance. When Lance first started, his personal

goal was to sell enough furniture and appliances to meet his monthly quota and even meet bonus qualifications, but with the economy so bad he was lucky if he even sold one chair a day. His boss tried to work with him, but after poor sales figures four months straight, he had no choice but to let him go. Even though a week had already passed Lance had to hurry up and find something else before Alyse found out, or even worse, before their $1,100 rent payment was due.

Later that evening, the three of them all sat down for dinner. However, Alyse watched as Lance played around with his food. He seemed at times in deep thought and in another world. He would then stare at Brie for seconds at a time. Even though he was acting a bit strange, she loved the fact that Lance loved their daughter unconditionally. Lance never knew his father, so when they found out Alyse was pregnant, he vowed to always be there for them no matter what. He was a firm believer that children needed their father's in their lives. He even stopped doing a lot of things he used to do like selling dope, drinking, and smoking weed because he wanted to be a positive role model for her.

After continuing to watch Lance push his chicken around on the plate, Alyse couldn't take it any longer. She'd been married to him long enough to know that something was wrong and she needed to know what it was so she tried to pry it out of him.

"So baby, how was yo' day? Even though the shit was short." Alyse let out a slight laugh.

Lance's voice cracked. "It was a'ight. How was yours?" he asked trying to be more attentive.

"It was okay, but I'm sick of Jackie's ass." She covered her mouth when Lance gave her the famous look. He hated when she cursed in front of Brie. "Sorry about 'dat. So…you only sold one lil' couch today, huh?"

"Yep. We were pretty slow today," Lance responded. He looked down at his plate so he wouldn't have to look Alyse in the eyes and lie to her again.

Alyse kept asking questions during dinner and Lance kept vaguely answering her. Alyse could tell it was a waste of time trying to get Lance to open up to her, so she finally decided to just leave it alone. She figured when he was ready to talk to her he would.

After dinner, Alyse and Brie went into the living room to watch television, while Lance went straight into the bedroom. Lying across the bed, he wondered how they were going to live off his last paycheck, especially with the rent due in a couple of days. He didn't want his wife to think of him as a loser, and he certainly didn't want her friends to put that shit in her head either.

Lance knew that Roslynn always thought Alyse could've done better, especially since he was only a small time weed dealer when they met. He didn't have half the paper some other niggas had. Alyse being a beautiful Puerto Rican and black mixed chick with brick house measurements, could've been with any dude she wanted, but had chosen him.

In the beginning, Lance often thought that he was only a rebound romance, since she'd just broken up with a well known crack dealer named, Cordell two weeks before meeting him. However, all of that changed when they found out she was pregnant with Brie. Ten months after meeting, they had a brand new baby girl and were shopping for wedding rings. It was a fast romance, but none of that mattered since they loved each other so much. That's why Lance was determined to make things happen for his wife. She deserved the best.

After reminiscing with what seemed like forever, Alyse came into the room, plopped on the bed and immediately cuddled up next to his half naked body.

"Where's Brie?" he asked.

"I put her in the bed. Did you take a shower?" Even though she was enticed by the beads of water still resting on his body, she wanted to get on him about the wet towel around his waist, but decided to give him a pass.

"Yeah, I needed to relax."

She placed her hand on his chest. "Look, I know somethin' is wrong, but I'm not gonna pressure you to talk to me about it. I just want you to know that I'm here if you need me."

Hearing Alyse say those words made Lance feel a lot better,

but he still couldn't bring himself to tell her that he'd lost his job.

"Thank you, baby. That means a lot."

"I missed you today," she said.

"I missed you, too."

With one hand on his right nipple, Alyse leaned over and gently kissed the other nipple using her long tongue. She licked in a slow circular motion then proceeded to move down to his navel.

"Dis should make you feel better," she said, opening the towel.

By this point, his dick was at full attention, and harder than a steel pole. As always, Alyse stopped to admire her husband's enormously thick pipe. An attribute that she loved about him. She began to massage his shaft up and down with her hands before applying long wet strokes from bottom to top. She repeated this a few times before stopping at the head, then sucked her cheeks in to make more saliva.

"Damn…baby… that feels good," Lance whispered.

Satisfied with his reaction, Alyse positioned herself to take part of him in. She opened her mouth slightly and allowed the tip of his head to enter her mouth. As she continued to suck on his head, her jaws tightened, causing Lance's pole to grow harder. She then placed her hands below his manhood to play with his balls. A technique that absolutely drove him crazy.

"Oh, shit," Lance moaned.

Giving oral sex to her husband and watching his reactions was a complete turn on to her. Stroking his dick even faster now, Alyse widened her mouth to devour him entirely. Even though she wasn't a deep throat type of girl, Alyse took in all she could without gagging. Lance held onto the back of Alyse's head while she worked her jaws overtime. She would stop ever so often and suck on his balls again, but only a few seconds would pass before her lips were wrapped back around his manhood. He wanted to explode, but not before he felt her juices.

"I want to feel you baby," Lance said motioning for Alyse to stop.

Immediately taking charge, he quickly jumped up and removed all of her clothes, followed by her panties then entered her

**19**

pulsating vagina, pushing deep into her walls. Like a pro, Alyse threw her honey coated legs up and rested them on his shoulders, which was another thing that drove Lance wild. With each thrust, he gained more and more strength, causing Alyse to scream in painful satisfaction. She began winding her hips and pushing her pussy up and down his dick.

With forceful pumps, he leaned down and sucked her breasts while Alyse used one of her hands to tickle her clit.

"Fuck…I'm cumming!" Lance yelled out.

"Me too, baby," Alyse said. "Work 'dis pussy."

Seconds later, they were both reaching a climax in perfect unison.

# Chapter Three

Two days later, Alyse and Roslynn were enjoying a warm, beautiful day at The Ridgewood Golf & Country Club in Paramus. Sitting at an outside table on the clubhouse's rear terrace, the girls talked about old times as they waited on Jazmine, who was late as usual. They always made it a point to meet at least twice a month for lunch or shopping whenever Roslynn felt like treating.

Alyse kept looking at her watch. "Where's Jazz? We been here for over thirty minutes."

Roslynn looked around before answering in a low tone. "I know. I'm tired of always waitin' on her. Why are you and Jazz always late? Y'all take turns doin' that mess."

"Why you talkin' so low?"

"Girl, you know we ain't supposed to be talkin' all loud in here. That's ghetto," Roslynn announced. "The rules are pretty strict. These white people don't tolerate that kind of stuff."

"I don't even understand why you chose 'dis spot for lunch if we can't be ourselves. 'Dis place is too damn stuffy anyway."

Roslynn looked around the clubhouse again like she was embarrassed. "Why you usin' that type of language in here? Lower yo' voice, before they put us out."

"Good, let them put us out. I'm not feelin' this place anyway. Ro, just because you married to a successful dude, don't mean you gotta act all booshie. Shoot, I don't know who you tryna fool. You ghetto just like me," Alyse said with a wide smile. "Ms. Preacher's daughter, Jazmine, is the least ghetto if anythin'."

Roslynn flashed the four carat emerald cut ring on her French manicured hand. "Well, obviously my man didn't think I was ghetto, bitch."

Alyse grinned so hard, her checks began to hurt. "I thought

**21**

we won't supposed to curse. I knew the real Roslynn would come around sooner or later."

"Forget you, Alyse. Besides, I was just tryin' to give y'all bitches a polished environment to come to. You have to be a member here."

*Wow, when did she start using words like polished*, Alyse thought. She knew that regardless of where they were, eventually Roslynn would curse her out. The real Roslynn had a quick temper, and didn't take shit from anybody. However, she definitely put up a good façade in front of her husband, Adrian. He didn't tolerate her acting any way other than classy...never trashy.

"Fuck this. I'm about to order," Roslynn said. "We can't sit here and order strawberry lemonade all day." She lifted up her hand to motion for the waiter.

"No, don't do 'dat Ro. Let's wait a few more minutes."

Just as Roslynn was about to respond, they saw Jazmine walking toward them at a quick pace. However, the clubhouse manager was right behind her.

"Sorry I'm late," Jazmine said out of breath.

"Excuse me, Mrs. Washington. Do you know this woman?" The manager asked. "She didn't announce herself at the door with the Maitre D'."

Shocked by how horrible Jazmine looked, it took a few seconds for Roslynn to answer. In her white voice of course. "Oh, yes. This is my other guest. She's here to accompany me for lunch."

Alyse cracked up and mouthed the word booshie.

"Okay, that's fine, but you do remember the dress code, right?" the manager questioned.

Both Roslynn and Alyse looked at the baggy jeans and long black, oversized Obama t-shirt Jazmine had on. "Yes, I'm aware of the dress code, and I do apologize for her appearance. Apparently, my guest just forgot that I mentioned it to her," Roslynn said in a proper tone. She gave Jazmine a look of death.

"Mrs. Washington, to be honest we're already making an extreme exception for you. Remember you all are actually supposed to be in golf attire, but because Mr. Washington is such an excellent member, we bent the rules a little bit. However, denim is not permitted," the manager informed.

"I do understand," Roslynn replied, then tossed her long auburn weave over her shoulder.

Alyse shook her head in disgust.

"Again, I'll bend the rules just this once, and allow your guest to stay, but this can't happen again," the manager said.

Roslynn gave what Alyse hoped was a fake smile. "Thank you."

"Would you and your guests like to order now? I do realize you've been here for a while. Don't worry about your waiter. I can place the order for you."

Roslynn smiled. "Yes, give us three orders of crab cakes and asparagus."

Alyse frowned. "Asparagus. I don't want no damn asparagus." She looked at the waiter. "Y'all got any fried chicken or baby back ribs back there? Beef ribs though…no pork. I don't fool around wit' the swine."

The manager turned up his nose. "No, I'm afraid we don't have any beef ribs Ma'am. We do have chicken, but it's baked, and served with a mango chutney sauce."

"Mango Chutney? What the hell is 'dat?" Alyse asked.

Roslynn looked completely embarrassed. "Sir, just give us a few more minutes to look over the menu."

When the manager finally walked away, that smile quickly turned into a serious frown. "Alyse, don't you talk to nobody else up in here 'til we fuckin leave. Why the fuck you in here talkin' about chicken wings?" She then turned to Jazmine. "And you…why the hell would you come up in here dressed like a damn crack head? What you tryna do, get Adrian kicked out of this country club? I called and told you to put on somethin' decent. You look like shit," Roslynn said. "And why you got all that damn makeup caked on yo' face?"

Alyse spoke up. "Shut up, Roslynn. I can't believe you sittin' here actin' like 'dis. Tossin' yo' hair around like a damn white girl."

"Whatever, Alyse. I'm gonna toss my weave whenever the fuck I want. Shoot, I paid a lot of money for this hair. This ain't that regular beauty supply shit, you know" Roslynn responded. "Besides, everybody ain't got it like you."

She was referring to Alyse's good grade of hair that she'd recently cut into short layers and dyed a sandy brown color. It went well with her skin tone, and had turned out pretty good for a home job. Alyse couldn't afford to go to the salon, so she always experimented with her tresses.

Roslynn then started up with Jazmine. "When are you gonna stop wearin' that damn ponytail?"

"Here Jazz…sit down," Alyse said ignoring Roslynn. She stood up, hugged her frail looking friend, then pulled out a chair. "Do you want me to order you somethin'? It looks like you need to eat."

"No," Jazmine answered, taking off sunglasses.

Roslynn gasped and held her chest. "Oh my God!"

Embarrassed, Jazmine quickly put them back on.

"Girl, what the hell happened to you?" Roslynn asked.

Jazmine knew she had to come up with a good story because if her girls knew that Vince was responsible for her badly bruised face there would be hell to pay, especially from Roslynn. She hated Vince with a passion. She tried to be the picture of perfection now, but back in the day she was a fierce bitch as most people would say. Hell, all of them were off the hook at some point. The three women had been friends since elementary school, and grew up in the same grimey Newark housing projects called Baxter Terrace. They had a close knit bond that each of them vowed to keep.

"Y'all know how much I love my McDonald's sweet tea, right," Jazmine said laughing. "Well last night, I went to get a cup and I got robbed. The guy hit me in the face, and took my purse."

"What?" Alyse shrieked not finding any humor in what Jazmine said. "Girl, you could'a been killed."

"Robbed. See, what did I tell y'all about still livin' in the hood, especially you Alyse. You need to get the hell outta Newark," Roslynn said.

Alyse immediately defended herself. "Shut up, Roslynn. Everybody ain't got money like you. Besides, Jazmine's neighborhood is nice. It's not bad."

"East Orange…I beg to differ," Roslynn replied in a proper tone again.

"You know what Roslynn, forget you. I got robbed and could've gotten really hurt," Jazmine replied, on the brink of breaking down. She felt bad for lying to her friends, but was too ashamed to tell them that she was being beaten by her own husband, especially when she was warned by everyone not to marry him.

"Did they catch the asshole?" Alyse asked, sipping on her lemonade.

"No…but Vince will find the guy. He has some officers on it," Jazmine stated without eye contact with either one of her girls.

"Well, I'm glad to know that you okay even though yo' ass look like crap. You need to start takin' better care of yourself, Jazmine," Roslynn advised.

Jazmine played with her ponytail. "Yeah, I know." She looked around the room. "I don't like this place. Why are we eating here?"

Alyse sucked her teeth. "Well, Ms. Roslynn here said she wanted us to be in a *polished* environment.

"Polished. The hell with that," Jazmine said, pulling on her t-shirt. "I got enough rules at home. I don't wanna eat here. Let's go."

Alyse nodded her head. "I agree. Let's blow 'dis camp."

Roslynn was pissed. "Y'all some ungrateful bitches. It's not like y'all were gonna pay for the meal any damn way." She went into her Chanel purse, and pulled out a twenty dollar bill to pay for the lemonade. "Let's just go to the mall and eat there. That way we can do a lil' shoppin', too. Y'all can ride wit' me if you want. I wanna show off the new wheels that I got this mornin'."

Alyse's eyes widened. "You got another new car? What happened to the Mercedes you just got? Man, I hate yo' ass sometimes."

Roslynn flashed an 'it's good to be me' smile. "I traded in the Benz. The summer is comin' up, so I wanted a convertible."

"I wish Vince was like Adrian. He's so good to you,"

Jazmine chimed in.

Roslynn nodded her head. "Yeah, that's true, but he don't know 'bout the new car yet. He didn't want me to get it, but I got the shit anyway."

"Are you serious? Adrian's gon' kick yo' ass," Alyse said as Jazmine shifted in her seat.

"Shit, you got this all wrong. As soon as I put this thang down on him, he'll forget about everything." Roslynn smiled. "Come on y'all, let's go. I'm hungry."

Jazmine looked at her watch. "I only have time to grab something to eat. Besides, Vince didn't give me any money to shop."

Roslynn sighed. "I hate Vince. He always gives you tight-ass allowances and time frames like you fifteen years old. How much time you got today, forty- five minutes…thirty?"

Jazmine looked at her friend, then lowered her head. Roslynn was right. Vince had managed to isolate her from every single person in her family. However, the strange thing about it was the fact that he still allowed Jazmine to see her friends some-times. It was weird.

"Well, y'all can shop all you want. I don't have two damn nickels to rub together, so I just gotta window shop," Alyse men-tioned.

Just as the girls stood up to leave, Alyse's cell phone rung. When she saw it was her daughter's school, she threw her hand up and yelled, "Wait."

Alyse answered the phone as Jazmine and Roslynn sat back down. They couldn't hear what was going on, but they could tell it wasn't good news because of the terrified look Alyse had on her face.

"What do you mean?" Alyse asked, on the verge of drop-ping her phone. After a few more seconds, she quickly hung up. "I gotta go. Brie fainted at school."

Both Jazmine and Roslynn immediately stood back up. Roslynn's tall 5'9 frame always loomed over her friends. Not to mention her big D cup breasts, tiny waistline and huge round ass made her look like a professional porn star.

"Oh my God. Do you want us to go with you?" Jazmine asked.

"No…go shoppin'. I'll call ya'll later," Alyse replied.

Roslynn spoke up. "Go and see about my God baby. Tell her Auntie Ro said get better."

Alyse looked grateful. "Thanks." She grabbed her purse and walked out the clubhouse at top speed.

"I hope she's gonna be alright," Jazmine said with concern. "Maybe we should do this later. It's not right if Alyse is not here."

"Yeah, you right. Well, call me if you hear anythin'," Roslynn responded.

After giving each other huge hugs, the two women left hoping that the goddaughter they both shared would be okay.

✳✳✳

An hour after taking Brie to the emergency room at University Hospital, a nurse finally called them to an examining room in the back. After taking Brie's temperature and vitals, the nurse left the room and told them the doctor would be in shortly. Alyse tried to call Lance twice, but he didn't answer. She really didn't want to bother him until she knew exactly what was wrong with Brie, but she knew he would never forgive her for not telling him that his "Little Princess" had fainted.

Besides, even though the emergency room attendant hadn't said anything about the insurance deductible when they registered, she knew it would only be a matter of time before they did. Alyse needed to know how they were going to get the money. She pulled out her cell phone and dialed his number, but again it went straight to voicemail.

"Hey, baby. I just wanted to let you know I'm at the hospital wit' Brie. I'll try you again in a few. I love you," she said, before ending the call.

Suddenly, a tall grey haired man entered the room and told Alyse his name was Dr. Wells. Alyse extended her hand and greeted him.

"Hi, I'm Alyse and 'dis is my daughter, Brie."

"Well, let's take a look here," Dr. Wells said, putting on a pair of gloves. "Brie, I'm going to poke around a bit so I can see what's making you so sick alright."

Brie shook her head up and down. "Is it gonna hurt?" she asked.

"No, not at all," Dr. Wells responded. He made sure to use a soft assuring tone.

He felt Brie's neck and then examined her eyes, ears, and throat. He then took off his gloves and wrote something down in Brie's chart. "How long has she been sick? What symptoms does she have?"

Alyse hated the fact that his exam was over so quickly. It almost seemed as if he was rushing.

"Well, she's been sick off and on for a while now. She's always tired and complains about her body achin' a lot," Alyse replied. "Is she okay?"

"Well, Brie does have a slight fever, and with the rest of her symptoms I think she probably has some sort of viral infection, because of her flu-like symptoms."

"You can get the flu in the spring?"

"It's uncommon, but not impossible. An acetaminophen, which is basically Children's Tylenol should help."

"I been givin' her Tylenol for a while now, and it don't seem to be workin'," Alyse informed.

"Well, I could give you a prescription for Tamiflu. However, I gotta tell you, that medicine works best within the first forty-eight hours of experiencing symptoms. You said Brie's been sick for a while, so the medicine might not be as effective."

"I'm willin' to try it."

"But if she starts to get a fever, go back to the Tylenol. Only use the Tamiflu when the fever breaks."

"What about her faintin' in school, Dr. Wells?"

"That could've been a case of dehydration. Just make sure she gets plenty of liquids and lots of rest. It might even be a good idea for her to stay inside for a day or two."

Alyse wanted so badly to ask the doctor if he was sure, but didn't want to offend him. She really didn't care for the doctors at

University Hospital, but it was the closest medical facility to Brie's school.

"Okay. Thank you," Alyse said even though she wasn't completely satisfied.

Dr. Wells tore off the prescription from his pad and handed the paper to Alyse. "Bye-bye Brie. You take care," he said then quickly walked out of the room.

After helping Brie down from the table, Alyse let out a small sigh of relief then proceeded toward the door. As they were walking past the registration desk, a fat woman with a bright blond wig waved Alyse down.

*Damn, I know she's gonna ask me about 'dat deductible,* Alyse thought to herself. "Yes, is somethin' wrong?" Alyse asked.

"Yeah, it is. We seem to have a problem getting authorization for today's visit, so we need to confirm your insurance information," the woman said in a loud and obnoxious tone.

Alyse looked around at the other patients in the waiting area. She hated that the woman had put her business out there in front of everybody.

Alyse played it off. "There must be some sort of mistake." She wanted to tell the woman that she knew about the deductible, but was afraid to bring it up.

The woman typed something in the computer, then looked back up. "No, it's not a mistake. Your insurance seems to be canceled."

When Alyse looked back again and saw people staring like she was their entertainment, she became heated.

"Canceled…now I know you made a mistake. Besides, my daughter has already seen the doctor so now what do I do?" Alyse asked.

"Well, for starters you need to get your insurance straight before you come in here wanting services. If you don't have the funds to pay for the visit today, then we'll just have to bill you. However, just make sure you pay it, so we don't have to waste our time with collections," the rude fat woman had the nerve to say.

Alyse lost it. "What? Yo' fat-ass is way out of line. I tell you what, bill me then bitch!" Furious, she grabbed Brie by the hand and walked out.

"Ooohhh…mommy. You said a bad word," Brie said, looking up at her mother.

Alyse stopped dead in her tracks and knelt down. "You right, Brie. Mommy did say a bad word. It's just 'dat I hate 'dis hospital." When she looked down at her daughter's confused face, she smiled. "I'm sorry, baby. It won't happen again."

Alyse and Lance were very careful about saying things around Brie because her little brain was a sponge. She only needed to hear something one time for it to stick with her. Next thing you know she would be trying to repeat it in her class. There were enough kids in Brie's school, who obviously didn't have the right guidance, so Alyse didn't want her daughter to be one of them.

As Alyse buckled Brie in the back seat, she noticed that her daughter was starting to become hot. After feeling her forehead, Alyse quickly got behind the wheel and drove straight to the pharmacy. She tried to call Lance on his cell phone to let him know what was going on, but again it went straight to voicemail.

"Lance you need to answer the damn phone! I took yo' daughter to the hospital, now we on our way home. Call me!" After ending the call, Alyse continued to fuss. "Lance knows better than to cut his fuckin' phone off."

"Mommy, you said another bad word," Brie said in a weak tone.

"Sorry, baby. Mommy is just tryna find Daddy, 'dats all."

It was Lance's idea to always call him on his cell phone, and never at work in the first place. Up until now, Alyse never had a problem with that, but today was different. Dialing the number to the furniture store, Alyse placed the small flip phone up against her ear, only to hear a busy signal a few minutes later.

"Dis is really gettin' annoyin'," she said, throwing the phone in the passenger seat.

When Alyse got to the pharmacy a few minutes later, she unfortunately ran into the same problem with their insurance card when she tried to pay for the prescription. Boiling hot by this point, but not wanting to start an argument in front of Brie, she pulled out four twenties to pay for the eighty dollar medicine and stormed out of the door. Eighty dollars that was supposed to go toward her already overdue cell phone bill. As bad as Alyse wanted to call Lance again, she decided not to because she knew the conversation wasn't going to be pretty. She needed to know what the hell was going on. She also needed a stiff drink.

***

As soon as the movie let out, Lance slowly walked to the car and checked his voicemail. He knew it was risky turning off his phone, but didn't want to run the possibility of Alyse hearing any nonsense in the background. His wife was nosy when it came to things like that, and was known for asking a thousand questions about his whereabouts, so he felt safer just not answering at all. After going on a stressful job hunt earlier that morning with no luck, Lance decided to go somewhere to get his mind off of his towering pile of problems. To him, the movies was much better than drowning his sorrows at a bar or even worse jumping in front of a car on the New Jersey Turnpike.

"You have two new messages. To listen to your messages, please press one," the animated voice announced.

Pressing one, Lance hoped like crazy that one of the messages would be from a job. However, once he heard Alyse's voice, and the message she left, his hope turned to fear. Picking up his speed at this point, Lance damn near sprinted to his car, jumped in and hurried home.

By the time he got there, Alyse had fallen asleep on the couch. Trying not to wake her up, he tip toed into Brie's room to check up on his baby. However, after giving her a kiss on the cheek, he quickly went back into the living room and immediately woke up Alyse.

"Honey…Brie's burning up." Lance looked uneasy.

Alyse shot straight up on the couch, then rubbed her eyes. "I know. She can't seem to break 'dat fever. I already gave her the faithful 'ole Tylenol."

"What happened when you took her to the hospital?"

"The doctor said Brie probably has the flu because of her

31

symptoms, but I can't give her the prescription medicine until the fever go down."

Lance looked back toward Brie's room. "My poor little princess."

"Little Princess…well yo' Little Princess fainted at school today, and I couldn't even get in touch wit' you. Where were you?"

Lance started to stutter. I…I…was at work."

"I called yo' cell phone several times, but it went straight to voicemail. You know better than 'dat shit, Lance. I even called yo' job."

Lance's heart felt like it had fallen into his shoe. "My job? What happened when you called there?"

"Nothin', the line was busy, and I never called back."

Lance tried his best to let out a sigh without Alyse noticing. "Oh, well we had a lot of people calling up asking about a sale today. You know with this recession everybody wants a deal. Just hit me up on my cell for now," Lance said, headed to the bathroom.

"I'm not finished. When I took Alyse to the hospital today, the insurance company wouldn't authorize the visit or the prescription. She said the insurance was canceled. What's up wit' 'dat?"

Again, Lance's heart began to race. He had to come up with something quick. "Shit, I forgot to tell you my boss said they are having problems with the insurance company, but it should be fixed soon," he said fidgeting. "Don't worry. I'll take care of it."

"So, what we supposed to do in the meantime? What if Brie has to go back?"

"Honey, don't worry. I'm sure all the kinks will be worked out by then."

Alyse placed her hands on her hips. "You been actin' really weird lately. Do you need to tell me somethin'?"

Lance shook his head. "Naw baby. I'm just tired."

Alyse looked at him suspiciously then mumbled. "Yeah right. Tired my ass."

# Chapter Four

Pulling her new 650i convertible BMW directly in front of The Shops at Riverside in Hackensack, Roslynn stepped outside then handed her keys to a bald headed parking attendant. Walking a long distance in her expensive four-inch Manolo Blahnik heels wasn't an option, so she always chose the valet. Hell, Roslynn only shopped where she knew they provided the special service anyway. She was a diva in every sense of the word. With beautiful mocha colored skin, Roslynn was very beautiful, and always looked like she'd just come from Fashion Week. If her appearance wasn't on ten she wouldn't even come out of the house.

After reminding her favorite parking attendant not to scratch her car, she strutted to the entrance.

"Don't worry, Mrs. Washington. I'll be very careful. I see you got a new car!" he yelled.

Roslynn turned around and slid her Bottega Veneta sunshades down a little so he could see how serious she was. "Yes, it is new James. You know I like you and all, but if you put one scratch on my shit, that's yo' ass," she said, referring to the silver metallic beauty.

Roslynn always talked shit to the attendants every time she came to the mall, but they loved it. Of course, they loved the huge tips she gave them even more. With her black Chanel handbag thrown across her shoulders, Roslynn sashayed straight into the Louis Vuitton store like she'd helped start the company. As soon as she walked in, her regular sales clerk, Heidi's face lit up. She almost broke her neck trying to get to Roslynn before anyone else did.

"Mrs. Washington...how are you?"

Roslynn tossed her weave and used her proper voice. "I'm

doing grand. How about yourself?"

The petite white woman looked concerned. "Well, it's been a little slow lately. A lot of my customers have told me that because of the economy their husbands have put them on a budget."

Roslynn frowned. "Budget…honey, I don't even know the meaning of that. Besides, if my husband even formed his lips to say that word he would be on punishment for weeks. If you know what I mean."

The two women laughed just before Roslynn began to browse the store. As Heidi continued to chuckle, little did she know the joke had been one big lie. Just like so many other husbands, Adrian had also put Roslynn on a budget recently in order to control her spending habits, but so far it hadn't been working. Roslynn wasn't trying to hear the word budget, and usually used her sexual charms to make him forget all about those kinds of conversations.

She was a compulsive shopper, who hated to be labeled as a shopaholic whenever she and Adrian discussed her addiction. Roslynn was what one would call an "I deserve it" shopper. She felt as if she was entitled to everything she wanted regardless of how much it cost, and had to have the latest fashion must haves.

Being very well off wasn't always the case for Roslynn. In fact, just like her best friends she'd grown up dirt poor with a crack head mother, who financed her habit by turning tricks. Hell, her mother even tried to sell Roslynn a few times for a hit. Roslynn learned at an early age how to hustle and scheme for everything she wanted, and Adrian was no exception to the rule. Whenever he would come to a hole in the wall strip club called, The Furnace, where she worked a few years ago, he would bring her little gifts like flowers and perfume. They called it The Furnace because it would get so hot in the building that people would literally pass out.

After the gifts, Roslynn always felt obligated to give Adrian a lap dance, which worked in her favor anyway because his tips were generous. He loved when she would make him feel like he was the only guy in the club. So much so that he got up the nerve to ask her out. Roslynn said no a couple of times, but caved in after he bought her a gorgeous diamond necklace.

With her money radar on high at that point, as soon as Roslynn found out Adrian had inherited a bank from his parents who were deceased, she swung right into action. Plus, by Adrian being fifteen years older than her, he was an instant sugar daddy. Throwing her pussy on him at least two times a day, Adrian caved in, as well and asked for Roslynn's hand in marriage, when she was only twenty-one years old. Six years later, they were still together and Roslynn was in love with Adrian's money more than ever before.

Roslynn continued to browse the store until an older white woman, who had redneck written all over her face, shot her a snooty look.

*What bitch? You think I can't afford to be in here or some shit? Well, let me show you.*

"Heidi, I'll take the large Trevi Damier Canvas bag. It's still a little over two thousand, right?" When Heidi shook her head, Roslynn continued to show off. She walked over to the case of accessories. "I'll take this, too," she said, picking up the matching wallet.

Heidi flashed a gleaming smile. "I'll be glad to get those items, Mrs. Washington. Would that be all?"

"For today, I guess." Roslynn went in her purse. "Would you be a doll and put everything on my American Express *Black* card," Roslynn emphasized, as she pulled out the card. She looked over at the older woman and gave a mischievous grin.

The woman rolled her eyes in return then gave a little smirk before leaving.

Heidi laughed. "I'm so glad you did that. That lady always comes in here like she owns the store, but never buys anything."

"The nerve of some people. This is not a place to window shop."

As Roslynn watched Heidi walk into the back of the store to get a fresh bag, and to ring up everything, her cell phone began to ring. Pulling the new touch screen Blackberry from her purse, Roslynn let out a huge sigh as soon as she looked at the caller ID. She wasn't in the mood to take the call, but knew that the person would just keep calling back, if she didn't answer.

"Make it quick," Roslynn said.

"Make it quick. Don't be talkin' to me like 'dat," her ghetto cousin, Kamilla, responded.

"Kamilla, what the hell do you want?"

"You know exactly what I want. Why you actin' all dumb? What, bitch you caught a case of amnesia or somethin'?"

Roslynn looked around the store. She wanted to go off, but had to keep her composure. "I'm not gonna be too many bitches, a'ight."

"Why…what you gonna do? Don't make me place an important phone call. I got da fuckin' number on speed dial."

As Roslynn was about to respond, she saw Heidi walking back toward her. "Look, I gotta go."

"So, when should I expect da…" was all Kamilla was able to get out before Roslynn hung up on her.

She quickly turned her phone off, because she knew her irritating-ass cousin would call back.

"Thank you so much for being a valued customer, Mrs. Washington," Heidi said, handing Roslynn her shopping bag.

"My pleasure," Roslynn replied as she signed the receipt. "Have a nice day, and tell that broke bitch to stay out the store."

As Roslynn headed toward Bloomingdales, she paused momentarily to admire a rectangular shaped diamond studded watch in the Tiffany and Co. store window. It was another one of her favorite places to shop. Saliva damn near oozed from her mouth the more she stared at the beautiful timepiece.

"Damn, I gotta get a closer look at that beauty," she said to herself just before walking inside.

However, unlike Heidi, the only clerk in Tiffany's wasn't as eager to help her. Instead, she acted like she didn't even see Roslynn when she walked over to the counter.

*Another old white bitch who's trying my nerves. She must don't know how I roll,* Roslynn thought. *What the hell is up with these racist bitches today?* "Excuse me. Can I see that diamond watch that's in the window?" she asked the woman.

"Which one, there's more than one watch in the window

you know."

Shaking her leg back and forth, it took all of her not to go off. Under normal circumstances the clerk would've gotten cursed out, but Roslynn was trying to control herself. Adrian had asked her on several occasions to be more lady-like in public, so to please her husband, that's exactly what she was trying to do. However, this lady was pushing it.

"The rectangular one with the black strap. It has two rows of princess cut diamonds."

"I'm sorry but, that's our 18K white gold Resonator Cocktail Watch. It retails for twelve thousand, six hundred, and we're not having a sale," the clerk responded in a nasty tone.

"I didn't ask you how much the shit costs. I just need you to walk your old snooty-ass over there and get it out of the window so I can see it."

The nice Roslynn had left the building.

The woman was shocked. She knew from Roslynn's tone and language that she meant business, so to avoid confrontation, the woman strolled over to the window and removed the watch. Roslynn could tell the woman didn't want to do it, but with no other sales clerks around, she didn't have much of a choice.

Just as the woman handed the watch to Roslynn, the gay manager of Tiffany's walked from the back of the store. He was known for always wearing the Tiffany-blue colored tie and matching pocket square. Sometimes he even wore the socks. Quickly, he rushed over in true gay style as soon as he spotted Roslynn.

"Oh, Mrs. Washington. Where have you been daaarling? I haven't seen you in months." He kissed Roslynn on both sides of her cheeks.

"I've been fine, Clark. My husband buys me so much jewelry these days that I haven't felt the need to come in here for a while."

"Okay, my dear what can we do for you today?" Clark asked.

"Well, the lady right here was just about to be a doll and fasten this diamond watch for me. Weren't you?" Roslynn asked, giving the clerk a devious smile.

The clerk didn't smile back, and looked at Roslynn with the question 'Can't you put it on yourself' but instead, she grabbed the two watch straps and secured it on her wrist.

"Umm…that's too tight," Roslynn announced. She held onto the same grin, as the woman looked at her then at the manager.

"Well, you heard Mrs. Washington. The band is too tight. Readjust it," Clark ordered.

Again, Roslynn smiled. She knew the band wasn't too tight, but just wanted to fuck with the old coon for being a bitch earlier.

The woman looked like she wanted to spit fire as she followed Clark's demands. "How does it feel now, Miss?" She was fake and Roslynn knew it.

"Umm, you can call me Mrs. Washington, or Ma'am actually," Roslynn taunted. She was getting a kick out of fucking with the old woman. "Yes, this is fine. I like it. Ring it up."

"Excellent. Mrs. Washington daaarling you certainly have good taste," Clark said. After helping Roslynn take the watch off, he gave her two more kisses on the cheek. "I'm so glad you found something. That watch is so exquisite."

Roslynn looked at the iced-out watch again. "Yes, it is."

"Please ring Mrs. Washington up," Clark ordered then handed the jewelry to the woman.

Going through her wallet, Roslynn eyed her many credit cards. "You can put it on this one," she said, handing the clerk the American Express card again.

As soon as the woman walked away, and Clark excused himself to go and greet another customer, all Roslynn could think was, *Oh my God. Adrian is gonna have a fit when he finds out how much money I spent. Maybe I need to start using cash so my purchases are harder to detect.*

"Oh well, I guess I gotta go home and turn on the sexual charm," Roslynn said to herself then pushed up her bra.

Her body was her best asset and she was damn proud of it.

\*\*\*

Three hours into her shopping, Roslynn looked down at her old watch and noticed that it was 5:20 p.m. It was almost time for Adrian to get off of work. Although he was the president of his bank, and didn't have to necessarily punch a clock, he always came home around six. However, if Roslynn had it her way, she would definitely want him to stay at work even later. Adrian coming home before the malls closed would sometimes put a damper on Roslynn's shopping sprees, especially if she didn't get home in time to hide all of her bags.

This time, not only did she have bags to hide, but she also had a brand new car that he didn't know anything about. It wasn't gonna be as easy hiding that shit. Her plan was to park the BMW in their four-car garage, then call Adrian to tell him their garage door opener wasn't working. Adrian wasn't what you would call *Bob The Builder*, and he didn't do any manual work around the house. Knowing that, Roslynn figured he would just park his car in front of the house, then call someone to fix the problem. Until she had a chance to break the news, her plan had to be successful.

While waiting for the valet to bring her car, Roslynn glanced around the parking lot then suddenly stopped when she spotted a familiar looking face. Curious, she lifted her sunglasses up to get a better look. The further the man walked across the lot, the more he looked like the Vice-President of Adrian's bank, Jerry, but there was only one problem. This particular guy looked as if he was holding another man's hand, and she knew Jerry wasn't anywhere near gay.

*Shit, I'm trippin'*, Roslynn thought to herself as the valet jumped out of her car.

Placing her sunglasses back down, she walked over to the driver's side, threw her shopping bags in the backseat, then handed the guy a tip.

"Thank you for getting' my car so quickly, James."

"No, *thank you* Mrs. Washington," he said smiling when he saw the fifty dollar tip. "See you in a day or so."

39

As Roslynn sat behind the wheel, she glanced at the clock again, and noticed that it was now 5:30. Even though she only lived about ten minutes from the mall, Rosylnn still didn't want to take any chances on running into him, so she quickly pulled out of the parking lot like she was competing in a drag race.

With her top down and the wind dancing through her long weave, Roslynn sped down Hwy 17 trying to beat her prompt husband home. Instead of coming to a complete stop at every stop sign she came across, Roslynn just slowed down or decided to run them altogether. It was a dangerous and reckless way of driving, that continued until she entered her upper class neighborhood. However, as soon as she made a right onto Nevada Street and pulled up into her circular omni stone driveway, her eyes immediately widened.

"Fuck!" Roslynn yelled then began to beat the sterling wheel. "Fuck!"

Adrian had beaten her home. Roslynn had to think quickly as she stopped her car and watched Adrian pull his S Class Mercedes Benz into the garage. At this point, her entire plan had failed. She needed to go to Plan B right away. If Adrian knew just how much she'd spent, especially with the car after he'd specifically ordered her to cut back, he would shit bricks.

With her mind running a mile a minute, Roslynn quickly decided to put the car in reverse, then park on the street directly in front of the house. For now, this spot would just have to do until she found the perfect time to break the news to Adrian.

Jumping out of the driver's seat, she opened her trunk and threw all her bags inside after making sure she didn't have any of the receipts in her purse. She looked around to make sure her nosy white neighbors weren't watching before heading to her 4800 square foot home.

After walking up to her front door, Roslynn reached into her purse, pulled out a container of tic-tacs, then shook about four into her mouth. For some reason, she was nervous about Adrian's response to her spending, and the way he might react this time.

"Here we go," she muttered softly then rolled the mints around on her tongue. Roslynn took a deep minty breath before placing her key in the front door, and turning the knob. "Honey, I'm home!" She had to remember to drop her hood voice immediately.

Roslynn immediately took off her heels when she stepped into the foyer. She'd just convinced Adrian to get her new Italian marble floors a week before, so she didn't want to scuff them up.

"Honey, did you take off your shoes when you came in?" she asked, then placed her purse on the round cherry wood table.

"Yes," Adrian replied. He walked up to her and flashed his charming smile. "How did you know I was home anyway?" he asked, greeting her with a kiss. Roslynn loved his thick full lips.

She also loved the way he reminded her of basketball star, Grant Hill, with his tall 6'4' frame, pecan skin, big eyes and smooth goatee, which now had grey hairs sprinkled throughout. At age forty-one, he didn't look a day over thirty.

"I saw you pull up just before I did."

"That's funny. I didn't hear you pull into the garage," Adrian said with a confused expression.

Roslynn had to think quickly. "Oh...no I didn't park in the garage. My opener wasn't working, so I parked out front." She hoped like hell he didn't look out the window.

"Really, well remind me to call someone about that because my opener works fine. Do you want me to move your car?" Adrian walked closer to the door, but Roslynn stepped in front of him.

"No honey, that's okay. It'll be fine." Small beads of sweat began to form on her forehead.

"Are you sure? You never park in front of the house."

When Roslynn shook her head, Adrian finally left the issue alone, then turned around and headed toward the family room, his favorite place to relax. Feeling a small sigh of relief, Roslynn followed closely behind.

"So, where have you been?" Adrian asked before unloosening his Armani tie.

"Oh, I went to drop off a few things at the cleaners and a couple other places."

Adrian looked at her like a worried parent. "Would one of the other places happen to be the mall?"

"Honey, I don't have to go shopping every time I step out of the house," Roslynn said, trying to play it off.

"Good, because you've been spending way too much money. You have enough shoes, enough perfume, enough of that makeup and we certainly don't need this house redecorated for the third time. I'm sick to death of faux paint."

Roslynn looked at her abstract painted walls then back at her husband. From his response, she knew her new purchases weren't gonna go over well. "Honey, please. Do we have to talk about this again? Let's just relax. I know you've had a long day."

Before Adrian could respond, their personal chef, Ramon walked into the room. "Excuse me, Mr. and Mrs. Washington, would you like me to start dinner now?"

Roslynn walked over and whispered in his ear, "Actually, you can take the night off. I'll be cooking dinner tonight," she said, winking her eye. She needed to butter Adrian up and what better way then making him a romantic dinner.

The chef wanted to laugh in Roslynn's face. He'd been working for them since they moved into the custom built home six years ago, and had yet to see her boil a pot of water. He wasn't even sure if she knew where the forks were.

"As you wish," Ramon said, walking out of the room. He silently said a prayer for Adrian.

"Ro, what are you up to?" Adrian asked.

"Nothing much," she said with a smirk on her face. "Now, I'ma go get out of these clothes so I can make us some dinner. Why don't you go take a shower?" she said, sticking her tongue in his ear. It didn't take much to turn Adrian on.

"Umm…umm. Forget dinner, let's just have dessert."

"Down boy! You can have dessert later."

✱✱✱

Roslynn stood in the kitchen dressed in a sheer black La Perla camisole with sexy matching shorts. Having no idea how to cook the things Adrian liked, she paced around her huge gourmet kitchen like a lost child. Growing up in the hood, the only thing

42

she did know how to fix were Ramen noodles and grilled cheese sandwiches, with the famous government cheese of course, so preparing dinner might've been more difficult than she thought. At that point, she even contemplated warming up leftovers from the night before, but dismissed that idea as well.

"No, this has to be special so I gotta figure something out," Roslynn said, grabbing her autographed G. Garvin cookbook from the easel.

A book that hadn't been opened since she met the famous chef at a booksigning, at least three years ago. Thinking of Adrian's favorite food, she quickly found the page for seafood, then spotted a simple recipe for Shrimp Alfredo.

"Oh, this seems pretty easy," Roslynn convinced herself. She turned around and began to look through a few cabinets. "Now, where the hell does Ramon keep the pots?"

After looking in even more cabinets, she finally found a pot to cook the Fettuccini noodles, then walked over to her LG stainless steel refrigerator. A refrigerator that contained an LCD flat screen T.V in the door panel, which was another one of Roslynn's many luxuries. Grabbing some shrimp from the freezer, Roslynn was just about to place the bag in the sink when she was suddenly startled by a loud noise.

"Adrian!" she called out.

After receiving no response, Roslynn figured that she was probably hearing things, then began to get back to work. However, little did she know, Adrian was standing in the doorway, watching her every move. He especially admired her body, not to mention, her paw print that was very visible in the booty shorts.

"So, where were you earlier today?" Adrian questioned. Why the hell did you lie to me about where you were earlier?" Adrian questioned.

"Oh, shit. You scared me."

"What did I tell you about using that kind of language? It's so unattractive for a *real* lady to do that."

Roslynn never understood why Adrian never wanted her to curse when he cursed all the time. She also didn't understand why he wanted her to be someone she wasn't. In that case, he should've married a Harvard graduate, not an ex-stripper.

Roslynn immediately stopped what she was doing. *Damn. What does he know*, she thought. "What...are you talking about?"

He walked further into the kitchen until they were able to make perfect eye contact. "Don't act innocent Roslynn. I just checked the voicemail. American Express left two messages. When I called them back, they informed me that they just wanted to confirm the purchase you made at Tiffany's today."

The palm of her hands began to sweat like crazy as Roslynn racked her brain about what she was going to say. Just like before, she had to act quick. "Honey, I can explain."

"Explain? How the hell can you explain spending twelve thousand dollars on a watch that you don't even need. Hell, I just bought you a brand new Rolex for your birthday three months ago. You're gonna put us in the damn poor house if you don't stop spending!" Adrian ranted.

"Sweetheart, please don't be upset," Roslynn pleaded.

However, she knew that he would be very upset. Adrian didn't have a problem spoiling Roslynn because he'd been doing it since they'd met, but he did have a problem every time she went overboard. It had been that way ever since they'd gotten married, and Roslynn knew how he was. She just chose to ignore it most of the time. Adrian was obsessive when it came to their finances and investments, so she was used to this lecture by now.

"Roslynn, we've talked about this shit over and over. I mean, this is the reason why I give you a certain amount to spend every month. Don't you understand? I want us to have a certain amount of money at all times."

She shook her head. Hell, Roslynn understood exactly what Adrian was saying. They couldn't even have children because of his strange way of thinking. As soon as Adrian asked Roslynn to be his wife, he made it very clear that he never wanted to have children. He said that children were too needy and cost too much money. He also said that he'd rather spend his hard earned money on something more valuable like a Fairline 50 foot yacht. Roslynn never understood how he could compare the life of a child to a boat, but never questioned him. Even after being married for six years, he still hadn't changed his mind about starting a family, and it was obviously not a situation where he was willing to compromise.

"The watch needs to go back," Adrian informed her.

Roslynn hoped like hell she'd heard wrong. "What?"

"You heard me. The watch needs to go back."

Roslynn taking something back to the store was unheard of. He'd never asked her to do that before. "Are you serious, honey? But that's embarrassing."

"Well, you should've thought about that shit before you bought something without my permission, especially when I pay all the bills."

Roslynn walked over to her husband. If he was this upset and had asked her to return the watch, she could only imagine how he'd react about the car. She had to hurry up and put in some major work.

*Maybe playing the guilty role will do the trick*, Roslynn thought. "You're absolutely right Adrian. I understand everything you're saying." She began to rub his chest in a seductive manor, then made her way to the back of his neck which was *his spot*.

Just like she suspected, in a matter of seconds, Adrian's whole demeanor began to change. "Umm…what are you doing?"

"Nothing, just trying to make you feel better."

He was mesmerized by her fragrance. She wore Lovely by Sarah Jessica Parker most of the time. It had a soft sweet smell to it.

"I've been a bad girl, so I should get punished."

"Yeah, you should," Adrian replied. It never took much to get him in the mood.

As Roslynn rubbed the back of his head, Adrian ran his hands over her body and down to her thighs while kissing her neck. She tilted her head back further as she guided his hands to meet her paw print. She spread her legs like she was being frisked by the police. Adrian in return, removed her cami, then licked her back down to her ass. He then tickled her clit with his fingers until he felt her moistness.

"Damn, you wet," Adrian announced.

"Only for you, Daddy," Roslynn replied in a sexy tone.

She grabbed the buckle of his Prada belt, then unloosened it before unbuttoning his pants. As the custom suit pants fell to the floor, Roslynn didn't waste anytime pulling down his boxers and exposing his big dick. His ten inch manhood, was one thing that she loved about him. For an older guy, Adrian still had a nice physique.

Seeing his dick stand at attention, Roslynn slowly began to make her way down so she could give him the head of his life, but Adrian stopped her.

"No, I wanna feel you," he said pulling her back up.

After turning Roslynn around, Adrian slowly positioned her upper torso over the sink, then guided his thick shaft inside her pussy. He spanked her ass with each thrust as she pounced on his dick and repeatedly bumped her head on the cabinet.

Without any other solution, Roslynn placed her hands on the handle of one of the cabinets to prevent from getting a concussion. Her body also began to scrape the kitchen sink, but she was determined to engulf this painful pleasure until he burst all his babies in her cave.

"Fuck me harder, Daddy," she moaned.

During sex was the only time Adrian allowed her to curse.

"Oh shit!" Adrian yelled. He spun Roslynn back around, placed her on the cold granite countertop, then entered her from the front.

She wrapped her legs around his waist and bounced on his dick as fast as she could, hoping that the sex would allow her to keep the watch. Seconds later, he began to squeeze her nipples until his volcano finally erupted.

"I'm cumming!"

"Yes...cum for me, baby," Roslynn whispered. She was a little upset that she didn't get a chance to reach an orgasm, but this time it wasn't about her. It was about a watch and a car that didn't need to go back.

As Adrian's body began to jerk, she ran her hands up and down his back until he finally spoke. "Damn baby, you got the best loving."

Roslynn smiled. "I certainly hope so."

"Trust me…you do," he muffled.

Adrian began to rub his wife's nipples again until his manhood slowly became stiff. Round two was certainly on the way, and it was now or never for Roslynn to break the news to her husband.

"Oh, by the way baby, I bought a new car today," she said, kissing his chest.

His dick immediately went limp.

# Chapter Five

Jazmine made sure to pull into a parking spot that was close to the front door of the East Orange Police Station so she wouldn't be noticed. Doing her wifely duties, and after receiving several threatening phone calls earlier that morning she'd stopped by Vince's job to bring his lunch, but wanted the visit to be as quick as possible, especially since her bruises still hadn't healed. Jazmine had a fair complexion so it seemed as if her marks took forever to go away. Checking her appearance one last time, she glanced into the rearview mirror to make sure the sunglasses were covering her bruised face, then exited her car. However, as soon as Jazmine walked through the front door, she bumped right into Miles, an old friend and one of Vince's co-workers that she'd known for quite some time.

Both Miles and Vince had entered the academy at the same time, but only Miles had moved on to become a homicide detective. Since Vince failed the standard test to become a detective every single time, he took the lame way out and somehow blamed Miles for his failures. He was still an officer…an officer that now pushed paperwork at the station, so to say that he was bitter is an understatement. It was the ultimate hater move, and since then they had nothing to do with each other. Because of Vince's childish behavior, Jazmine wasn't allowed to talk to Miles, so she always tried to avoid him at all cost. This day was no exception.

"Hey, sorry bout that Jazmine," Miles said, with a slight grin. "I didn't see you."

"Don't worry about it," Jazmine replied. She quickly readjusted her sunglasses that had fallen down then turned around to leave.

"Wait," Miles said, grabbing her by the arm. "I haven't seen much of you and Omari around here lately and now I know why." He pulled the glasses down the bridge of her nose, and examined her eye.

Jazmine quickly moved his finger from her face. "It's not what you think." She refused to give Miles any eye contact. Not only because of her bruises, but because he was a very attractive man. Even though he was a red bone just like her, Miles had a pair of green colored eyes that seemed to mesmerize Jazmine every time she looked at him. Not to mention, he dressed very nice, and always treated her with respect. Qualities that Vince lacked at the moment.

"If it's not what I think, then why are you so defensive?" Miles asked.

Jazmine knew she couldn't keep making up excuses for Vince's attacks, but what could she do. Vince told her over and over that if she told anyone he would take Omari and she would never see him again. She nervously looked around the station, to see if anyone was watching them.

"I have to go."

"Look, Jazmine I'm not trying to get into your business, but I'm concerned about you."

Tears formed in the corner of her eyes. "There's no need to be. I'm fine. Now, I have to go find Vince."

At that very moment, Miles' attention was diverted. "Speak of the devil," he said.

Jazmine turned around and was stunned to see Vince standing there with a disapproving look on his face.

"Jazz was just asking me if I'd seen you," Miles said trying to cover for her.

"Was she now?" Vince said with his thick eyebrows raised.

Trying not to arouse suspicion, he wrapped his arm around her waist and planted a passionate kiss on her lips. Fooling people had become an art for Vince, but Jazmine's uneasiness made it so obvious to Miles that something was definitely not right.

"Alright, well you two love birds have a nice day. I've got to get back to work. Gotta lot of unsolved murder cases to work on," Miles stated with a smirk.

Even though it seemed like hard work, Vince smiled as

Miles walked off and a few other officers walked past. However, that smile immediately disappeared once everyone was out of sight. Grabbing her tightly around her arm, he quickly escorted Jazmine to a secluded area of the station.

"What the fuck are you doing?" Vince said, throwing her up against the wall.

Jazmine's head hit the cement block wall with a hard thump. With her eyes widend, she was in disbelief that he was abusing her right at the police station. Then she slowly muttered the words, "You told me to bring you lunch," she said, handing him a sealed Tupperware bowl. "It's baked chicken and rice."

Vince snatched the bowl, placed it on the floor then began to scold Jazmine like she was a child. "Yeah, I told you to bring my damn food, not come in here and flirt with that high yellow muthafucka. What the hell are you doing here so early anyway? It's only 11:00 a.m. You know I don't like to eat until 1:30. I should make your dumb-ass leave and come back at the right time."

"I wasn't flirting with him. I just asked him if he'd seen you."

"Don't ask that nigga shit bout me. The last thing I need is for his bitch-ass to be all up in my business. And what the fuck was up with him callin' you *Jazz*? Huh…what the fuck was that?" he asked, grabbing Jazmine by the arm again.

He looked around to make sure the coast was clear before delivering a quick hard blow to her abdomen. Jazmine collapsed to her knees in pain. Vince was content to let her stay there until he saw some fellow officers walking in their direction. He quickly pulled her up then started kissing and hugging her like they were a couple of teenagers making out.

"Get a room, Anderson," one of the officers yelled out, calling Vince by his last name.

Vince laughed. After they were gone, he grabbed Jazmine by her hair and whispered, "The next time you come up here, call. I'll meet your dumb-ass outside. Under no circumstances are you to come in here again. Do you understand me?"

Trembling like a leaf, she nodded "Yes".

"Now go the fuck home," Vince said, shoving her out of the door. "And you better be there when I call."

✳✳✳

Jazmine drove around for about an hour, not really headed anywhere in particular, but not headed to her house either. Despite Vince's threats, she just didn't want to go home. At this point, she didn't know where to go or who to turn to, but she had to talk to someone about what was going on. The further she drove, the more she began to think about Vince and what went wrong.

When she first met Vince, he was so caring, and treated her like a queen. Jazmine's mother, on the other hand, despised him from the very beginning. She told Jazmine constantly that Vince was putting on a good front, and that he was the devil in disguise. Her mother warned Jazmine not to marry Vince especially only after dating him for three months, but she didn't listen.

Vince was a rookie officer at the time, and already established financially. He also had a nice car, and was an impeccable dresser, so all of that was a turn on, especially when Jazmine was tired of dating thugs and living in the projects. Not to mention, both of her best friends had found men who they wanted to be with, so she had to keep up. When Vince proposed marriage to Jazmine, he told her that she could have whatever she wanted. He promised her a beautiful home, and a chance for a better life. He was offering her the chance of a lifetime, and after living in poverty for so many years she accepted his proposal. It's just too bad he'd failed to keep those promises.

Distraught, Jazmine drove straight to the person she knew could help her get out of this and that person was Roslynn. Pulling up in her friend's driveway, Jazmine was just about to put the car in park, when her cell phone rang. All she could do was let out a huge sigh just before answering it.

"Where the fuck you at?" His pitch was so loud she had to move the phone away from her ear.

"Umm…I'm at a friend's house," Jazmine replied.

She could hear Vince breathing hard. "What friend? I told

you to take your ass home!"

Jazmine didn't want to tell him, but when he repeated the question, screaming at the top of his lungs, she got scared.

"I'm at Roslynn's house."

"Jazmine, you better get your ass home now!" he yelled.

"Please, Vince. I just need to get out."

"Bitch, did you hear what the fuck I just said. Get your ass…" Vince never got a chance to finish before he was cut off.

Surprisingly, Jazmine had pulled out her brave card for a second, and took it even further by turning off her phone. Of course, she knew she would have to pay for her actions later and more than likely with an ass whooping, but right now she didn't care. Sitting in Roslynn's driveway for a few minutes, Jazmine wondered if she was doing the right thing by finally letting her friend in on her secret. It was something she'd kept to herself for so long and she really didn't want to be judged, but letting it out was better than having a nervous break down. A few more moments passed before Jazmine finally got out of the car, walked up to the door and rang the bell.

Roslynn opened the door with a huge smile. "Hey, girl. What you doin' here?"

Jazmine broke down…instantly. "I didn't know where else to go."

"Oh my goodness! Sweetie come in," Roslynn said, grabbing Jazmine by the arm. "What's going on?" She looked at her friend's dingy sweat pants and soiled t-shirt and shook her head.

Jazmine took a seat on the beautiful antique sofa in the family room. Roslynn took a seat next to her.

Jazmine didn't know where to start so she just blurted it out. "Vince has been hitting me!"

Roslynn's face balled up with anger. "What? That muthafucka! I knew he won't shit!" She embraced Jazmine. "So, that's why you been wearin' so much makeup lately, huh?"

Jazmine shook her head. "Yeah."

"Don't worry, I'm here for you." She grabbed Jazmine by the shoulders and looked her in the eyes. "When did this start?"

"A little over a year ago. I started suspecting that he was

cheating on me because he was acting really crazy and hanging out all times of the night. When I confronted him about it, he slapped me."

"Did you go to the police?"

Jazmine shrugged. "How can I? Shit, he is the police."

"So fuckin' what?"

"Ro, police look out for their own. I can go and file as many reports as I want, but they're not gonna do anything. Especially to Vince. He's one of their best officers. Besides, he said that if I ever told anyone he would take Omari away from me."

"Fuck that cock-diesel muthafucka! No judge in the state of New Jersey would give him custody of Omari."

Jazmine stood up and looked out the window. "I don't think he would go through the judicial system. Vince is crazy and I think he would just take Omari and leave. Roslynn, if he does, I might not see him again," she said sobbing.

Roslynn got up and hugged her friend. "Jazz, the only way to stop Vince from doin' that is to go file a police report and get a restrainin' order against him."

"Okay. You're right."

"Or we can go over to Baxter Terrace or Bradley Court and find one of our old homeboys to send his bitch-ass a message. Oh, remember that rough nigga Cordell, Alyse used to date? He still sell drugs around there. I know he'll be willin' to put in some work for a small fee." Roslynn loved it when she could get hood.

"No, if I do it, I want to do it the right way."

"What about yo' mom, Jazz? Couldn't you leave him, and go stay wit' her for a while until you get on yo' feet?" Roslynn knew that Jazmine hadn't spoken with her mom in almost two years, but hoped that they'd spoken recently.

"Ro, you know me and my mom stopped getting along once I married Vince. Besides, he doesn't allow me to talk to her anyway."

This time Roslynn jumped up. "See that's the damn problem. Why the hell do you allow that nigga to run yo' life like that? He can't tell you who you can and can't talk to! I mean look at you, Jazz." Roslynn walked over and pulled on Jazmine's dirty t-shirt. "You don't even care about yourself anymore. It's time to start takin' care of you again. Actually you know what…fuck this."

Roslynn told Jazmine to give her a minute so she could get dressed. She had every intention on taking her friend to Newark so she could finally talk to her mom because at a time like this, Jazmine needed her family for support.

As Jazmine waited for Ro to get dressed, she wondered around the large family room wondering how she got to this place in her life. A few minutes later, Roslynn came down the staircase at top speed, and told Jazmine she was ready to go.

"Where are we going?" Jazmine asked.

"You'll see," Roslynn replied grabbing her Gucci bag along with her keys.

When the two women opened the door and stepped out, they saw a patrol car driving erratically down the street. Once the driver of the car was in clear view, Jazmine started to lose her nerves.

"Oh my God. It's Vince. What are we gonna do?" Jazmine said terrified.

"Girl, calm down and get in my car. I'll handle him." When Roslynn deactivated the car alarm, Jazmine quickly ran toward the passenger's side and hopped in.

Fuming, Vince emerged from his patrol car and ran up to the house. He walked up to the side of the car and banged his fist on the hood.

"Oh, so you gon' turn your fuckin' phone off. Get your ass out of this car and go home!" he roared.

"Muthafucka are you on medication? Stop bangin' on my new shit! Besides, she's not goin' nowhere wit' yo' Ike Turner ass!" Roslynn shouted

Vince walked over to Roslynn. Standing toe to toe, he looked her in eyes. "Bitch, you need to mind your own business."

"She is my business," Roslynn replied. She held a boxer stance to let Vince know she wasn't bullshitting. "Vince, get the fuck off my property. You got me out here actin' all ghetto in my upscale neighborhood!" she yelled looking around.

Vince grabbed Roslynn by the arm. "I'm warnin' you. Stay

the fuck out of this or…"

Roslynn snatched her arm back. "Or what? I ain't scared of yo' cocky- ass. You know me Vince…you know I'll fuck yo' ass up."

Vince placed his hand on his gun. He looked at Jazmine then back at Roslynn. "Or I promise you…you're gonna be sorry."

Roslynn wasn't fazed at all by Vince's threat, but Jazmine knew he meant what he was saying. Not wanting her friend to be harmed, she jumped out of the car and told Vince she would go home. "Just leave Ro alone!" Jazmine yelled.

Roslynn watched in horror as Vince yanked Jazmine by her hair away from the house and then shoved her in the backseat of his patrol car like she was a rag doll or even worse...a criminal.

"We'll get her piece of shit car tomorrow, trick," Vince yelled before pulling off.

"Trick, who you callin' a trick ass…" Roslynn stopped in mid sentence when she saw one of her neighbors pull up in their driveway.

It took all of her not to run behind the car and curse Vince out, as she raised her hand in true Ms. America fashion and gave the neighbor a wave. The fake Roslynn was back.

# Chapter Six

Later that afternoon, Roslynn exited off the 280 highway, turned onto Sussex Avenue, then did her normal routine of making sure her doors were locked. Roslynn was from the hood, so she knew how niggas in Newark operated. Even though she was born and raised in a crime-infested area, there were a lot of people who didn't give a shit, especially when it came to carjacking so she didn't want to take any chances.

It was a typical day of sneaking to the hood for Roslynn. When she wasn't with her girls, she usually spent most days shopping or pampering herself at her favorite spa. However, whenever those things weren't on the agenda, she would drive back to her old hood just to keep herself grounded. Roslynn was definitely booshie now, but was also a hood chick at heart. When she was around Adrian and his friends, she was the perfect classy wife, but when she was around her friends she liked to talk shit and keep it real. She loved living in Paramus, but it could be boring at times. Like when she had to attend fancy social galas with Adrian and his associates. She hated all that nonsense but she had to play the part in order keep her man happy.

As soon as Roslynn made a left onto Orange Street, she shook her head in disbelief. Her old projects, the infamous Baxter Terrace was definitely not the same. It looked like it was a small foreign country at war with its run-down three-story brick buildings accompanied by black R.I.P markings on every wall. The garbage and crack vial littered grounds didn't help either. Because of all this, apparently, the city had decided to tear down the dangerous and drug ridden property, and in a matter of months replace all the residents to other housing projects in the Central Ward like Felix Fuld Court and Seth Boyden Terrace. When that finally happened, it was going to be sad for Roslynn not to be able to see her old building where she grew up, or the concrete courtyard where she and her girls used to hang out, but at least Roslynn still had the memories to hold onto. Driving slowly, she suddenly began to watch as a crack head lit up a pipe right on the sidewalk.

*Damn I miss this crazy shit sometimes,* she thought. *All that's missin' now is a police chase or a shootout, and that'll really bring back old times.*

"Ro, what you doing round here?" a guy yelled interrupting her thoughts.

She rolled down her window halfway. "What...you own Newark now, nigga?" she yelled with a smile. Roslynn didn't even recognize the guy right away, but knew she had to have a sharp comeback. She could see the guy laughing and yelling something as she kept it moving.

Roslynn still had a lot of street creditability, and was what most people would call a ride or die chick. Back in the day if she was with a guy and he got into a gunfight, she would be right next to him popping off as well. Not to mention, the large amount of fist-fights she was involved in. Mothers, aunts, sisters, cousins...it didn't matter who it was, and she damn sure didn't discriminate. Fighting was her passion, and her specialty was fooling people with an angelic look, a misleading feature that Roslynn used to her advantage. Whoever thought she was nice and timid always let their guards down, causing Roslynn to issue some serious beat downs.

After driving past Rutgers University, Roslynn made her way over to Waverly Avenue. She pulled over in front of a Felix Court project building and placed the car in park. She stopped right by a group of guys who where huddled in a small circle. Some were smoking weed, while others were playing a game of dice.

"Montee. Montee, come here!" she yelled out the window.

Montee turned around and smiled showing a mouth full of gold teeth. "Yo' Ro, what's up, Ma? You ain't been to see me in awhile," he said rolling up on Roslynn's car with a stack of money along with the dice in his hand. "Damn, you still fine. When you gon finally let me hit dat?"

Roslynn got out of her car and hugged the slim man. "Please. You can't afford to hit this."

"Shit, you probably got dat right. The cost of yo' pussy been high since back in '99," he responded with a slight laugh. "Where you been hidin'?"

Roslynn looked at her friend, who was black as midnight. "Well, you know how I do. You see me...then you don't."

"See, dats what I be tryna tell 'dese niggas 'round here. You gotta let people look fo you sometimes. Dat keeps 'em guessin'," Montee said banging his fist up against his hand.

Just then one of the guys playing dice yelled at Montee. "Yo' Montee, what the fuck you gon' do? You playin' or what nigga? Bring da fuckin' dice back. I need to win some money!"

Montee clenched his jaw. "Nigga, who da fuck you think you talkin' to? I'll come back ova dat mufucka when I get ready. As a matter of fact." Montee quickly threw the dice on the ground before walking toward the guy. He then lifted up his shirt, and pulled out a black .45 caliber gun. "How 'bout I give you 'dis instead nigga?" Montee yelled. He placed the gun up against the man's face. "Don't you eva fuckin' disrespect me!"

When the guy slowly shook his head, Montee removed the gun. "Now get da fuck away from me before I pop yo bitch ass."

As the man walked away without hesitation, Roslynn just shook her head.

Montee was a dude who Roslynn would definitely give her last to. When she, Jazmine, and Alyse were growing up, he was one of the biggest dope dealers in Baxter Terrace, and gave each of them money whenever they needed it. He also called the three girls his little sisters and kept them safe from dudes in the streets. He was a good provider and substitute father-figure until he served an eight year bid in prison for drug possession and sale of a controlled substance. After getting out, he went right back to doing what he knew best. This time on top of selling drugs, he was also involved in all types of scams. If there was a scam going on, Roslynn would bet any amount of money that Montee was in on it.

When Montee walked back over to her, Roslynn smiled. "I see you still stayin' on top of yo' game around here," she said, sitting on the hood of her car. Normally, she wouldn't have treated her two-hundred dollar Hudson skinny jeans so badly, but this wasn't the time or place to think about material things.

"Shit, dat ain't gon eva change. I gotta keep niggas in check," he replied. "Now, like I said, what you doin' 'round here?"

"Nothin'. I'm just chillin'. I decided to swing through the old hood to see what's up, that's all. What you been up to?"

Montee looked around. "You know me, Ma. I'm on my damn grind. As a matter of fact, I'm workin' on a top secret deal right now. Lookin' to make at least six figures off dis thing."

"Damn, six figures. What kind of deal you got goin' on?" Roslynn asked intrigued.

"Now, you know I can't tell you dat, Ro. Just know it's definitely gonna be my biggest payday when da shit go down."

Roslynn knew that was all she was going to get out of Montee. He never told anyone what his plans were. Most of the time the people who were involved in the scams didn't even know what the plan was until the last minute.

"Yo' Montee, you ready to roll," another man yelled from a nearby alley.

"A'ight! I'll be there in a second," Montee yelled back. He diverted his attention back to Roslynn. "I gotta go take care of somethin', Ma. Holla at me if you need anythin'."

Roslynn smiled. "Montee, you still the same."

"Well you know, I fucks wit' you, so I'ma always look out," he said walking away. He quickly turned back around. "Oh, but shit what da fuck am I talkin' bout. You a balla now. You don't need me no more," Montee said teasing her.

Roslynn laughed. "Stay out of trouble, nigga."

"Dat shit is easier said than done, baby."

Jumping back into her car, Roslynn picked up her cell phone and decided to give Alyse a call before she headed back home. Not only did she want to check on her Goddaughter, but she also wanted to see where her friend was.

"What's up girl?" Alyse mumbled.

"Why the hell you whisperin'?"

"Because I'm at work! You know my bitch of a boss don't

like us usin' our cell phones."

Roslynn made a strange face. "You need to quit workin' at that damn flea bag hotel."

Alyse wasn't in the mood for her shit. "And then do what? I ain't got it like you. Look, I gotta go."

"Wait, I got a present for Brie. Maybe it will make her feel better."

"Oh, 'dat was nice of you, Ro. I hope it makes her feel better because she's still strugglin' wit' 'dat damn fever."

"I'll call you when I get there so you can come outside."

"Bitch, 'dis ain't curb-side service. You gonna have to bring the gift to me cause I got work to do. I'm on the third floor."

"Fine, I'll be over at the roach motel shortly," Roslynn said before hanging up.

Ten minutes later, Roslynn pulled up to the Howard Johnson. She didn't even bother parking in a spot. She just rolled up to the front and put her hazard lights on. "I damn sure won't be here long," she said to herself looking at the hotel and wondering why it was still even in business.

Swinging her weave across her shoulders, Roslynn quickly strutted to the elevators in her four inch Christian Louboutin platform pumps. Her nose was so far up in the air that she walked past several people and didn't even bother to make any eye contact. It was funny how one minute Roslynn didn't mind being in the hood, and the next minute she despised it.

When she finally got to the third floor, Roslynn looked in each room that was open, until she finally found Alyse in room 318.

"Damn, this what you do all day," Roslynn said when she saw Alyse dusting the small desk inside the room. She eyed her friend's unattractive maid uniform.

Alyse threw the small hand towel at her. "What the fuck do you think?"

Roslynn looked around the room and frowned at the outdated flowery comforter and numerous stains on the carpet. "There ain't no way in hell I would be caught dead doin' this shit. Put some damn gloves on before yo' ass catch somethin'.."

**61**

"Ro, you act like you were born wit' a silver spoon in yo' mouth or some shit. Don't ever say what you wouldn't be caught dead doing. I guess you forgot all about the times you had to get on your knees and clean yo' momma's kitchen floor," Alyse said laughing.

Roslynn took off her Prada sunglasses. "Forget you!"

"What you doin' in Newark anyway, Ms. Booshie. I thought you hated this side of town?"

"I went around the way, to Baxter Terrace."

Alyse looked at her friend in shock. "Baxter Terrace. What the hell you doin' around there? Shit, I don't even like goin' back to 'dat hell hole anymore." Alyse smiled. "Girl, Adrian would kick yo' ass if he knew you were hangin' out in the hood."

"Yeah, I know, but Adrian needs to understand that I like goin' back there sometimes. I just feel like I don't wanna forget where I came from. Shit, his ass met me in the hood."

"Bitch, yo' ass is so fake. You do act like you forgot where you came from. Look how you acted at lunch the other day, and how you acted when you came up in here just a few minutes ago."

Roslynn knew her friend was right, but wouldn't dare give her credit. She handed Alyse the gift for Brie. "Give this to my baby. It's a new Ipod Touch."

"A Ipod. Are you serious? Brie is too young for something like 'dat. She's only four, remember?"

"I wouldn't care if she was only two. My Goddaughter de-serves the best. Now, make sure she gets it." Roslynn put back on her glasses. "I'm gettin' outta here before someone sees me in this dump. Come walk me to the elevator."

"Ro, don't you see I got work to do."

"Damn, ungrateful bitch, you can't even walk me to the el-evator. That Ipod was two hundred dollars."

Alyse was so blown. "Well, I didn't tell yo' ass to buy it." She now wished she would've just met Roslynn's ass downstairs. "Come on girl," she said sucking her teeth.

With Roslynn walking slightly ahead, she suddenly stopped like she'd seen a ghost when two men emerged from a room. Two men who were holding hands and kissing each other like they were celebrating something special. They were so caught up in the moment, that they didn't even see the women standing there.

Roslynn was stunned. The guy with the dreads was equally shocked when he finally came up for air and saw Roslynn standing there with her mouth hanging open. Quickly coming out of her trance, she lifted her Blackberry and snapped a picture of the two lovebirds with her phone.

She looked back at Alyse. "I had to take a picture of that sickenin' shit."

When the dread head saw her reaction, he put his hands on his hips and asked, "Honey, is there a problem?"

As soon as he said that, the other guy looked in Roslynn's direction and damn near fainted.

"As a matter of fact, there is a problem because it seems as if yo' lil' boyfriend here works for my husband." Roslynn looked at the Vice President of Adrian's bank, Jerry, with disgust. "Damn, how could you do this to yo' wife?" She could care less about talking proper around him at this point.

"I'm not...It's...not what...you think," Jerry managed to say.

"Not what I think? How the fuck is kissin' another nigga, not what I think? Do you *think*, I'm stupid? You know what, now I know that was you I saw in the mall parkin' lot the other day. You were holdin' that nigga's hand," Roslynn said, pointing to the man with dreads. "I hate a punk muthafucka in the closet."

At that moment, Alyse also realized that Jerry was the man she'd recognized when cleaning the rooms a few days earlier. *Damn, this must be his creep spot*, she thought to herself. She'd seen Jerry plenty of times whenever Roslynn had cookouts over at her house.

Roslynn looked at her watch. "Jerry ain't you supposed to be at work? What the hell you doin' in Newark anyway?" When Jerry didn't answer she continued. "Actually, I was on my way to the bank to see Adrian anyway. Maybe he'll want to know why you ain't at work."

She walked away shaking her head as Alyse followed closely behind. Jerry's first thought was to run after Roslynn and plead for her not to say anything, but he figured that would just be a waste of time.

"So, you have a wife?" Both Roslynn and Alyse could hear the dread head asking Jerry as they made their way to the elevator.

Once Roslynn hit the down button, Alyse asked Roslynn if she knew Jerry was gay.

"Hell no. Shit, I know his wife very well. All of us been on double dates together and them some. I can't believe this."

"Girl, you just don't know who to trust these days. You gonna tell his wife?"

Roslynn wanted to, but then she quickly smelled a strong case of blackmail. "No. Somethin' tells me this information might be more valuable to me at a later time."

Hearing her friend say that, immediately reminded Alyse of the old Roslynn. "Now, why don't I find 'dat shit surprisin'?"

# Chapter Seven

"Mr. Washington, your wife is here to see you. She's walking back to your office," Adrian's secretary announced through the speaker phone.

Adrian looked surprised because Roslynn hadn't said anything about coming to see him. "Really? Okay thanks, Sabrina," Adrian replied just before Roslynn walked in wearing a short black trench coat and red stilettos.

Relaxing in his leather executive chair, Adrian took off his reading glasses then gave his wife a strange look "It's seventy degrees outside, don't you think it's a little too warm for that coat?

Roslynn ignored his question and stood with her hands on her hips. "Why the hell does Sabrina have to announce me like I'm some stranger?"

"Roslynn, haven't I told you before…classy women don't use that sort of language. And remove your hands from your hips. All of that stuff makes you look like a damn hood rat."

"Adrian, did you forget where you met me?" Roslynn walked over and sat in the chair across from her husband's desk.

He rubbed his goatee. "Oh, I know exactly where I met you, but what does that have to do with the way you're supposed to act now. Who in the hell acts like their proud to be from the hood? Besides, the way I look at it, you should be glad I came and took you from that place. It's no telling where your life would be without me."

However, that was just it. Roslynn was proud to be from the hood. She just wished Adrian understood that. "Look, Adrian I appreciate everything you've done for me, but if you just allowed me to be myself sometimes I wouldn't have to…"

Adrian appeared to be hanging onto her every word.

**65**

"Wouldn't have to what? Spend all my damn money, what? Who the hell do you want to be, a fucking hood chick? Well, that's never gonna happen if you wanna be married to me." He played with his diamond cufflinks for a second. "Speaking on money, did you take that damn car back? I called the dealership this morning and told them to be expecting you. Oh, and the watch?"

Roslynn thought Adrian's actions were so embarrassing. Just as she was about to respond, his speaker phone made a loud beeping noise, then Sabrina's voice came through. "Mr. Washington, Jerry wants to know if he can come into your office. He said it was an emergency, but I told him you were in there with your wife."

Adrian looked at Roslynn. "Oh no, send him in. My wife and I aren't talking about anything important."

Roslynn gave Adrian an evil glare as Jerry walked into the office with several folders. By the small beads of sweat on his forehead and the bridge of his walnut colored nose, he looked as if he'd ran up fifteen flights of steps. Walking up to Adrian's desk, Jerry nervously looked at Roslynn with fear in his eyes then began to bite down on his bottom lip.

"What's going on, Jerry?" Adrian asked. "How was lunch? You were gone a pretty long time."

Roslynn looked over at Jerry with a devious grin. Thinking about his poor wife, she wanted to whisper the word dick sucker so bad, but couldn't. "Oh, you just came from lunch. Where did you go? You know they have really great food in Newark. Do you ever go there sometimes?"

As she waited for him to answer, she couldn't believe how such an attractive man could be gay. Jerry was tall, with a medium build and rocked a bald head. He also looked damn good in all his suits, which was another great quality.

One of the beads of sweat, rushed down Jerry's face. "Umm…"

"Roslynn, what difference does it make where he went to lunch," Adrian butted in. "What can I do for you, Jerry?"

Jerry looked at Roslynn again before focusing on his boss. "Well, I know we're getting ready for the audit, so I came to see what things you need me to get on top of, but I can just come back later," he lied. He'd really come into the office to feel Adrian out, and to see if Roslynn had said anything.

"Oh, so that's the emergency. Well, actually we can discuss that now. It's okay to talk in front of my wife," Adrian informed him.

Even though he still seemed nervous, Jerry finally took a seat.

Adrian pulled out a stack of paperwork. "So Jerry, what's going on with the dormant accounts? Have you been in contact with the estates?"

"No, but I'll get on it tomorrow. I've been so tied up lately," Jerry replied.

*Tied up? Shit, the only thing you've been tied to is another niggas dick*, Roslynn thought.

Adrian continued to sift through the paperwork. "None of the dormant accounts have had any activity in over two years and at least four of the accounts have over six figures in them. This bank's reputation was built on customer service, so make sure you contact the estates right away. We need to know the status of each account before the audit."

Jerry shook his head. "Yes sir."

"So, how's your wife Jerry?" Roslynn asked with a smirk on her face.

Jerry choked a little then told her his wife was doing great.

"I'm going to have to call her and see if she wants to do lunch sometime soon. Maybe I'll take her to Newark."

"Why do you keep talking about Newark?" Adrian asked looking back and forth between his wife and Jerry. Roslynn didn't respond.

"Well, I'm gonna leave you two alone now," Jerry said as he stood up. He didn't even wait for a reply before he quickly exited the room. When he left, Roslynn stood up and went over to lock the door.

"Aren't you hot in that damn thing?" Adrian asked referring to the coat again.

"I guess so. Maybe I should take it off." She began to unbutton the coat in a slow manner.

"Okay, what are you up to?" Adrian asked when he saw his wife's naked body.

"Nothing. I just wanted to come and apologize again for getting the car after you told me not to. I'll go turn it in tomorrow," she said, standing in the middle of his office with her breast exposed and swollen.

"So, you came to my office completely naked to tell me that?" Adrian might've hated the ghetto side of Roslynn, but absolutely loved the freaky side.

She walked over to Adrian, turned him around in his chair and sat on his lap. "So what was that you and Jerry were talking about?"

It was hard for Adrian to concentrate. "What are you talking about?"

Roslynn stuck her tongue in his ear. "Something about dorm accounts." She really wasn't interested in their conversation, but had to play it off. The truth was, she'd planned all along to come to his office and seduce him so he'd stop being pissed about the car. Driving home, taking off all her clothes and putting on the trench coat was all apart of the master plan.

"Ro, they're called dormants not dorm. Why are you so interested anyway?" He gave her a surprised look. "Are you thinking about taking me up on my offer to work here?" Adrian had asked Roslynn to become more involved at the bank for years, but she always declined his invitation.

"Umm…no. I just wanted to broaden some of my knowledge about the business."

He went on to explain that dormant accounts were savings accounts that held unclaimed money and had no activity for a specific amount of time. "Do we have to talk about bank accounts right now, though?" he asked, grabbing both of her breast.

"You know how horny I get when we talk about money. Look, see how wet I'm getting," Roslynn said, placing his hand between her legs.

Adrian's dick became rock hard. "Now I know we need to talk about something else," he said, kissing his wife's neck.

Adrian's hands seemed to have a mind of their own by this point. While his fingers caressed her clit, he suckled at her right breast, teasing her at first with gentle licks before nibbling at her nipples.

"That feels good, daddy," Roslynn moaned seductively.

Seconds later, Adrian stopped. "You're still taking your birth control pills, right?" he asked

Roslynn was surprised. "Of course. Why would you ask me that?"

"Because I just want to make sure. The last thing I want is a little snotty nose kid running around."

"You don't have to worry about that, baby."

She began to lay soft kisses on his forehead, then licked his ear lobe before unzipping his pants to release his suffocating penis. That was all it took before Adrian stood with Roslynn holding on and placed her on his desk. Entering her bikini-waxed vagina with a deep thrust, they began to fuck as if he'd just been released from jail. As his shaft filled her inner walls, she clenched her pussy tightly, which made his dick throb. Grabbing both of her ankles, Adrian began spreading Roslynn's legs as far as they could go before giving her several rapid paced strokes. Strokes that eventually caused his body to jerk out of control.

"Shit...I'm cumming," he said slowing down his speed.

Never before had Roslynn felt him climax so acutely. It was as though she could feel every ounce of sperm that he'd released into her body.

Minutes later, Adrian fell back into his chair. "Baby, that was incredible," he said out of breath.

"You know...there's more where that came from," she replied. Hopping off of the table, Roslynn dropped to her knees in front of him, then licked the tip of his manhood nice and slow.

"Oooh...shit," he coaxed.

"How does it feel?" she asked.

"Okay...okay...you can keep the car."

As soon as those words left this mouth, Roslynn smiled then thought to herself, *mission accomplished.*

# Chapter Eight

A week had gone by and the girls were so caught up in their problems that they'd barely spoken to one another. Roslynn, in need of another girl's lunch date, called Alyse and Jazmine on a Thursday, and told them to meet her at Brasilia Grill, a Brazilian restaurant in Newark known for its lavish buffets and live music. She figured that the girls would rather eat in a place less formal and closer to their homes this time. So after finally getting Jazmine to agree, the women decided to meet at the restaurant at 12:00 p.m. sharp.

For the first time since they'd known one another all the girls arrived on schedule, and after greeting each other with hugs and kisses, they settled into three seats at the bar. A bartender took their orders right away. Roslynn and Jazmine ordered grilled salmon, while Alyse, who was on a budget settled for chicken tenders and fries off the kids menu.

"So Jazz, how you been?" Roslynn asked sipping on a margarita. "I ain't seen or talked to you since yo' deranged-ass husband showed up at my house. By the way, why didn't you call me when you came to get yo' car?"

"I didn't come and get it, Vince did. He said I wasn't allowed at your house anymore," Jazmine replied. She played with her usual ponytail. "Honestly, I don't know how much more I can take of this."

"Jazmine, you need to leave his crazy-ass," Roslynn said.

"What's goin' on?" Alyse asked with a confused expression. "Did I miss somethin'?"

Jazmine cleared her throat. She couldn't seem to get the words out.

"Do you wanna tell her or do you want me to?" Roslynn

asked.

Jazmine ran her hands down her face. "Vince has been hitting me."

Alyse's eyes bulged. Not only was she angry at Vince, but she was also angry at Jazmine. "Why didn't you tell me 'dis shit sooner?" Alyse loved Jazmine like a sister so the thought of Vince laying his hands on her made Alyse's blood boil.

It wasn't until Jazmine started crying that she calmed down. When she saw how upset Jazmine was, her heart ached. "Look, we need to pray," Alyse said.

Jazmine and Roslynn both looked confused. Alyse wasn't the religious type, so her statement came as a surprise.

"Don't look at me like 'dat. We need to pray," she repeated.

"A'ight, what the fuck we prayin' for?" Roslynn asked.

"We need to pray 'dat I don't kill his ass," Alyse responded, grabbing their hands.

Jazmine and Roslynn were so tickled. They both pulled their hands back.

"No. I'm serious. He has to be dealt wit'," Alyse admitted.

"See, that's what the fuck I been tryin' to tell her!" Roslynn shouted. "I told Jazz we could call that nigga, Cordell, that you used to mess with Alyse 'cause we know how he get down. Shit, Jazz might not be able to recognize Vince when Cordell finish with him."

Alyse's eyebrows wrinkled. "Cordell. Why even bring him up? I'm done wit' 'dat nigga."

"I didn't say you had to fuck 'em Alyse. I just know that nigga is crazy and…" Roslynn stopped talking when Alyse gave Roslynn a look that said 'no way'. "Fuck it then. We can call Montee and his crew. I just seen his ass the other day."

"Montee would probably be better," Alyse replied. "Plus I heard a few dudes he be runnin' wit' blew some people up in a house about two months ago, and they walk around braggin' 'bout the shit."

"I say we call 'em," Roslynn reiterated.

"I don't want to get him killed. I just want him out my life," Jazmine finally said. She was shocked that Roslynn would suggest getting some thugs to take Vince out. Besides, he was still the father of her son.

"I knew there was somethin' 'bout him I didn't like. I just couldn't figure it out," Alyse said.

"I second that shit. He always looked shifty to me. You sure that muthafucka ain't on somethin'? He was lookin' crazy as hell the other day. His eyes were all red and he was sweatin' like he was meltin' and shit. I mean damn, I know it was hot that day, but that shit was ridiculous," Roslynn added.

Jazmine began to wonder if Roslynn was right. "Well, his outbursts have been random lately. Plus, he'll be sitting in the basement quietly then all of a sudden he'll come upstairs like Jason from Friday the 13th."

"Oh yeah, somethin' shady. I say you go to the basement and find his stash," Roslynn said laughing.

"I've been down there a few times when he's at work to see if I can find something, but nothing ever pops up," Jazmine informed.

"After we eat, we goin' to the police station," Alyse replied in a stern tone. "I mean it."

Jazmine hesitated, but finally agreed. It was time for her to stand up to Vince and she knew her friends would be there to support her. They always helped her deal with any problems, and this time was no different.

They didn't waste anytime digging into their food when it arrived about fifteen minutes later, and of course Roslynn had to mess with Alyse when she placed a chicken tender into her mouth.

"How's yo' happy meal, boo?" she asked placing a well seasoned piece of salmon in her mouth. "Want some ketchup?"

All of the women laughed even though Alyse did roll her eyes.

"So, how's Brie?" Jazmine asked.

"Girl, she drivin' me crazy wit' this bug. Every other day she has a fever which makes her whine all the time. What about Omari? How's he doin'?"

"He's okay. He's getting to that age where he asks a lot of damn questions all the time, but other than that, he's fine."

Roslynn snickered. "See, that's why I don't have any kids. I can't deal wit' all that mess."

"Ever since your baby died a few years ago, you've never wanted to have anymore children?" Jazmine asked.

"Nope," Roslynn replied.

"What about Adrian?" Alyse questioned.

Roslynn shook her head. "He definitely don't want any. He said the only reason he married me was 'cause I didn't have any kids."

"Damn, 'dats deep," Alyse replied.

"Children do get on your nerves at times, but there's no greater feeling than being a mother," Jazmine emphasized.

For the next hour, the girls talked about everything from their families to the latest fashions. Even though they lived very different lifestyles, they had a bond that couldn't be broken.

"So, Alyse, what's goin' on over at the roach motel. You seen Jerry's gay-ass over there anymore?" Roslynn asked.

"Girl, no. Neither one of them gay blades been back. What ever happened wit' 'dat? Did you tell Adrian?" Alyse asked.

"What's going on?" Jazmine inquired.

"Me and Alyse saw Adrian's Vice President from the bank kissin' another nigga," Roslynn informed.

Jazmine's eyes bulged. "You lying. You mean the cute bald headed dude?"

"Yep. That nigga is obviously a fruit cake," Roslynn confirmed. "I didn't even mention that shit to Adrian. I was so busy tryin' to seduce my husband that day, I wasn't even thinkin' 'bout him."

"Yeah, that whole situation was crazy," Alyse responded. "I haven't really been to work 'dat much since then because Brie keeps gettin' sick."

Roslynn laughed. "Maybe she's allergic to livin' in the hood."

"We don't really live in the hood," Alyse said in her defense.

"Umm…I don't know Alyse. Y'all apartment building is not in the best area. Why don't ya'll move out to East Orange with us?" Jazmine asked.

"Lance ain't movin' out there," Alyse shot back.

"How in the hell is his broke-ass gonna tell you where to live?" Roslynn said rolling her eyes. "I don't know why both of y'all ain't let me hook y'all up wit' one of Adrian's rich friends."

Jazmine smiled. "You mean gay friends. No, sorry I'll pass."

"Yeah, I'm fine, too," Alyse added.

"Shit, being broke ain't never fine," Roslynn replied with a smirk. She then went into her purse and pulled out two crisp one hundred dollar bills before handing them to Jazmine.

"What's this?" Jazmine asked.

Roslynn shrugged her shoulders. "If you ever get up the nerve to leave that pshyco fuckin' husband of yours, I know you'll be leavin' wit' nothin'. At least that will get you a hotel room at Alyse's roach motel for a few days. She can even clean yo' room."

Alyse punched Roslynn in the arm. "Shut up."

✳✳✳

After they finished eating and it was time to go, both Alyse and Roslynn were pumped about going to the police station. Jazmine on the other hand was torn about the situation. Going to file charges against her husband would no doubt cause some serious drama in her family and maybe even risk Vince taking Omari away from her. On the other hand, she would be escaping a terrible ordeal that had caused her heartache, disappointment, and physical pain so she decided to go with it.

Fifteen minutes later, each woman pulled up to the station in their individual cars and parked. After exiting the vehicles, they all rallied around each other before going in.

"Maybe we should've gone somewhere else. I mean coming to the same station where he works might not be such a good idea now that I think about it," Jazmine mentioned. "Can we at least come back on a day he's off?"

"Fuck him! His co-workers need to see what kinda' man he

really is," Alyse said, swinging her Target purse across her shoulder. "Besides, he don't even allow you to be out the house when's he's off most of the time."

Jazmine was definitely starting to have second thoughts. "I can't do this. He's gonna take my son! He's gonna take Omari from me I know it."

Roslynn and Alyse were both at a lost. They wanted desperately to help Jazmine, but couldn't if she didn't help herself.

"Jazz, we know you scared, but you gotta do 'dis," Alyse pleaded.

"Look, do you want to keep livin' like this? If you do then let's go, but if you don't then you need to do somethin' about it," Roslynn said, tired of all the bullshit.

A tearful Jazmine didn't answer.

"Jazz, I know 'dis is hard for you, but you have to stand yo' ground. You have to do 'dis not only for you, but for Omari. He shouldn't have to grow up in a house where his father is beatin' his mother. And who's to say his crazy-ass won't start hittin' Omari. You've got to protect yourself and yo' son," Alyse said, hugging her.

Jazmine agreed with her friends then looked at her watch. "It's two o'clock. Vince goes to lunch at the same time everyday, so he'll be back by 2:30. We need to hurry up." She took a deep breath then told them she was ready. With that said, the three ladies walked slowly down the spiral sidewalk and entered the police station.

As soon as the desk sergeant saw Jazmine, he smiled and asked if she was there to see Vince.

Jazmine looked nervous. "Umm…no. I'm not here to see Vince. I'm actually here to file a police report."

The sergeant looked confused. "You want to file a police report?"

His question made Roslynn frustrated. "Ain't that what she said?"

The cop cut his eye at Roslynn then looked back at Jazmine. "I guess what I'm trying to say is why do you want to file a police report? Should we wait for Anderson to come back from lunch? "

"Hell no, we ain't waitin' for him. Plus, it don't matter why. Just find someone to take the damn report, and hurry up!" Roslynn yelled.

Jazmine asked Roslynn to calm down. She was already a nervous wreck and Roslynn was making things even worse.

The sergeant stared coldly at Roslynn. "Ma'am watch your language or I'm going to ask you to leave."

Roslynn was about to start flapping her gums again, but Jazmine quickly told her to stop making a scene. "I'm sorry about my friend, but could you please just hurry and get someone to take my report?"

The sergeant gently patted Jazmine on her hand. "Sure."

He left the desk shortly after, but quickly came back. When Jazmine saw the sergeant walking toward them with Miles of all people, she wanted to ball up and hide.

"Damn. Who is that?" Roslynn asked out loud.

"Umm…you married remember?" Alyse stated.

"I'm married…not dead bitch!" Roslynn countered.

"Jazmine, you know Detective Miles Gardner don't you? He insisted on taking your report," the sergeant said.

Jazmine tried to force a smile. "Of course."

"Hello Mr. Gardner. My name is Roslynn. Nice to meet you," she held out her right hand so he wouldn't see the ring on her left.

"Nice to meet you too, Roslynn," Miles said.

"Umm…how can I get in contact with you? You know, just in case I need a copy of this report." For some reason Roslynn felt like flirting just to see if she still had it. She had no intentions on ever calling Miles. It wasn't worth the risk. Besides, there was no way she would ever fuck with someone with a cop's salary.

"Sure." Miles pulled out his business card.

"Thanks," Roslynn said batting her eyes.

Alyse, on the other hand, rolled her eyes and hoped her friend was only playing.

"Come on, Jazmine. Right this way," Miles said extending his hand. "Your friends can wait here."

After Alyse and Roslynn gave their friend two supportive hugs, Miles led Jazmine down the hall toward his office. However, she suddenly stopped right before walking inside. Scared the whole situation was going to blow up in her face, she turned around and proceeded to leave.

"Jazmine, I promise you. Everything's gonna be okay. Have a seat," Miles assured before pointing to an empty chair.

Jazmine looked back down the hall just to see if Vince was anywhere in sight, then finally walked inside.

Miles closed the door behind him. "Well, the last time I saw you…you insisted that everything was alright, but of course I didn't believe that. So now you can tell me what's really going on." He had a compassionate tone.

Up until now, Jazmine couldn't even imagine telling any-one out of her circle what she'd been going through with Vince. Now she was about to spill her guts to a man she barely knew.

"Vince has been hitting me," she muttered.

Miles grabbed a pen and started to write. "When did this start?"

"Over a year ago," Jazmine answered. "Can I ask you a question?"

"Of course," Miles said listening attentively.

"If I file a report against Vince, will he be arrested?"

"More than likely."

Jazmine sat quietly for a moment before asking her next question. "Will he be held in jail until we go to court?"

"I'm gonna be honest with you. I doubt it. He'll probably post bond and it's up to the State's Attorney's office if there will even be a trial. In the meantime you can get a protection order."

"What about my son? Can he take him?"

Miles didn't want to tell Jazmine that she couldn't stop Vince from seeing their son, but he was obligated to be straight up with her.

"So you're telling me that even if I press charges he may not get locked up until the trial, if there's even a trial and I still have to let him see his son."

"I'm just saying there are no guarantees," Miles replied.

The odds were not in Jazmine's favor and she was beginning to think that no one could help her, especially the justice system. Just when she was about to ask Miles another question, Vince came busting threw the door like he was raiding a house. The depth of his anger almost made her heart stop.

"What the fuck is going on in here?" Vince asked. He looked at Jazmine with piercing eyes. "The desk sergeant told me y'all muthafuckas were back here."

"Like you don't already know," Miles replied sarcastically.

"What the hell are you talking bout?" Vince asked. He inched closer to the desk, but Miles gave him a look that said, 'try it.'

"Look, don't come in my office with all that nonsense. I know what you're doing and you know what you're doing. Now everyone else is gonna know, *Officer Anderson*," Miles said obviously clowning him.

"Nigga, fuck you!" Vince yelled. "You don't know shit 'cause it ain't shit to know. Is it?" he asked, staring coldly at Jazmine.

In a panic, she ran quickly out of Miles' office at top speed, then straight out the front door of the station. Seconds later Roslynn and Alyse ran behind her, but Jazmine never stopped. By the time they made it to the parking lot, Jazmine was already in her car and speeding off like she was a Nascar driver.

# Chapter Nine

Wanting to get away from everyone, Jazmine peeled down Lincoln Street in the opposite direction of her home. She'd gained an instant headache and was sweating profusely. Not wanting to kill herself or anyone else, she pulled into a gas station and sat in her car. *What the hell am I gonna do now,* she thought. *I can't go home. Vince is going to kill me.* All she could think about was getting a serious beat down for pulling that stunt.

"Why the hell did I let them talk me into this shit?" she yelled out loud.

Numb, Jazmine got out of her car and starting walking down the street in a complete daze. She was in such a daze, that she didn't even notice that she'd stepped right into the street and was almost hit by a car. It was like everything was moving in slow motion, and she was like a walking zombie. It wasn't until she heard the sounds of a police siren that she finally snapped out of her trance. A concerned stranger who'd witnessed the incident walked right up to her.

"Ma'am, are you alright?"

Jazmine glared at the stubby man, but didn't respond.

"Do you want me to call someone for you?" he asked. "You walked right out into that traffic."

She looked around. "No, no. I'm fine." She pulled away from the strange man. "I'm fine."

In reality she wasn't fine. Back in the day when she thought of the word psycho, she thought about Anthony Hopkins character in the movie, *Silence of the Lambs* or the lunatic who ate people, Jeffrey Dahmer, but never in her wildest dreams would she consider Vince to be one. It was as if he had no sense of guilt anymore...no conscience, like he was emotionally blind, and that to

**81**

her represented someone willing and capable of doing any damn thing. She couldn't remember the last time he apologized for his behavior or seemed the least bit remorseful, so she knew she had to get her and Omari out of their situation before things got worse. She just had to find the courage somehow to do it.

Speaking of Omari, Jazmine panicked when she looked down at her watch and realized it was 3:02 p.m. Time had slipped away, and she was late picking him up from school. Running back toward her car, all she could think about is if her baby was wondering where she was. Ever since his first day of kindergarten, Jazmine had never been late picking him up, so she could only imagine what he was thinking.

Once she reached her car and opened the door, she jumped inside and grabbed her cell phone so she could call his school and let them know she was on her way. She wasn't surprised to see she had over twenty missed calls. Most of them were from Roslynn and Alyse, the rest were from Miles. What did surprise her was there were none from Vince.

After receiving a busy signal, Jazmine decided not to call back, but to just drive over there, especially since the school wasn't too far away. Making a u-turn in the middle of the street during rush hour, Jazmine gunned the gas pedal for the second time that day. Weaving in and out of traffic at a high rate of speed, she honked her horn in an effort to get the other drivers to move out of her way. It wasn't until she turned onto the street leading to Omari's school when she finally slowed down. The last thing she wanted to do was embarrass him.

Jazmine began to worry when she didn't see Omari standing outside where he usually waited for her to pick him up. She rolled her window down and yelled to Ms. Jenkins in a panic.

"Hey, have you seen Omari Anderson, Ms. Jenkins?" When Ms. Jenkins ignored her, Jazmine got even louder. "Ms. Jenkins, have you fucking seen Omari?"

She finally looked in Jazmine's direction. "Who you cursin' at? If he ain't out here then I ain't seen 'em. He ain't in my back pocket!"

Putting her car in park and turning off the engine, Jazmine

jumped out of the car and ran toward the front entrance. She wanted so badly to punch the ghetto aide right in her face as she passed by, but didn't want to stir up any trouble. Besides, Langston Hughes was a decent public school, and she didn't want to risk getting Omari kicked out.

"You can't park yo' car in front of the school like 'dat!" Ms. Jenkins yelled. "Dats the pick-up drop-off zone only!"

Ignoring the blonde headed woman, Jazmine rushed toward the school's office. As she was made her way through the hall, she spotted a group of Omari's friends from their neighborhood.

"Have you guy's seen Omari?" Jazmine asked.

When the group of friends shook there head no, she was about to lose it. *Maybe he's still in his classroom,* she tried to reason with herself.

When Jazmine rushed into the classroom, the room empty except for Omari's teacher, who was seated behind her desk.

"Hello, Mrs. Anderson," Omari's teacher said, smiling.

"Mrs. Sinclair, where's my son?" Jazmine screamed.

The teacher seemed surprised by Jazmine's reaction. "Calm down Mrs. Anderson. You and your husband must've got your signals crossed. He picked Omari up about a half hour ago."

"Oh my God!" Jazmine said scared. "Why did you let him take my son? He's never been here to pick him up!" In three years, Vince had never stepped foot inside the building, so no one even knew what he looked like.

Now the teacher really seemed concerned. "I'm sorry Mrs. Anderson, I didn't know. Your husband's name is on your son's list, and he had I.D."

Jazmine instantly broke out into a cold sweat as she ran out of the room. Her worst nightmare had come true. Vince had taken her son away from her.

Driving down the street like a bat out of hell, Jazmine proceeded to her house. Worried to death that Vince may try to leave town with Omari, she called his cell phone to try and smooth things over with him. When he didn't answer, she threw her phone down. After driving erratically and honking her horn at a white couple who were driving like they were sight seeing, Jazmine drove her car right up on the curb in front of their house. It didn't matter that she'd fucked up what little grass they had, because instead of landscaping, Vince was only into beating ass. She jumped from her car, and unlocked the door, as fast as she could.

"Omari! Omari," she screamed, running throughout the house. No one was home. She walked over to the cordless phone in the kitchen and called Vince again, but there was still no answer.

Jazmine paced the floor back and forth like a mental patient. She was at a loss, and wasn't sure what to do next. She picked up the phone again, but this time she was calling Roslynn.

"Maybe she was right about calling Montee," Jazmine said to herself. However, just as she was dialing, the front door opened. It was Vince and he had a sneaky look on his face.

"Hey, baby! You look like you had a rough day," he said, laughing his ass off.

"Where is he?" Jazmine asked shaking. Vince ignored her. "Where the hell is Omari?" she yelled.

Vince laughed, then walked away from her. He sat down in the living room and plopped his feet on the coffee table like he didn't have a care in the world. Jazmine followed and told him that if he didn't tell her where Omari was she was going to call the police.

"Bitch, I am the police. Besides, you gonna call'em and tell'em what?"

"I'm gonna tell them that you took my son, you bastard!"

"Don't you mean *our* son?"

"Vince, you better tell me where he is or I swear to God…"

Vince jumped up and got in her face. "Or what?"

Seconds later, the front door opened again. "Hi, Mommy," Omari said walking into the living room with a big grin.

Jazmine ran over to Omari and hugged him like she hadn't seen him in years. She kissed her son over and over. "Are you okay?"

"Yeah. Why?"

"I was just looking for you that's all," she said trying not to cry.

"I was outside. Daddy told me to wait out there for a little while before I came in." He looked at Vince. "Was that long enough, Daddy?"

Vince held a smirk. "Not really. You could'a stayed a little longer. Oh shit! I forgot to tell you Jazmine that I took off from work early and picked him up from school today. Then we went to Cold Stone in South Orange for some ice cream."

Jazmine wanted to shoot Vince with his own gun. She couldn't believe he'd played that type of game. "Honey, why don't you go and do your homework," she said to Omari.

"Okay. Dad you picking me up tomorrow, too?" He seemed excited that his father was finally showing him some attention.

Sitting back down, Vince turned on the television and flipped through the channels. "Maybe son.We'll see about that cuz you…just…never…know…what's gonna happen," he emphasized

Omari left the room confused by his father's comment, but Jazmine knew exactly what he meant.

✳✳✳

Later that evening, Vince went downstairs into the basement, which he called his man cave. It was a place where only Jazmine was allowed when she did the laundry, and where Omari wasn't allowed at all. In the room where Vince hung out, where numerous cob webs in every corner, a dusty couch, coffee table, and an old CD player where he listened to his West Coast rap music. He was a big fan of Dr. Dre, Mac-10, Snoop, and Suge Knight, even though his ass didn't even rap.

After turning on *The Chronic* CD, he went into the bathroom where no one was ever allowed to use and locked the door. Taking a picture of the famous Death Row Vibe magazine cover off the wall, he dug around in the hole that he'd made in the plaster until he found his jackpot. Carefully removing the black sock, he placed it on the sick, then pulled out the only thing that he loved at the moment…his drugs. His secret for two years. Vince had used drugs off and on back in the day, but now it was a consistent habit. Using up to two times a day when he had a stash. Seeing the product made his eyes beam, and just like the functioning addict he

85

was, Vince sat down on the toilet seat, pulled up his sleeve, and wrapped the rubber band around his arm. After filling the syringe with the brown powder, also known as Superman on the street, he plucked his arm to find a good vein. Once a big green one was in sight, he pricked it with the needle and injected the contents.

Within seconds, his eyes rolled in the back of his head as the drug took total control of his body. Once the syringe was empty, he slid it out of his arm and sat back on the toilet. He sat dazed for a few minutes as a delicious warmth spread throughout his body…totally satisfied about the feeling of relaxation he was experiencing. No more fears, no more painful memories of his father striking him and his mother everyday. No more excruciating memories of his father sneaking into his bedroom almost every night. Memories that he hadn't shared with a single soul…memories he would take to the grave.

After sitting there and nodding for what seemed like forever, Vince placed the dirty needle and the rest of his drugs back in the sock. He stood up, reached inside the hole and carefully placed the sock back inside. Also in the hole were tubes of Mederma, and Ambi Fading Cream which he used to keep the scaring down on his arms. High or not, Vince always pulled out the cream and placed it on his arm just before placing the picture back on the wall.

When he finally went back upstairs and into the kitchen to get something to drink, Jazmine was preparing dinner. Stumping around, he kept going on and on about how he could take Omari and make sure Jazmine never saw him again if she came to his job.

Jazmine saw how red Vince's eyes were and just thought he was drunk. She knew he was doing something down in that basement, but just didn't know what it was. "Maybe you need to go lay down 'cuz I'm not arguing with you tonight."

"Fuck you, bitch. You go lay down."

Trying not to get him started, Jazmine immediately left the kitchen and went into the living room.

"And I'll tell you something else. You pull another fucking stunt like you did today and the next time I'ma pick Omari up and keep going." Vince started laughing and dancing around the living room.

Without warning, all of Jazmine's pent up frustration came to a head.

"You know something is wrong with your crazy-ass. I don't give a fuck how you feel bout' me, just leave my son out of it!" she belted. Fuming, she turned around and walked upstairs to their room.

Vince was surprised at Jazmine's bold speech. He thought after all the beatings she would be too scared to speak to him that way, but he was wrong. She was obviously a woman fed up and she was letting him know it.

"Like I said before bitch, you can leave but my son ain't going no fuckin' where," he said following her into the bedroom.

"I know. I know. You make the money. I'ma leave here broke. Save it because I am gonna leave and I'm gonna take Omari with me. Little do you know, I wouldn't dream of leavin' my son here with your psychotic-ass!" Jazmine hated arguing with Vince with Omari in the other room, but she was sure, her son was used to it by now. She pointed to his work-out area. "Vince, just leave me alone. Go over there and lift some weights like you always do!"

Running up on her like a ragging bull, Vince slammed Jazmine up against the wall and reached into his pants and pulled out his small Micarta pocket knife. After opening it, he placed the sharp nine inch blade up against Jazmine's face.

"Bitch, how bout' I kill him then neither one of us will have him."

Jazmine couldn't believe what she was hearing. She was absolutely horrified at Vince's threat.

"How could you threaten your own child's life?" she said, staring at the tip of the knife.

Vince moved the knife to the side of Jazmine's neck. When he started licking her face and barking like a dog she knew something was definitely wrong with him.

"I wouldn't have to if you would just keep people out of our fuckin' business and stop tryin' to turn him against me."

Jazmine cut her eyes at Vince. "You think he doesn't know

what's going on. He sees how you threaten me, so if anyone's to blame it's you!"

Vince grabbed her head and smashed it against the wall. "Shut the fuck up!"

Breathing heavily, Jazmine responded, "The truth hurts, doesn't it." Even though Vince could've cut her at any moment, she didn't care. Jazmine was tired of living in fear.

Vince lost it. Throwing the knife down, he started punching Jazmine in the face. Omari could hear his mother screaming from his room, so he ran to her aid.

"Daddy stop!" he yelled, as he tried to grab his father by the waist.

Vince swung from Omari's tiny grip and shoved him to the floor.

"Oh, you want some too!" Vince yelled. He raised his hand to strike Omari, but Jazmine threw her body over him to block the blow.

"Get away from him!" Jazmine shouted.

Vince told her to shut up as he grabbed the knife again, then cut her ponytail completely off. Afterwards, he threw it in her face and laughed. Adjusting his clothes, he looked down at his crying wife and son before leaving the room. "Now, carry your ass downstairs, and finish cooking my dinner, and that shit better be done by the time I get back."

Jazmine stayed on the floor, until she heard the front door to the house close. She immediately helped Omari up on the bed and asked if he was okay. With his eyes filled with tears he nodded yes.

"It's okay, baby," she said, hugging him. "It's alright."

Omari sat closely to his mother, holding on to her for dear life. He hated seeing his mother hurt. He was starting to hate his father.

"Mommy, let's just leave," he whispered. "I have some clothes in my backpack already."

Jazmine kissed Omari on the forehead. Seeing him so upset, made her realize that it wasn't just Vince's fault, she was partly to blame too for not leaving when the beatings first started.

Tears began to race down her face as she looked on the floor at her ponytail. She'd been growing her hair since Omari was born, and now she had to start all over.

"We will, honey. I just have to get a few things ready first, but I promise you we're gonna leave soon."

Omari was so glad to hear his mother say they were leaving, he just wondered when she would keep her promise.

# Chapter Ten

"Oh, that's my shit!" Roslynn yelled as she turned up the radio in her car and sung the lyrics as loud as she could.

Up early for a Friday, Roslynn was on her way to a hair appointment, which always made her feel good. Besides, she needed a little pampering after dealing with Jazmine and her drama the day before. With her convertible top down, she loved the way the wind whipped through her hair. She also loved the fact that Adrian had allowed her to keep the car.

*If this is love, real, real love, then I'm staying no doubt*
*But if I'm just a prisoner, then I'm busting out*
*Is that true? Is that true? Is that true?*
*Well, I don't like living under your spotlight*
*Just because you think I might find somebody worthy*
*Well, I don't like living under your spotlight*
*Baby, if you treat me right, you won't have to worry*

Roslynn absolutely loved the song, *Spotlight* by Jennifer Hudson and turned it up every time it came on the radio or when she played the CD. The girl could definitely sing, and she'd asked Adrian to book the Oscar winner for her birthday party next year, but he said no of course. Instantly, Jennifer's recent family tragedy began to invade Roslynn's thoughts, and she wondered how well her favorite artist was doing.

Just as Roslynn was about to sing the chorus again, her cell phone rang. When she looked at the caller ID she didn't recognize the number, and was reluctant to answer it, but decided to answer it anyway.

She turned the music back down. "Hello."

"Yes, may I speak to Mrs. Washington?" the woman asked in an annoying tone.

"Speakin'. Who's this?"

"Mrs. Washington, this is Paige from FIA Card Services. I'm calling about your April payment, which we didn't receive."

*Oh shit,* Roslynn said to herself. She'd completely forgot to pay her platinum Visa credit card bill. Just one of four credit cards that Adrian knew nothing about. "Yes, it's in the mail."

"Do you know what day it was mailed so I can document it? This way you don't receive anymore calls from our office."

"I actually just mailed it yesterday. I'm sorry it's late."

"That's fine. We understand these are stressful times for everyone," the woman said trying to be pleasant.

"Thank you. Have a good day," Roslynn said before hanging up.

"I forgot to check my damn Hotmail account," Roslynn said to herself. She'd opened up an email account that Adrian wasn't aware of, so her paperless credit card statements could be routed there, but she'd been slipping lately. With an $18,000 balance on that card alone, her minimum payment was a little over four hundred dollars a month, so she couldn't by any means, get behind. It was bad enough every time she withdrew the cash to pay the bill, Roslynn had to lie and say the money was for spa treatments, new weaves, the list goes on. One time she even acted like two of the tires on her car had slow leaks, and needed to be replaced. Roslynn used any excuse whenever she needed cash in order to cover up her hidden debt, but she had to admit…the games were getting old.

Roslynn arrived at First Class Hair fifteen minutes later. With a Caramel Frappuccino from Starbucks in one hand and her Hermes Birkin bag in the other, Roslynn walked in like the diva she was. Ty, her gay stylist had been doing Roslynn's hair for years, but he was much more than that. He was more like a brother. Whenever Roslynn needed to talk, he was there to listen and vice versa.

"What's goin' on?" she asked, kissin' him on both cheeks.

"Oh, nothing much just being my usual wonderful self," Ty said, swinging his long weave. "And honey, I must say you're still the flyest bitch in New Jersey besides me of course."

"You are so damn crazy," Roslynn said, taking a seat in his chair.

Ty ran his hands through her weave. "It's about time for this mess to come out. You've been rocking this style and color for too long."

"Adrian would probably love that shit. He hates fake hair."

"Honey, that husband of yours is a mess. So, are we taking the weave out and giving you a short chic cut today?" Ty asked. "I mean Daddy does pay my tab."

Roslynn laughed then did her signature move of tossing the weave over her shoulder. "Hell, no. I like my hair. Just take this out, and give me something new."

The two chatted some more, but Roslynn seemed distracted when she saw a number come across her cell phone screen. She didn't answer. From that moment on, Roslynn seemed preoccupied. Even Ty noticed how distant she was, especially when he started removing the weave from her hair. Roslynn was extremely tender headed and usually complained when he pulled on her scalp the least bit. This time she didn't say a word.

"Ms. Thang, what's up with you today? You're not your usual diva self," Ty mentioned

"I just have a lot on my mind today."

Ty laughed. "I knew something was wrong with your ass because you're usually a little chatter box up in here."

"Shit, even Diva's have rough days," Roslynn replied.

"Hell, everyday is a rough day for me, especially when I gotta deal with simple minded folks like that cunt in the booth next to me."

Roslynn looked up at Ty. Luckily the new stylist next to him wasn't there, so they didn't have to talk in codes like they normally did. She was a young girl, fresh out of hair school, who obviously hadn't learned much. Every time she did someone's hair, they complained. She also didn't like Ty for whatever reason, causing them to argue all the time.

"I thought she got fired when she fucked up that ladies perm," Roslynn inquired.

"Honey, the owner ain't gonna fire her. You know they

fuckin', right?"

"Ty, shut up."

"Yes, girl. The owner slippin' his dick all in and out that coochie."

"Ooo…Ty you need to stop."

"And I'm mad 'cause I been trying to get that dick for the longest. Now that little skank gonna bring her lack of talent ass up in here with us professionals and get a hold of that meat. I'm pissed."

Roslynn laughed so hard she spilled some of her coffee. "Oh shit, I just bought these jeans."

"Child, please. Just take that Amex Black card out and swipe it at Saks again."

"Yeah, you right. I'll just go buy me another pair. Hell, I need to buy three more pairs," she said trying not to let him in on the fact that her spending was being monitored.

While Ty continued to take out her weave, Roslynn checked her emails on her Blackberry. When she saw an email from yourpartner@yahoo.com, she got irritated. *What the hell does she want,* Roslynn thought. *I wish she would just leave me alone.*

When she opened the email, her eyes widened. She almost went ballistic.

I see you wanna play fuckin' games by not answerin' yo' phone so in dat case I want 5 thou by next week. If not, then I'll be visitin' Adrian over at Washington Savings & Loans. By the way I already got a account there so if you want, just tell him to transfer it.

Roslynn shook her head. *This bitch has completely lost her damn mind.*

Ty had just taken out another track when Roslynn told him she had to make an important phone call outside. Her mind was spinning as he asked her several questions.

"What…I didn't hear you," Roslynn asked. She stood up to leave.

"I said I ain't finished yet," Ty said, standing with his hands on his hips. He couldn't believe she was willing to go outside with exposed corn rolls in the front of her head and weave along the sides and the back.

"I know, but I gotta make this call."

Roslynn rushed out of the salon and quickly walked to her car. After getting inside, Roslynn dialed a familiar number. When the woman picked up, she immediately started yelling into the receiver.

"What the fuck was that email about?"

"Oh my…you can take da girl out of da hood, but you definitely can't take da hood out of da girl," her cousin, Kamilla, sarcastically replied.

"You got that shit right and don't forget it."

"Da email shoulda been clear. I need some mo' money."

Roslynn looked at her phone as if she was hearing things. "Bitch, you must be crazy or something. How am I supposed to get that kind of money from Adrian? He monitors our accounts like a fuckin' prison guard. Plus, I just gave yo' ass two thousand a few weeks ago. Do you know every time I give you money, I have to lie and say I blew it on shopping?"

"So what. I got bills to pay. I don't give a shit what you have to do to get da money."

"Hell no! I'm tired of you tryin' to hustle me!" Roslynn yelled.

"Hustle you? Bitch, I did you a favor. I could've exposed yo' lil' secret a long time ago, but I didn't. Let's face it. I'm runnin' dis shit. One word from me and yo' husband will have you in da first cab back to Baxter Terrace."

As bad as Roslynn hated to admit, Kamilla was right. If Adrian ever found out about her past he would leave her for sure. Suddenly, Roslynn felt an urge to tell Kamilla to go to hell, but she didn't want to antagonize her any more than she'd already had. As much as she hated her cousin, Kamilla had gotten Roslynn out of a jam when they were teenagers. Kamilla told Roslynn that she would never tell anyone about the deep dark secret, and kept her word. That is, until Kamilla found out Roslynn married someone with money, and was living well. From that point on, Kamilla started extorting money from Roslynn in exchange for her silence.

Annoyed with Kamilla's threats, Roslynn decided to pull her card. "Just think about it. You tell my husband about our deal and he leaves me, then yo' ass will end up broke and on the streets, too. So you see, I'm not the only one who will lose out on their luxurious life."

Kamilla was quiet. She really hadn't thought about that, but she still felt that Roslynn had more to lose than she did so she shot back. "Since you wanna play fuckin' games make it ten thousand and I want it by next week, or kiss dat beautiful big house you live in good-bye," she said before hanging up the phone in Roslynn's ear.

Panicked, Roslynn tried to call Kamilla back, but her phone went to voicemail.

"Shit!" Roslynn yelled, slamming her phone down. She had no idea where she was going to get that kind of money without Adrian realizing it was gone, but she had to figure it out.

# Chapter Eleven

That same day of Roslynn's drama, Alyse was having a few problems of her own. She was running late for Brie's doctor appointment and Lance was nowhere to be found. They'd discussed him accompanying her to the doctor's office, but when she woke up and found him gone, she assumed he couldn't take the day off. Hell, Alyse's bitch of a boss, Jackie wouldn't give her the day off either, so she had to call out sick earlier that morning. Jackie viewed Howard Johnson like a Fortune 500 company, and undedicated employees were huge pet peeves. If Brie didn't get better anytime soon, Alyse probably wouldn't even have a job to go back to.

Once Alyse and Brie were ready to go, they made their way to the car and climbed inside. However, when Alyse tried to start it, the engine wouldn't turn over.

"Shit!" she screamed, then hit the steering wheel.

Waiting for a few seconds, Alyse tried to start the Toyota Corolla again, but it still wouldn't budge. She was pissed because she'd told Lance about the problems with her starter a week ago and he promised to have it checked out. With no time to waste, she had no other choice, but to pull out her cell phone and call a cab. It wouldn't have been such a pressed type situation if Brie would've been going to her regular pediatrician, because that hood spot didn't even care if you showed up. However, this was a new doctor that Jazmine had referred her to, so Alyse wanted to be on time.

Waiting for the cab to arrive, Alyse stood outside her apartment building and called Lance's cell phone again. When he didn't pick up, she got even more annoyed with him and hung up.

"His ass ain't never available when I call," she mentioned to herself in a low tone. Alyse had no idea what was wrong with

Lance lately, but she'd made it a point to get some answers as soon as they talked.

Within a few minutes, the cab driver was in front of the apartment blowing the horn as if he didn't see them standing there. As Alyse grabbed Brie by the hand and started toward to the car, he had the nerve to blow the horn again.

*We comin' asshole*, Alyse thought as she opened the back door and helped Brie inside.

"Why the hell you keep blowin' the horn? Didn't you see us there?" Alyse asked.

"Where you headed?" the rude cab driver asked, looking over the seat. He never answered her question.

"30 Bergen Street. We runnin' late too, so if you don't mind, can you hurry," Alyse inquired.

"It depends if there's traffic. I can not break the law Ma'am," the cab driver said in a thick Arabian accent.

"A'ight just drive." Alyse rolled her eyes and started muttering under her breath. *Fuckin' foreigners.*

The driver started the meter, then drove off. Traffic was surprisingly light that morning, so Alyse started to relax a little, especially after glancing down at her watch. So far they were making good time. She reached over to braid one of Brie's ponytails that had come undone, then stared at her daughter as she played with her new Ipod.

"I hope 'dis doctor can tell us what's wrong wit' you, pumpkin," Alyse said. "I know you tired of being sick."

Brie shook her head, but never once took her eye off her new electronic toy. The Ipod hadn't been able to help with Brie's health, but it certainly helped with her spirit. Alyse reminded herself to have Brie call and thank Roslynn for the expensive gift. She was thankful for her friend as well. Roslynn's ability to buy Brie things that she could never afford was a blessing, and their friendship was priceless.

Tears began to form in Alyse's eyes and she turned to look out the window. As the cab made a right onto Springfield Avenue, her watery eyes almost popped out of her head when a familiar face caught her attention. It was her husband Lance and he was coming out of a movie theater.

"What the fuck?" she said out loud.

Brie finally looked up. "What's wrong, mommy?"

"Nothin', baby."

Alyse turned and looked out the rear window to make sure she wasn't seeing things. Sure enough it was him. She couldn't pull the cell phone out of her purse fast enough. Calling him for the third time, she prayed to God that he would pick up. A few seconds later her prayers were answered.

"Hey baby. What you doing?" Lance asked.

Alyse's first instinct was to tell the cab driver to turn around so she could get out and beat his ass. Here she was trying to get their daughter to the doctor and he was at the movies without a care in the world.

"What the fuck you think I'm doin'?" she snapped. "Where are you?" she asked already knowing the answer.

"I'm at work. Why?"

Now she really wanted to tell the cab driver to stop. "Oh, so you work at the fuckin' concession stand now? You askin' people do they want butter on they popcorn and shit?"

"Alyse, what are you talking about'?" Lance asked, playing dumb.

"I'm talkin' 'bout yo' ass. I just saw you walkin' out the Newark 6 movie theatre on Springfield Avenue!" she yelled. "I can't believe you lied to me. What the hell are you doin' off in the middle of the day?"

Lance couldn't say a word. He just sat quietly while Alyse cursed him out in what seemed like seven different languages.

"Did you forget 'dat Brie had a doctor's appointment today?"

"Oh shit. I'm so sorry, honey."

"Dat sorry shit ain't gonna help Lance. Do you know that me and yo' daughter are in a damn cab right now? My car wouldn't start. I asked you to get it fixed!"

Lance paused. "I know, Alyse. I guess I forgot about that, too."

Alyse was silent for a moment. She couldn't believe how

Lance was acting. Moments later she could see the cab driver pulling up to the office building.

"Look, I gotta go. We pullin' up at the doctor's office. Oh, by the way is 'dat insurance stuff taken care of?"

"Yep." Lance couldn't bear to let his wife down a third time.

"You know, I can't believe that you forgot about this appointment. Thanks for lettin' me know 'dat you don't wanna be a responsible fuckin' father anymore."

The statement cut Lance deep, and it was at that moment, when he thought to himself that lying probably wasn't the best decision.

"You don't need to say nothin' else to me until you figure out what the hell is goin' on wit' you," Alyse said before hanging up the phone.

Lance had obviously let his pride cloud his judgment and now he was about to pay for that decision. Just like the last time, Alyse would soon find out that the insurance company wasn't going to pay for this visit either, which was going to put him in a serious bind. Lance knew eventually he would have to tell his wife the truth. Have to tell her that he was behind on all of their bills, but he just wasn't ready. The whole predicament made him feel like a failure.

✳✳✳

When Alyse and Brie walked into the office, they were greeted with a warm smile from an older, grey haired, African American woman who was obviously the receptionist. They hadn't even been there five minutes and already the experience was different from their regular doctor. She asked Alyse her name then gave her a few forms to fill out. When Alyse was finished, she handed the forms along with her insurance card to the receptionist, then said another quick prayer to God, hoping that everything would work out. After making two photocopies, the receptionist handed the card back to Alyse.

"The doctor will be with you two shortly," the receptionist

announced with another smile.

"Thank you."

Alyse took a seat next to Brie, who was back into her Ipod again and began to wait. To her surprise, she hadn't even gotten to page four of the People magazine she was reading before a nurse called Brie's name.

"Wow, I like 'dis place already. Normally I can read 'bout four magazines before we're called," Alyse said to herself. She put the magazine down, then grabbed Brie's hand.

Walking to the back of the office, the nurse led them to a colorful room that was painted with Disney cartoon characters. She took Brie's blood pressure, temperature and weight, before telling them the doctor would be in momentarily. While they waited, Brie finally put her Ipod down, and played with the numerous toys in the room. A few seconds later, the doctor walked in.

"Hello, I'm Dr. Salter," he said, shaking Alyse's hand.

"Hello, Dr. Salter. I'm Alyse Greffen and this is my daughter Brie."

He grabbed the end of Brie's nose and gave it a playful pinch. "Well, hello Ms. Brie."

Brie smiled from ear to ear.

"So, Mrs. Greffen, what's the reason for your visit today?"

Alyse began to describe Brie's symptoms and told him all the medication she'd been taking recently. After telling Brie to hop up on the table, the doctor began to examine her lymph nodes, tonsils, then listened to her heart and chest cavity with his stethoscope.

He looked at Brie's chart. "Did she have any blood work done at the hospital?"

"No, not at all," Alyse replied.

"Well, it might not be a bad idea if she does at this point, especially since she can't seem to shake her fever. I'm going to send in a nurse to give Brie some medicine to reduce the fever as well as take a few tubes of blood."

Brie looked straight at her mother. She was only four, but she knew what the word blood meant. Relating the word with pain, she started crying before the doctor even left the room.

"Don't worry, Mrs. Greffen. We have a new technique we use which should only cause minimal discomfort."

Alyse shook her head. "Okay."

Alyse held her daughter in her arms and tried explaining to her how important it was to have her blood taken. "Honey please stop crying. The only way for Dr. Salter to find out what's making you sick is to look at your blood."

Brie wasn't trying to hear a word Alyse was saying. As far as she was concerned it just wasn't happening and when the nurse came in she made it known in no uncertain terms. She kicked and screamed in dramatic fashion until the nurse drew the last tube. One part of Alyse was ashamed at the way Brie was acting, but the other half understood because she hated needles, too.

When Dr. Salter returned to the room, Brie was still sobbing. "Because Brie has been so sick, I do realize the urgency to find out what could be the problem. In this case, we can put a rush on the blood work."

"How long does a blood test normally take?"

"Usually, it can take anywhere from two to four days, but my wife works in the laboratory, which is not too far from here, so I can put in a call." Dr. Salter smiled, then winked at Alyse. "I'll have a courier rush over and pick up the blood work."

"Thank you so much." She was grateful for his concern.

"We have our own little cafe in the building. I think it might be a good idea to get Brie a bite to eat so she doesn't get weak."

Alyse agreed. She left the doctor's office and took the elevator down to the first floor where the café was located. It was a small but comfy place that served mostly coffee and pastries. She ordered a ham and swiss sandwich with fruit juice for Brie and an apple Danish for herself. By this time, Brie started whining, which was an instant indicator that she wasn't feeling good anymore. Alyse hoped the blood work would show the cause of Brie's illness.

Alyse unwrapped Brie's sandwich and put a straw in her juice box, but she refused to eat. Instead, she laid across her mother's lap and moaned. Alyse felt her forehead and once again she was burning up.

"Oh my goodness, Brie. What's wrong wit' you?" she asked her daughter, as she rubbed her back.

"I wanna go home," Brie cried.

"I know honey, but we have to wait for yo' tests. It shouldn't be long, okay."

Brie didn't respond, she just kept whining until Alyse finally had enough and took her back up to Dr. Salter's office. When she opened the door, the receptionist asked if she could speak with her for a moment.

Alyse had heard that tone before. *Here we go again,* she thought.

"Your visit will be three hundred and twenty five dollars today."

Alyse almost passed out. "Three hundred and twenty five dollars? Why? I have insurance."

"Well Ma'am, when we contacted the insurance company, they informed us that your policy was canceled."

Alyse wanted to cry. She couldn't believe that Lance had lied to her once again. "Is there anyway to bill me?" she asked in a lower voice. The longer she stood there, the more embarrassed she became.

The receptionist shook her head. "No Ma'am. We need the payment made today."

Alyse had to think of something quick. She went into her purse like everything was under control. "Do you take checks?"

"Yes we do."

Alyse pulled out her checkbook. *This check is gonna bounce all over fuckin' Newark,* she thought as she wrote the check. "Here you go."

"Thank you. I'll get you a receipt."

"My daughter is feelin' really bad and needs to lie down. Can I take her back to one of the examinin' rooms?"

"Of course. Let us know if we can do anything else for you," the woman said.

Despite her insurance drama, Alyse found the receptionist to be very pleasant, which was definitely appreciated, especially compared to the receptionist in her regular doctor's office. They all came to work with a stank attitude, but Alyse made it her business to tell them off every time she went there.

Alyse picked Brie up and took her back to the examining room. After sitting there for at least twenty minutes, Alyse couldn't take it anymore. She got up and started pacing the floor.

"I wish they would hurry up," Alyse said, rubbing her hands together. The longer she waited, the more nervous she became.

In the middle of one of Alyse's paces, Dr. Salter walked in and told her that he wanted to admit Brie into University Hospital for more tests.

Alyse panicked. "Why, what's wrong?"

"I wish I could answer your question, but I don't want to speculate prematurely. I'm going to call the hospital and set up everything, but you need to go straight there."

Alyse began to cry. "We can't wait 'til tomorrow? I need to let my husband know what's goin' on."

"I really think you should go today. I'll set everything up for you."

"Okay, but there's one problem?" Alyse said, looking over at her daughter who had fallen asleep. "I don't want her goin' to University Hospital. One of the doctor's over there was the one who told me everything was okay. 'Dat she probably had the flu. He obviously doesn't know what he was talkin' 'bout." She was very emotional.

"Please calm down, Mrs. Greffen. We can go over to Children's Hospital if that makes you feel any better."

"Why…why does she need to go to the hospital anyway? Why today?"

"The reason I'm suggesting you go today is because your daughter's blood work came back abnormal. I feel that she should be hospitalized immediately for further testing. They should be able to give you more precise answers after they run the tests I suggest. Would you like to drive her there or would you like for me to call an ambulance?" Dr. Salter asked. "I have to be honest though. Insurance companies are starting to lower the amount they pay toward paramedic fees, so you may have to come out of your pocket a little for the transportation. If I were you, I would just drive myself."

As frustrated as she was, Alyse wanted to say 'Sir, I don't even have any damn insurance or a car'. Instead, she pulled out her cell phone to call Lance. There was no way in hell she was about to take a cab to the hospital.

Alyse felt like she was in the middle of a nightmare. Her daughter was seriously ill and no one knew why, and her husband was a fucking loser. However, even though she was pissed at Lance, at a time like this he needed to be there. Along with calling him she also called Roslynn and Jazmine so they could meet her at the hospital. Right now, Alyse needed all the support she could get.

# Chapter Twelve

By the time Alyse, Brie and Lance got to the hospital, Roslynn had already been there for fifteen minutes pacing the floor like Alyse was doing earlier. Because she'd gotten the call before Ty had a chance to finish her new weave, Roslynn looked like Cousin It from the Adams Family. You could barely see her eyes from the way the uncut, virgin Indian hair laid in her face.

"It's about time y'all got here," Roslynn said, when she saw Alyse and Brie walking through the automatic doors of the hospital.

Alyse was so shaken up, she immediately broke down as soon as she saw her friend. "I don't know what's goin' on," she said, wiping the tears.

Roslynn pushed the hair out of her face. "Well, this is a good hospital. They'll find out what's wrong wit' her." She turned to Brie. "You're goin' to be fine sweetie. Roslynn was even sympathetic. It was no secret that she wasn't the maternal type, but seeing Brie looking so sick melted her heart.

"Auntie Ro, you have new hair," Brie said.

Roslynn smiled then removed the hair again. "Yes, baby. Auntie Ro didn't have time to cut it though. As soon as I heard about you, I rushed right over."

"Where Jazmine at?" Alyse questioned.

"Where you think? Locked up in the damn house. Vince took off from work today, so she can't sneak out. I'm so sick of his ass." Roslynn sucked her teeth.

"Oh. Well, can you watch Brie for me? I'm gonna go register her," Alyse said. "Lance is parkin' the car, but he should be here in a minute."

"Okay." Roslynn took Brie by the hand and led her to the

waiting room.

When Alyse took a seat at the registration desk, she told the registrar her name and immediately pulled out her fake insurance card. At this point, it was fake because the policy was canceled and she knew it. However, that wasn't gonna stop Alyse from trying to get her daughter some medical attention.

"Oh, Mrs. Greffen. Dr. Salter called, and told us that you'd be coming. I just need you to fill out this form giving us permission to treat your daughter along with your ID and insurance card. No need to fill out any other paperwork right now."

While Alyse signed the paperwork and the registrar made copies of her ID and insurance card, Lance walked over and placed his hand on her shoulder.

"There you go," the registrar said, handing the items back to Alyse.

When Lance saw the insurance card, he and Alyse looked at each other for a brief moment before he lowered his head. Alyse on the other hand rolled her eyes.

When the registrar called for a transport, it only took a few minutes for a tall hefty man to come over with a wheelchair. "Mrs. Greffen, he's ready to take your daughter up to the pediatric unit," the registrar informed.

"Can me and my husband go wit' her?" Alyse asked. "Oh, and her Godmother."

The registrar smiled. "Absolutely."

Alyse motioned for Roslynn to bring Brie over to her. Roslynn sat Brie down in the wheel chair before kissing her on the forehead. It was a very emotional moment for all of them.

"You ready little lady," the transport said as he wheeled Brie to the elevators with everyone following.

A minute or so later, the elevator doors opened to the fourth floor, which was decorated with bears and multi colored wall paper. He then rolled Brie into a room and helped her onto the bed.

"A nurse will be with you shortly," he said before leaving.

"Mommy, I want to go home," Brie spoke quietly.

Looking at her husband and friend for support, Alyse had no idea how she was going to explain to Brie that she was going to have to stay in the hospital until they released her. How could she explain it to her daughter when she didn't understand it herself?

Surprisingly, Roslynn took matters into her own hands. "Brie, the doctor needs to find out what is makin' you feel so icky. The only way they can do that is if you stay here tonight. You understand?"

Brie nodded. "Okay."

Alyse thanked Roslynn, then sat on the bed next to Brie. A nurse came in moments later and asked Alyse if she could take all of Brie's clothes off and put the hospital gown on. She also gave them a pair of footies before leaving the room.

"Where the hell did she go? Is that all she gonna say? I need some more damn information," Alyse said frustrated.

"Calm down baby. You go find the nurse. I'll take her clothes off," Lance stated.

After gaining her composure, Alyse left the room in search of the nurse to ask her a couple of questions. Meanwhile, Lance held up the little footies so Brie could see they were Sponge Bob. "Wow, Sponge Bob socks. Look at that Brie."

Roslynn was clueless. "What the hell is Sponge Bob?" she whispered to Lance.

Lance looked at Roslynn. "You playing right." When Roslynn didn't reply, he smiled. "Oh, shoot. I forgot you don't have any kids."

"Auntie Ro, do you like Sponge Bob?" Brie asked as Lance got her undressed.

Roslynn had a confused expression. "Umm…I don't know."

"What about Dora the Explorer?" Brie continued.

Lance laughed when he saw the look on Roslynn's face. "Honey, yo' Auntie Ro has no idea who you talkin' about."

"Hey, Roslynn do you think I can talk to you for a second?" Lance asked.

"Yeah."

As the two walked closer to the door, Roslynn wondered what Lance wanted.

Lance seemed hesitant to speak. "Umm…I'm sorta in the

dog house with Alyse right now, so I wanna go downstairs to the gift shop and get her some flowers. I also wanna get Brie a gift. Something that will cheer her up."

Roslynn smiled. "Oh, that sounds like a good idea. I'll stay wit' Brie until you get back." When she turned around to walk away, he grabbed her arm lightly. Roslynn instantly gave him a crazy look. "Is somethin' wrong wit' you?"

Lance lowered his head for a second. "Umm…I'm sorta in a bind right now, so I was wondering if you could loan me the money to get the gifts."

Roslynn's eyes became two sizes bigger. Never in her twenty-seven years had a man ever asked her for money. "Are you serious right now?" Lance reluctantly shook his head. "What kind of shit is this? So, you don't even have money to buy some damn flowers and a teddy bear?"

Lance was completely embarrassed by Roslynn's tone. "Can you please lower your voice?" He looked over at Brie, who was studying them like an exam. "Brie is watching us."

"This is ridiculous, Lance," Roslynn whispered. She walked over to her purse, pulled out her wallet and pulled out a fifty dollar bill before walking back. "I'm not sure why yo' ass don't have any money, but regardless of what it is, you need to get yo' shit together. The next time you ask me for money, Alyse or Brie better need a damn lung." She handed Lance the crisp fifty dollar bill. "I gave you a lil' bit extra just in case yo' broke-ass don't even have money to feed my friend."

Lance wanted so badly to give Roslynn the money back, but had to swallow his pride. It was degrading to sit there, and let someone talk to him that way, but he couldn't even get upset. Everything Roslynn said was completely true, so he couldn't argue with that.

"Hey baby, Daddy is going downstairs. I'll be right back," Lance said to Brie before walking out. He snuck past Alyse as she stood patiently at the nurse's desk in order for his gift to be a surprise when he got back.

"So, can you tell me what's goin' on wit' my daughter," Alyse asked when the nurse finally put the phone receiver down.

When the nurse told her that a doctor would be in to speak with them shortly, Alyse was about to get hype.

"Here's the doctor now," the nurse said, pointing behind Alyse.

The doctor walked up and introduced himself as Dr. Atkins. He then suggested they go into a conference room on another floor so they could talk.

"Yes, of course," Alyse replied.

As they walked past Brie's room, Alyse stuck her head in. "Where Lance at? It's time to talk wit' the doctor."

*Hopefully he askin' somebody for a fuckin' job application,* Roslynn thought.

"He went downstairs for a minute."

As nervous as Alyse was, she didn't even have time to get mad that Lance wasn't around for yet another important conversation. "Well, when he comes back just tell'em I'll be in a conference room on the first floor."

When Alyse and the doctor walked into the conference room, a few minutes later, she quickly took a seat at the table. The doctor sat directly across from her, and placed a green chart on the table. He didn't waste any time opening the folder and then began reading its contents.

"I see that Dr. Salter asked that a battery of tests be performed. We'll be running most of the tests today and the rest tomorrow," he commented.

"Will she be able to go home tonight?"

"I'm afraid not. We need to monitor her throughout the night."

"Okay…wait a minute. Monitor her for what?" Alyse asked, running her hands down her face. "No one is tellin' me what's wrong wit' her."

Dr. Atkins peeked up at Alyse with a grim look on his face.

Skimming through the report for Alyse's last name he said, "Mrs. Greffen, it seems as if your daughter has some abnormal blood cells."

"So, what does 'dat mean?" she asked, folding her hands against her chest.

**111**

"Well, in most cases it means some form of cancer like leukemia or Sickle Cell Anemia."

Alyse could feel her heart rate start to increase. "Are you tellin' me my daughter has cancer?" she asked in disbelief.

"We won't know for sure until we finish running some more tests. So I don't want us to get ahead of ourselves. Let's just get the test results before we push the panic button. I'm going to have additional blood tests performed which will give us a more definitive answer."

"I'm not leavin' my daughter here all night by herself."

"Oh, no we wouldn't want you to. If you'd like I can have the nurse bring you a rollaway bed. I'm going to take your daughter to another area of the hospital to perform the tests in about an hour, which should even give you some time to get comfortable."

"I can't believe 'dis."

Dr. Atkins stood up. "I know it's easier said than done, but try not to worry."

Alyse told the doctor thank you, then walked back to Brie's room. When she walked in, she scanned the room and saw that Brie had been hooked up to an IV. Staggering, she leaned across the bed and kissed her sleeping daughter on the forehead.

"I love you so much, baby girl," she said teary eyed.

Roslynn walked over to the other side of the bed and asked Alyse what was going on, but Alyse didn't hear a word she said. She just kept kissing her daughter and telling her everything was going to be alright.

Roslynn walked up behind Alyse and grabbed her by the shoulders. "What the hell is goin' on? You scarin' me!"

Barely able to get the words out of her mouth, Alyse slowly said, "They think she may have cancer, but they not sure yet." She hoped Brie didn't understand what she'd just said.

Roslynn covered her mouth. "Oh my God."

"I can't even think straight right now."

Roslynn embraced her and told her everything was going to be fine.

"Why don't you ahead go home? We won't know anythin' for sure 'til tomorrow."

"Absolutely not," Roslynn replied.

"I love you Ro, but there's nothin' you can do tonight. Besides, Lance will be here wit' me."

"Are you sure?"

"Yes, I'm sure." She sat down in the chair next to Brie's bed. "I don't know what I would do without her."

Roslynn placed her hands on Alyse's shoulder. "I promise you…you won't have to find out."

As the friends continued to embrace, Lance strolled back in the room carrying a vase full of yellow tulips and a huge white teddy bear. "Two gifts for my two favorite girls," he said with a wide grin. A grin that disappeared once he saw the look on his wife's face. Alyse immediately ran up to him.

Even though she was mad at Lance earlier, seeing him at that moment made her feel so much better. They'd been through so many things during their four and a half year marriage and they always managed to overcome them. Of course, those problems were nothing compared to the troubles of living from pay check to pay check, but Alyse had faith that they would get over this obstacle too.

Roslynn walked over to take the gifts out of Lance's hand, so he could embrace his wife. "What's wrong, honey?"

When Alyse filled Lance in on what the doctor said, he closed his eyes and took in a deep breath as if he was trying to soak it all in.

"They're wrong…they're wrong," he said over and over again until he broke down in Alyse's arms.

Alyse felt like someone had stomped on her heart, but she tried to be the strong one. "You right. They are wrong. She's gonna be fine. She has to."

# Chapter Thirteen

"Mr. Greffen," Dr. Atkins said, tapping Lance on the leg. "I need to talk to you and your wife. In private of course." He looked over at Brie who was already up and watching Saturday morning cartoons.

Lance looked at his watch and realized that it was only 7:45 a.m. He and Alyse had fallen asleep really late after sitting up and watching Brie sleep for what seemed like hours. He sat up, then shook his wife who was sleeping peacefully on the rollaway. "Alyse...Alyse."

Alyse slowly opened her eyes.

"Dr. Atkins needs to talk to us." Lance stood up and extended his hand.

After rubbing her eyes, Alyse reached up for her husband's hand, then immediately walked over to Brie. "Good morning, sweetheart. How are you feeling?"

Brie smiled. "Okay. My body hurt a little." She looked over at Lance. "Hi, Daddy."

"Hey, princess," Lance replied. He walked over and kissed her forehead. "Well, at least your fever finally went down."

"Mr. and Mrs. Greffen if we could meet in the conference room right away, that would be great. I'll have a nurse come in and check on Brie, then I'll meet you down there," Dr. Atkins said. He turned around and walked out.

"Brie, Mommy and Daddy have to go talk to your doctor. Be a good girl and watch cartoons until we get back," Lance instructed.

"Okay, Daddy. Can I have some orange juice when you come back?" Brie asked.

Both Alyse and Lance nodded at the same time. After kissing their daughter again, they walked out and headed downstairs. By the way Alyse began to bite her nails, Lance could tell she was a nervous wreck so he placed his arms around her waist.

"Don't worry, honey. Everything is gonna be okay." He tried to give a comforting smile.

"I sure hope so."

Once Lance and Alyse arrived in the conference room, Lance closed the door behind them, then took a seat next to his wife. They were surprised to see a red-headed woman sitting at the table as well, and wondered who she was. As Dr. Atkins opened up Brie's chart, he suddenly became nervous as well. When the doctor looked up and closed the chart, but didn't say anything, Alyse and Lance looked at one another in complete fear. They could tell it wasn't good news. They held each other's hand and awaited the results from the tests.

"Did you find out why Brie's so sick?" Alyse asked.

Dr. Atkins cleared his throat before giving them the news no parent wants to here. "Yes, we indeed found the problem. Mr. and Mrs. Greffen, I'm sorry to inform you of this but it appears as if your daughter has Sickle Cell Anemia," he said solemnly.

Alyse and Lance both looked at each other, but couldn't say a word. Seconds later, it was Lance who was finally able to speak. "Sir, did you say Sickle Cell Anemia?"

"Yes. I'm afraid so," Dr. Atkins confirmed.

"No! No! No!" Alyse began to repeat. Her tears were like a waterfall.

Lance was sure there was some kind of mistake as he consoled his wife. "Dr. Atkins are you sure? There's no way Brie can have Sickle Cell."

"Mr. Greffen, I assure you, we ran each test thoroughly, and they all came back with the same conclusion," Dr. Atkins guaranteed.

"But how? How did this happen? What is Sickle Cell anyway?" Lance asked.

"Sickle Cell Anemia is a disease in which the body makes sickle-shaped red blood cells. "Sickle-shaped" means that the red blood cells are shaped like a "C." Normal red blood cells are disc-shaped and look like doughnuts without the holes. Normal blood cells move easily through your blood vessels, but sickle cells don't. They're stiff and sticky and tend to form clumps and get stuck in the blood vessels and block them. This blockage ultimately causes serious pain, infections, and organ damage. Anemia is a ..." Dr. Atkins said, but was instantly cut off.

"Okay...okay. So, how do we make her better?" Alyse asked getting herself together. She wiped the tears from her eyes. "I'm not losin' my baby, so what are we gon' do to make 'dis right?"

"Well, for starters, both of you all need to be tested. In order for Brie to have the disease, both of you obviously have the trait," Dr. Atkins instructed. "Sickle Cell is unfortunately an inherited disease."

"I don't have a history of Sickle Cell in my family. What about you?" Lance asked Alyse.

"No! I mean I don't think so," she said, rocking back and forth in her chair.

They just couldn't believe it. None of what they'd just heard made any sense. For weeks they'd been told that she had a bug, but the real diagnosis was far from that. When Alyse informed Dr. Atkins what she'd been told, he tried to explain that some of the symptoms in Sickle Cell and the flu did resemble like fatigue, weakness, fever and joint pain.

"Dats why she always says her body hurts," Alyse mentioned.

Dr. Atkins shook his head. "Exactly. There are several ways we can combat this disease. For example, we can give her antibiotics to prevent any infections that may arise and pain medication. More effective treatments are intravenous blood transfusions and of course bone morrow transplants. However, I have to inform you that blood transfusions do carry some risks, especially in younger children. Blood carries excessive amounts of iron, which may damage patient's hearts, liver and other organs."

Lance and Alyse were in complete awe of what they were hearing. "What about 'dat bone marrow thing?" Alyse asked.

"I believe it's the best way to increase Brie's chances of

fighting this disease. Does she have any siblings? Healthy brothers or sisters are the best donors."

Both Alyse and Lance shook their head back and forth at the same time.

"Well, with no siblings, suitable donors are very hard to find, and even if we found a donor, there are still risks involved. Sometimes the transplant doesn't work or the recipient's body rejects the new marrow."

Lance and Alyse both lowered their head and held hands.

"Look, I don't want you all to lose your confidence. I'm just a firm believer that you should be aware of all the risks. This is not a death sentence. Every case is different. A lot of my patients go on to live normal, healthy lives after treatment," Dr. Atkins said.

"Well, Brie is gonna be one of those patients because she's a strong little girl and we're gonna see her through this. Right, baby," Lance said, putting his arms around his wife.

Alyse's tears didn't seem to stop. "Dats right."

"So, when could we get Brie started on some kind of treatment? I don't want her to be in pain," Lance pleaded.

Dr. Atkins finally looked at the red-headed woman. "Well, that's another thing we wanted to talk to you about."

"Hello, I'm the hospital's Chief of Staff, Jan Edwards," the woman said, reaching over the table. After shaking Lance and Alyse's hands she continued. "Mr. and Mrs. Greffen, we called your insurance company after you registered yesterday, and it appears as if your insurance has been canceled."

Lance's heart dropped. In the all the excitement, he'd completely forgotten that they no longer had insurance.

"Now, in a case like this, treatments can be very costly. Would you happen to have another insurance carrier?" Jan inquired.

Alyse never said a word, but looked at Lance.

"Well, we've had several problems with our insurance lately. Do you have the number so I can call them and straighten this out?"

"Yes, I do," Jan said, fumbling through her paperwork. She wrote the number down and handed it to Lance. "I'll give you a few minutes to make your call. You can use the phone over there," she said, pointing to the phone sitting on at the opposite end of the table.

As soon as she and Dr. Atkins walked out of the room, Alyse jumped up. "I'm so sick of 'dis shit. What the hell is goin' on Lance?"

"Baby, please sit down. I have to talk to you about something," Lance said, looking pitiful.

She crossed her arms. "No, I'm not gonna sit down. What's goin' on?"

Lance let out a huge sigh. "We don't have insurance anymore."

"No shit, Lance. People been tellin' us 'dat for a while now. The question is why. I mean I thought yo' job took the premiums right out of yo' paycheck."

When Lance didn't explain right away she tried to remain calm. "Well?"

"I lost my job! I haven't been to work in weeks."

Alyse had to sit down because she was feeling faint. She then stared at Lance as if he was speaking a foreign language. "What the fuck you mean you haven't worked in weeks. I don't understand. You left the house every mornin'. Where the hell were you goin'? So, all 'dat shit about you havin' good sales and not being able to receive personal calls at work was just yo' way of coverin' it up, huh?"

Lance's eyes welled up with tears. "I would go to the movies most of the time. When I wasn't at the movies, I would go to one of my boy's house." He waited for a reaction. When she just sat and looked at him with a deadly stare, he told her he was sorry for lying to her.

"Sorry…you sorry…they might have to put our daughter out because we can't pay for her treatments and you're sittin' here tellin' me you sorry!" She stood back up and walked over to Lance then began to pound on him catching him a few times in the face.

He grabbed her arms. "Alyse, I know I fucked up, but I'm gonna handle this."

"Muthafucka, you can't handle 'dis unless you got a stash

somewhere. I cannot believe 'dis shit!" Alyse walked back and forth trying to figure out what she was going to do now. She tried to stay calm because this was certainly not the time to be getting into this with him. "I want you to leave me alone."

"Alyse, let's talk about this."

"Muthafucka, did you hear what I just said?"

Just then, Jan walked back into the room without Dr. Atkins, but wondered if she should come back. Alyse put her anger for Lance on the back burner long enough to hear what the Chief of Staff had to say.

"I'm sorry, I should've knocked," Jan admitted.

"Oh no, that's fine," Lance said. He was grateful for Jan interrupting because it got him out the hot seat for a minute.

"So, did you all find out about your insurance?" Jan asked then sat down.

Lance cleared his throat. "Well…umm there seems to be a problem with our insurance."

Jan had heard that tone too many times in her career, and knew exactly what that meant. "Well, Mr. and Mrs. Greffen, this is a hard call for us because like I said before, these types of treatments can be well over two hundred thousand dollars, and the hospital can't afford to provide the services for free."

Alyse spoke up. "We gonna contact our insurance one last time. If 'dat don't work out, we gonna try and get the money."

For a few tense seconds, both Lance and Jan looked at her like 'how do you plan to pull that off'.

This time Jan cleared her throat. "Well…okay. I'm willing to give you all a few days to see what you can come up with, and hopefully things work out. If not, we'll have to talk about other options like transferring your daughter to another hospital. Unfortunately, the Board of Directors are very strict about patients without insurance coverage."

"Let me guess, you'll transfer her to University Hospital, right?" Alyse questioned.

"Yes," Jan agreed.

"Well, that won't be necessary," Alyse replied like she had everything under control.

Jan smiled. "That's great. You all are a wonderful family, so I'll talk to the board about giving you more time, but can't guarantee that they will."

Alyse walked over and hugged the red-headed woman. "Thank you."

"No problem. I'll do everything in my power to help. Now you all need to make your way upstairs. Dr. Atkins has prepared for you all to be tested for the Sickle Cell trait first then from there, you'll be able to give blood in the event a transfusion is needed," Jan informed them.

After receiving a hug from Lance, Jan walked out the conference room, and left the couple behind.

"How do you plan on getting the money?" Lance asked confused.

Alyse gave him the look of death. "What difference does it make? We know it won't be comin' from yo' broke-ass."

# Chapter Fourteen

After dropping Omari off at a friend's house, Jazmine rushed back home to change clothes, and to ask Vince if she could finally go to the hospital to support Alyse. Ever since she'd gotten the call from her friend the day before, all she could think about was Brie. Jazmine was worried whenever Omari even got a cut on his finger, so she knew it would kill her if he was ever laid up in some hospital. As a mother, Jazmine could only imagine what Alyse might be going through so her heart ached at the thought of her friend in pain. Jazmine wanted to be there, so she hoped and prayed that Vince would be in a good mood.

As Jazmine walked upstairs, she could hear Vince talking to someone. Trying to eavesdrop, she placed her ear up against the closed door, but the conversation wasn't clear. After straining for a couple more seconds, she finally decided to open the door.

"I'm going to have to call you back," Vince said to the mystery caller, then quickly hung up.

Walking over to the dresser, Jazmine mumbled, "Secret phone calls again, I see."

Vince threw the phone on the bed. "You always runnin' your damn mouth. What the fuck did you say?"

Not ready for a battle, Jazmine continued to pull out her light green v-neck t-shirt, ignoring his question.

"Don't act like you didn't hear me," he said, marching toward her. "Repeat what the fuck you just said, since you got so much shit to say!" he yelled

Instantly, Jazmine began to regret her comment. "Look, Vince. I didn't come in here to start with you. I'm just trying to change my clothes," she said brushing past him. "I wanna go to the hospital to see Alyse and Brie."

"You ain't going nowhere."

Jazmine frowned. "Why? I wanna go see how Brie's doing. She's sick Vince. You said I could go. You even gave me two hours this time."

"Well, I changed my mind. I don't give a shit how sick she is. You ain't goin'!"

"You know I'm sick of you treating me like this. I'm not your child!"

Annoyed by her lack of respect, Vince grabbed the back of her neck and pulled her to him. "I've had it with your smart-ass mouth and disrespectful behavior."

"Respect went out the door when you started beating me like a damn man," she said scolding him.

"Bitch, you gonna learn sooner than later who the hell you messin' with. I run shit around here and you better start actin' like you know." He forced her body over the back of his weight bench.

Not anticipating his unplanned actions, Jazmine tried to push her body up. "What the hell is your problem? I don't…" Before she could finish her sentence, Vince balled up his fist and popped her in the face.

"Get off of me!" she screamed, then grabbed her jaw.

"Shut up bitch. You asked for this shit." Vince quickly pulled his pants down to the floor then placed his huge hand around her neck.

"Oh no, please no," Alyse said as Vince pulled down her sweat pants and panties. "Vince please. I promise, I won't disrespect you anymore."

Not hearing a word she said, he rammed his thick shaft into her vaginal walls with excruciating force. She bellowed in pain with each thrust. As his pace multiplied, his grip tightened around her neck and she was hardly able to breathe. Fearing she may pass out, Jazmine tried to relax, but it wasn't coming naturally. Vince dug deeper into Jazmine and pulled her upper body back to him as he released his evil seeds into her damaged garden.

She began to cry like a homeless child, and wondered what kind of man Vince had become. He surely wasn't the same man she'd vowed to love until death do them part. Jazmine was at a loss for words, but managed to muffle something with the little air flow that remained.

"So, this is how you treat your wife and mother of your son, you fucking bastard!"

A puzzled Vince stared at the floor shaking his head in disbelief. "Oh, so you still talkin' shit. I guess that wasn't enough for you, huh?"

He reached for his police baton that was a few inches away from the bench and struck Jazmine twice in the back like she was resisting arrest. He forced her up against the wall with rage, then placed the hard baton up to her throat. "You don't get it do you! You'll learn how to respect me, you got that?"

Tears began to stream down her face as the baton moved from her neck, around her breast, to her stomach, and stopped at her damaged vagina. Vince forcefully spread her legs apart before teasing her clit with the black stick. Not waiting for her pussy to moisten, he gave Jazmine a little smirk before shoving the baton inside.

"Oww!" she hollered. "Noooo... what are you doing?" Jazmine hollered again.

Her screams filled the air as Vince pulled the baton in and out. Each time he pushed it inside a little harder, her insides felt like they were ripping apart. Blood dripped down her leg as he continued to pull out and re-insert his weapon of destruction. With each insertion, she bellowed in agony.

"Stop...please!"

As if he was finally listening, Vince removed the baton from Jazmine's pussy, then threw her on the bed. Flipping her over on her stomach in a matter of seconds, Jazmine never got a chance to resist before he spread her butt cheeks then plunged his shaft in her ass, with no lubrication.

"Nooooo!" she screamed in pain.

Ramming his dick in and out of her ass with each stroke Vince moved his body in a circular motion as if he was churning butter. He pumped and pumped for several more seconds, but before he released more evil seeds, he pulled his manhood out, yanked Jazmine's numb body off the bed and pushed her down to the floor.

"Get on your knees!" he demanded.

Unable to cooperate fast enough, Jazmine was hit in the face with Vince's open hand. He then sat on the edge of the bed and pulled her up on her knees with what little hair she had left.

"Suck it you ungrateful bitch!" When Jazmine didn't move, Vince got even louder. "I said suck it, dammit!" He pushed the back of her head to the tip of his dick.

Opening her mouth slightly, Vince crammed his dick inside and held onto the back of her head at the same time. As he pushed her head up and down at a rapid pace, Jazmine began to gag. However, that didn't stop him. Vince continued to move her head until he could feel himself about to explode

"You better fuckin' swallow, too," he instructed, then released his cum deep into her mouth. Reluctant, but ready for this to be over, Jazmine swallowed every bit of his sperm. With his dick still in her mouth, Vince pulled his wife by her hair, until their eyes met. "You'll respect me now, won't you?"

Hesitant, she nodded her head.

A slight smiled emerged on Vince's face as visions of his wife's painful experience crossed his mind. He loved to take her through all the agony and torture. It was a rush that he enjoyed. Finally pulling out, he wiped Jazmine's salvia from his dick on the unmade bed sheets. "The next time you get out of line I'm gonna kill yo' ass," he whispered, before he walked back toward the bathroom. "Oh, and don't even think you goin' to that hospital."

Jazmine laid on the floor motionless as a river of tears began to flow. After hearing the water in the shower come on, thoughts raced through her mind on how to escape. She badly wanted to escape the confines of the once warm and cozy place she called home, but didn't know if she had the strength to do it. Numb and in pain, she managed to get up and lay on the bed.

As thoughts of escaping continued to float around in her head, Vince's cell phone began to ring. Jazmine sat there while the annoying Snoop Dogg ringtone played *Sexual Seduction*. Once the music stopped, seconds later it started back up. In Jazmine's mind whoever it was must've wanted Vince to answer really bad, so she immediately thought about his secretive phone calls. Jazmine waited for Snoop to stop rapping again before she finally picked up the fancy Sprint phone and quickly made her way to the missed calls screen. Even though she knew if Vince caught her looking at his phone, she would get another beat down but at the moment she didn't care. Jazmine had to find out for herself, if another woman was the blame for her husbands erratic behavior.

Luckily, she'd played with Vince's phone when he first got it, so she knew her way around. After hitting the button to review the two missed calls, Jazmine's face frowned when she saw the name, Montee pop up.

"Why in the hell would Vince be talking to Montee?" she asked herself.

No sooner than she asked that question, Jazmine heard the shower water cut off. Quickly, she deleted the calls so Vince wouldn't see that she'd checked his phone. To Jazmine, it was better for her safety if Vince never knew that Montee called at all. After placing the phone back in the same spot, Jazmine laid back down and tried her best to play dead.

A few seconds later, Vince stormed out of the bathroom butt naked like something was on fire, then headed downstairs at top speed. Jazmine had no idea what was going on, until she heard the door to the basement slam shut. At that point, she knew exactly what was happening. Vince was headed down in his man cave to involve himself in yet another secret. Knowing he would be down there forever, it was now or never for Jazmine to finally make a move.

Slowly getting up from the bed, Jazmine managed to make her way over to her purse, then pulled out her cell phone. Making sure Vince was out of sight, she dialed Roslynn's number and waited for her to answer.

"Hey girl," her friend said on the third ring.

"I need you to come get me," Jazmine whispered.

"What did you say? Girl you gotta speak up. I'm at this damn mall gettin' ready to take back a watch that I bought. Can you believe Adrian pulled that shit? I mean…"

Jazmine cut her off. "He raped me! He raped me!" This

**127**

time hopefully she was loud enough.

Roslynn was quiet for a second. "Oh, my God. Are you okay?"

"No. Please go get Omari. He has a friend who lives in Walnut Park Apartments. The address is 151 North Walnut. Apt 209. After you get him, come get me. Park around the corner, I'll come outside."

"Hell no, I ain't parkin' outside."

Jazmine looked for Vince again. "Roslynn, please just do what I said and hurry up. He just might kill me next time."

✳✳✳

Roslynn couldn't even think straight. She knew if Vince was that out of control, she couldn't go to Jazmine's house alone so she made an important phone call on her way to East Orange. Anger built up in Roslynn every time she replayed Jazmine's words in her mind. Her body started trembling with rage. The thought of her friend being raped by her own damn husband made Roslynn want to kill Vince herself. It didn't make sense, and if she had anything to do with it, the shit was going to stop today. Knowing that it was going to take her at least twenty minutes to get to Omari's friend's house, Roslynn put the pedal to the medal so she could get there in ten.

Roslynn's eyes darted with anticipation as she passed each exit sign on the Garden State Parkway. When she saw the East Orange exit sign a few minutes later, her heart started pumping faster. After making several turns, she finally made it to Walnut Street in one piece. Parking her car right in front of the apartment building, Roslynn quickly jumped out and made her way to the second floor.

She could hear several kids playing and yelling to the top of their lungs when she knocked on the door.

A small framed elderly woman came to the door moments later. "Yes, can I help you?"

"I'm here to pick up Omari Anderson."

"And who might you be," the woman asked. She was old, but certainly feisty.

"My name is Roslynn and I'm a friend of his mom. She's sick, and asked if I could pick Omari up for her."

The old woman looked Roslynn up and down then sucked her teeth. "You betta not be playing no games girl." She then called for Omari.

While Roslynn waited, she peeped past the frail women when two of the kids in the living room started fighting. The two boys were screaming and acting like fools. "Keon and Kashaun. Sit the hell down before I put my foot up y'all ass!" the old woman screamed.

*See that's why I can't have no kids,* Roslynn thought taking notice of how the kids barely paid the woman any mind.

It wasn't until the woman grabbed a shoe off the floor and threw it at one of the boys that they finally calmed down. Roslynn couldn't believe that Jazmine allowed Omari to be in this crazy environment, but then again as crazy as his father was, he was probably used to this madness.

Moments later, Omari walked into the room looking just as bad as Jazmine had been lately. Roslynn eyed his dirty tennis shoes and faded jeans that had several holes near the cuffs. He was surprised to see Roslynn standing there, so he immediately went over and asked her why she was there. He'd known Roslynn all his life and she'd never picked him up from anywhere, so he knew something was wrong.

"Omari, who that?" one of the bad little boys asked.

"My auntie, Ro," he said softly, before opening the front door. "Bye, y'all. Bye, Ms. Gloria. Thanks for letting me come over."

Roslynn couldn't help but noticed how much Omari looked and acted like Jazmine while they walked down the hallway. Omari was truly his mother's child. He was mild mannered, polite and a bit on the timid side, the total opposite of his crazy father.

Hearing Omari say she was his aunt, made Roslynn feel bad. She never knew he felt that way about her and how could she when she never really spent any time with him. She decided right then that she would be more active in his life. Everything so far had been about Brie, but she vowed to quickly change that mentality.

When Omari climbed into Roslynn's BMW, he was amazed by all the gadgets it had. It was a lot more elegant than his mother's beat up old car.

"Are you taking me home?" he asked.

Roslynn wasn't exactly sure what to say. "I think we're gonna pick up your mom."

"Is she alright?"

"Yeah, she's fine," Roslynn said, pulling out of the parking lot. "Please put on your seatbelt."

After placing her own seatbelt on, Roslynn picked up the phone to call Jazmine. Being only a short drive away, Roslynn wanted her friend to get in place so they could make this a smooth transition.

A few minutes later, Roslynn waited two houses down and looked at her watch every other minute, wondering what was taking Jazmine so long. *She should be here by now,* Roslynn thought in a panicked state. *Fuck this shit.*

"Omari, I'll be right back. I want you to lock the doors. All you have to do is push this button right here when I get out. I don't want you to open this door for no one but me. You understand?"

Omari was starting to feel that something wasn't right. He asked Roslynn again where his mother was.

"Omari, please just lock the door. I'll explain everything to you later." After grabbing her phone, she got out and waited for Omari to follow her directions before she stooped down and crept toward the house. Then it hit her. "No, I better wait until he arrives just in case my girl is seriously hurt."

She quickly dialed the number. "Where you at?"

✱✱✱

Jazmine slowly walked down the stairs with Omari's duffle bag on her shoulder, two overnight bags for herself and her purse. A purse that no longer contained the two hundred dollars Roslynn had given her. Jazmine thought she'd done a good job at hiding it inside a pack of Trident gum, but now it was gone. Carefully look-

**130**

ing around the corner leading to the living room, she noticed that Vince was now sitting on the couch. She couldn't tell if he was asleep or not because his back was facing her. She leaned up against the wall and wondered what she should do. Jazmine wanted to make a run for it, but she was in too much pain. Then when Vince made a sudden movement, her heart starting beating so fast, it almost jumped out of her chest. She sat all the bags down and moved toward him, but when he didn't move again or even look her way when she called his name she assumed he was asleep.

Walking backwards, she grabbed the bags and tiptoed to the back door of her home. The closer she got, freedom only seemed a few footsteps away. Reaching out, she unlocked the door, then grabbed the doorknob. After opening the door slowly, she could smell the aroma of her fresh cut grass just before feeling a light tap on her shoulder.

"Going somewhere?"

Jazmine dropped the backpack instantly and turned around as Vince reached over her and slammed the door shut. He obviously enjoyed watching her squirm.

Her heart rate increased. "Umm... Vince. I was just going to pick Omari up from Ms. Gloria's house," she said, as Vince pulled her back toward the front of the house.

When Jazmine looked at him, she couldn't believe that he was still naked. She was also horrified at the sight of a needle still stuck in his arm along with the huge rubber band. She stood there in complete shock.

"Ha...ha...ha. Really? Out the back door?" Vince asked licking his lips. His eyes were dark and evil. "You goin' to Ms. Gloria's with three bags? Let me guess, you tryin' to leave, huh?"

"Oh, no...no."

"Yes, you are. You probably went lookin' for that two hundred dollars you stashed too, right? Well, don't look too hard 'cause I took that shit." He looked down at his arm. "I used it for this weeks supply."

"Vince please. I wasn't trying to leave."

"Stop lyin' to me!" he yelled.

He placed his hands around her throat and started choking her. When Jazmine's face started turned to turns colors from the lack of oxygen, suddenly there was a knock at the door. Vince released his grip long enough to look out the window.

"What the fuck is he doing here?" Vince asked out loud. He looked at Jazmine and frowned. "Take your ass in the kitchen and don't move. And if you do move, trust me, you'll regret it."

He managed to pull the needle out his arm, then took the rubber band off before placing it under the couch in the living room. Jazmine thought Vince would at least have the nerve to put on some clothes, but he walked right up to the front door and opened it.

"What's up?"

Miles' eyes widened. "Can I come in for a minute?"

"Hell, no. Now is not a good time. Me and my wife are in the middle of fuckin' as you can see."

Jazmine prayed that Miles wouldn't believe Vince's story.

"Well, I hate to bother you on a Saturday, but I really need to talk to you about a case," Miles insisted.

Vince looked behind him to make sure Jazmine was out of sight first before inviting Miles in. "A'ight. Since you obviously wanna see my dick nigga, come on in. See, I knew yo' ass was a fuckin' faggot."

The anger could be seen all over Miles' face as he walked in, but he didn't let Vince's comments interfere with what he was really there for. He immediately started looking around for signs of trouble without tipping Vince off.

"So, what's this shit about?" Vince asked.

Miles cleared his throat. "Man, are you alright? You're acting really strange."

"Hell yeah, I'm alright. Just get to the point, nigga!"

"Well, you know that case the prosecutor has me working on? He wants me to go over your report, so I was wondering if you could take another look at it before we go to court on Monday."

Vince wanted to get Miles out of his house, so he could finish tormenting Jazmine immediately. However, Miles had his own agenda. He kept Vince occupied until he saw Jazmine come from the kitchen and walk toward the back door.

"Man, get your ass outta my house talkin' about some damn report. That dumb shit can wait until next week!" Vince belted.

Wanting to give Jazmine a little leg room, Miles told him that he wanted them to put their differences aside and try to work together.

Vince laughed. "Fuck you. You weren't there when I needed you, so don't come up in here with that gay shit now. As a matter of fact, get the hell out my house."

"Maybe you're right. I apologize. We cool now," Miles said, extending his hand out for Vince to shake on it.

Vince declined and showed Miles to the door.

Roslynn was relieved when she saw Jazmine walking as fast as she could to the car. Still standing outside the car, she didn't waste anytime telling Omari to unlock the door. After helping Jazmine get inside, Roslynn ran to the driver's seat, jumped inside and quickly sped off.  She was just about to turn the corner when she saw Miles getting in his car. She blew the horn two times, just like they'd planned to let him know she had Jazmine.

"Ma, what's going on?" Omari asked from the backseat.

"I'll explain it to you later. Sit back for now and put your seatbelt on," Jazmine answered.

"Everybody is gonna explain it to me later," Omari mumbled.

"You called Miles?" Jazmine asked, still panicked.

"I sure did," Roslynn said. "Shit! I had to call somebody! Look at you, if I hadn't you probably wouldn't have gotten out of there alive. Boy I'm glad I flirted with him that day at the station."

"You're right."

Roslynn insisted on taking Jazmine to the hospital, but she wouldn't hear of it. There was no way she was going into a hospital and tell them her husband had just raped her with his baton. It would be too humiliating and there would be too many questions asked. Furthermore, she was worried Social Services might get involved and take Omari from her.

A few seconds later, Jazmine's phone started ringing. She

knew exactly who it was. However, when she grabbed the phone, she realized that it wasn't a call, but an actual text message that had come through. She instantly read the message that said.

```
Bitch I'm going to kill you!
Remember you can't hide!!
```

She showed Roslynn the text who once again suggested Jazmine let someone handle Vince. She was waiting for Jazmine to say no, but this time she was actually considering it.

# Chapter Fifteen

"God, what did I do to deserve 'dis? I know I'm not perfect and I should go to church a little more, but I'm not a bad person." Alyse kissed Brie's hand, who was fast asleep. After being bothered with doctors and nurses all day, she seemed worn out. Her little body had also been aching throughout the night, so the rest seemed like it was much needed.

"God please…please…take care of my baby." She wiped the tears from her eyes. "I can't stand to see her sick like 'dis." She paused from her heart to heart with God to straighten the blankets on Brie's bed. "God, I don't ask for a lot, but I'm askin' now. No, I'm beggin' you to help my child. Watch over her and give me the strength to get us all through 'dis."

"Amen," someone said.

When Alyse turned around, Lance was standing there with a Mountain Dew in his hand. "That was a great prayer."

Alyse tried to force a smile. "Thanks"

"Honey, why don't you get out of this room for a while? You need to get up and walk around."

Alyse shook her head. "No, I want to be here when the test results come back. I'm curious as to which one of us gave 'dis shit to our child."

Alyse and Lance had both been tested for the Sickle Cell trait earlier that morning, and were still waiting for the results.

"Honey, it's not like I'm gonna keep the results away from you. Just get some fresh air for me." Lance handed Alyse her cell phone. "Here, take your phone. I'll call you if Dr. Atkins comes in."

Alyse looked over at Brie then let out a huge sigh. "I guess you right. I'll go downstairs and get some air."

"Why don't you go to the cafeteria and eat something while you're down there," Lance suggested. "You haven't eaten anything all day."

"I don't have an appetite right now," Alyse replied then lifted her phone. "Call me if you find out anythin'."

When Lance agreed, Alyse finally made her way out of the room. The further she walked, the more faint she became. It was at that point she realized that getting something to eat might not be such a bad idea. On her way to the cafeteria, she called Roslynn to see where she was. It wasn't like either one of her friends not to come by or call.

"Hey friend, how's Brie?" Roslynn asked.

Alyse decided to take the staircase so the phone wouldn't cut off in the elevator. "She's not doin' so well. Where are you? Where's Jazmine? I thought y'all would come up here today."

"Alyse trust me, it's been a drama filled day. Both Omari and Jazmine are wit' me now. We can fill you in on the details later, but I don't think it's a good idea if we come up to the hospital right now. Jazmine has a lot of things to work out," Roslynn told her.

"Is everything a'ight?" Alyse asked.

"No…not really. But like I said, we can talk about that later. How's Brie doing? That's what we wanna know."

Coming out of the stairwell, Alyse knew their conversation was undoubtedly going to be very emotional. She started to tear up. "The doctor's found out why she's so sick," Alyse said, dabbing her eyes.

Roslynn could tell in Alyse's voice that it wasn't good. It wasn't going to be easy for Alyse to tell her friends but she knew it had to be done. If ever she was going to need them it was going to be now.

"Brie has Sickle Cell Anemia," Alyse said.

Roslynn was in complete disbelief. "Oh my goodness, Alyse I'm so sorry to hear that." She immediately relayed Alyse's news to Jazmine.

"Sickle Cell, that's hereditary, right?" Roslynn asked.

"Yeah, and 'dats why I'm so mad. Me and Lance ain't

**136**

never been sick from 'dis shit. Why did it have to make my baby sick?"

"That's crazy. So, what do they plan to do to help her?" Roslynn asked.

"Well, there are a lot of treatments, but the most effective ways to control the disease is a blood transfusion or bone marrow transplant. But the bone marrow is tricky 'cause siblings are the best donors, and we know she don't have a brother or sister. Since 'dat wouldn't work, she would have to get on a damn long-ass list for people who need bone marrow transplants," Alyse mentioned "Now, I know how you felt back in the day when yo' baby died, Ro. It's not a good feelin' to have a sick child."

The phone went dead for a moment, then suddenly Jazmine got on the phone. "I'm so sorry to hear this, Alyse. I can't even imagine what you must be going through. You tend to feel guilty because there's nothing you can do to protect them, but we just have to put everything in God's hands and trust that he will see you through this."

"Thanks, Jazz. 'Nothin' else matters to me at 'dis point. I just want her to be okay."

"And she will. Have you told her?"

As Alyse walked into the cafeteria, tears still flowed down her face. "I really don't see the purpose. It's not like she knows what Sickle Cell means. Besides I don't want her to panic."

Jazmine understood her reasoning. It also made her think about how precious life is. It could've just as well been Omari fighting the deadly disease. Once Roslynn decided to put the phone on speaker, all three ladies kept talking about all the new treatments available and what Alyse's options were.

"So, your insurance covering all this?" Roslynn asked.

The mention of insurance instantly reminded Alyse of her other problems. As she sat down at a table in the cafeteria, she asked if Adrian was nearby. When Roslynn told her no, she felt a little bit more comfortable with the things she was about to share.

"Lance got fired from his job. We don't have any insurance."

Again the line went silent for a few moments. "No insurance, so how are you all gonna pay for Brie's treatments?" Roslynn curiously asked. *That's why that nigga asked me for money yesterday.* "What about your job? Can you get insurance from there?"

"I called my boss, Jackie, 'dis morning to update her on what's goin' on, and to ask her for more time off, and the bitch said I was suspended for right now," Alyse stated.

"Suspended...what the hell is that supposed to mean?" Roslynn inquired.

"I have the slightest idea, and don't even give a shit. All 'dat's important right now is Brie." Alyse felt a lump form in her throat. She hated asking for handouts. "I have no idea, but I was wonderin' if you and Adrian could loan us a little money. Anythin' will help at 'dis point Ro."

Roslynn paused. As bad as she wanted to help her friend, she knew Adrian would never approve of it. She had to be honest. "Alyse, I would love to help you, and if it was my money, you know you could have my last to help Brie. I love you and Brie to death, but to be honest, I don't think Adrian would do it. Hell, y'all don't know this but I'm up to my neck in debt. I got three high-ass credit card bills right now that I've been hidin' from Adrian, and if he knew about it, he would kill my ass. I'm gonna have to sneak the money from our account, just to pay those bills."

Roslynn knew her friends sorta looked up to her because they thought she lived a fairytale life. A life that they wanted, but as it turned out, she had problems just like everybody else. At that moment, she wanted to tell them about Kamilla, but thought she'd confessed enough for one day.

When Alyse got quiet, Roslynn immediately felt bad. She didn't want her friend to think she didn't want to help. "But I'll still ask him Alyse," she lied. "Adrian is an asshole sometimes, so I might have to seduce him first." She wanted to say something a little more raunchy, but quickly realized that Omari was around.

"Thanks, Ro. I had no idea you where in debt," Alyse responded.

"Yeah, especially the way you shop," Jazmine added.

"We'll be grateful for whatever you can do for us," Alyse continued. "Shit, whoever or wherever it comes from. I gotta get some money from somewhere."

"Hell, it looks like we all need money," Roslynn chimed in. "If I don't get some money so I can pay these bills off before Adrian finds out I'm gonna be headed to divorce court. And Jazmine, if you don't get away from that crazy- ass husband of yours, we gonna be goin' to yo' funeral."

"Oh Ro...don't say that," Alyse replied.

"Well, it's the truth," Roslynn said. "Shit, I say we go buy three ski masks and go rob a muthafuckin' bank. Go straight Baxter Terrace on these fools. Some Set It Off, gangsta type shit!"

Both Jazmine and Alyse laughed, but Roslynn was dead ass serious. They waited for Roslynn to say she was just playing, but she never did.

"Y'all bitches laughin' but ain't shit funny. We all in fucked up situations right now, and gotta do somethin'," Roslynn stated.

Jazmine spoke up. "Don't make me laugh anymore, Ro. You made my damn side hurt. I agree with your crazy-ass. We need to do something, but robbing a bank ain't the answer.

Roslynn was so blown. "Okay fine, when yo' husband sends yo' ass to the hospital next don't call me!"

Jazmine was stunned to hear Roslynn say something so vicious to her, especially after what she'd just gone through. You could almost hear a pin drop, before Roslynn carried on. "You know I didn't mean that Jazz. I'm just so stressed out. I'm worried about Brie and I'm scared to death for you."

Jazmine didn't comment.

"What the hell happened?" Alyse asked.

"Don't worry about my problems," Jazmine finally replied. "Just concentrate on taking care of Brie. Her words hurt, but Roslynn's right. I need to stay the hell away from Vince."

At that moment, Alyse looked at her watch, and realized that she'd been gone for a while, but hadn't eaten a thing. She hopped up and told her friends that she needed to get back to Brie's room just in case the results from the blood test where in.

"I'll call y'all once I talk to the doctor," Alyse stated.

"Okay, love you girl," Both Roslynn and Jazmine said off beat.

"Love y'all, too," Alyse replied before hanging up.

After jumping on the elevator, Alyse's heart throbbed with each floor she passed. She was in so much pain. She wanted to rewind the time and have everything go back to when her daughter was running around driving her crazy. She'd taken all those times for granted, and would've done anything to get those precious moments back.

When the elevator doors opened she stepped off and quickly walked back to Brie's room. She found Lance sitting next to Brie's bed singing a Dora The Explorer song with her. Brie was so weak she could barely get the words out. Alyse stepped back out because she didn't want her daughter to see her crying. When she turned around she was greeted by Dr. Atkins, who didn't have a smile on his face.

"Hi, Mrs. Greffen. I can see that you're already upset, so I'll make this brief. Can you get your husband?"

From Dr. Greffen's expression, Alyse could tell that he was the messenger of even more bad news, and she'd had just about enough.

"I'll get'em Dr. Atkins, but I'm not going to no damn conference room. Whatever it is you gotta tell us, it's gonna have to be here. I don't wanna be away from my daughter no more."

"Okay, but I would prefer if we don't discuss this outside in the hallway. Can we at least go into the room? Do you want to discuss this in front of your daughter?"

"Dr. Atkins, what else can you say other than she got twenty-four hours to live 'dats gonna be so bad. I mean at 'dis point, I'm gettin' used to the bad news."

He shook his head. "Well, the news is definitely not that Brie has twenty-four hours to live. I just need to discuss the test results."

Dr. Atkins grabbed Brie's nurse and instructed her not to come inside until they were done, then followed Alyse inside the room. After closing the door, he walked up and shook Lance's hand. "How are you, Mr. Greffen?"

"I've had better days," Lance responded.

"Well, like I told your wife outside, I'm here to discuss the test results with you all."

Lance made sure Brie had something interesting to watch on television, then walked over and placed his arm around his wife. "Okay, Doc. So what did you find out? Which one of us passed the trait onto Brie?"

Dr. Atkins swallowed…hard. "Well, it appears as if Alyse passed one of the traits on to Brie, but Mr. Greffen you don't have the trait at all."

Both Lance and Alyse looked at each other with a confused expression. "What do you mean, Doc?" Lance asked.

"The tests confirmed that Mrs. Greffen does has the Sickle Cell trait, but I'm afraid you don't Mr. Greffen. See, it took two parents with the trait in order for Brie to inherit the actual disease."

Lance continued to drill the doctor. "Hold up. This shit don't make any sense to me."

Alyse was quiet as a mouse as Lance removed his arm.

Dr. Atkins paused then looked at Brie. Thankfully the T.V. show had her hypnotized. "Can I ask you all a personal question?" When Alyse and Lance shook their heads, he asked, "Was Brie adopted by any chance?"

For some reason Lance was hype. "Hell no. Alyse gave birth to Brie. I was in the damn room. What the hell are you saying Doc?"

Suddenly, Dr. Atkins began to turn a light shade of red. "Then my guess would be that Brie has another father."

Lance instantly stared off into space. He'd heard what the doctor said, but couldn't process it. "I am her father," he said adamantly. He gave the doctor an angry glare. "You better run that fucking test over again."

The doctor was in a very awkward position and didn't know what to do. He turned to Alyse, but she wasn't any help because she was in shock herself. He pulled out the results from a manila folder, then handed the two papers to Lance. Lance wasn't an expert at reading medical reports, but he did understand what zero percent probability meant. Instantly, the pictures of him cutting Brie's umbilical cord when she was born flashed through his head. At that moment, he felt like he was going to pass out. It was

**141**

like he was having a bad dream. He got up and stared at Alyse with an evil glare.

"So you been playing me for a fucking fool all this time?" Lance said on the verge of taking Alyse's head off.

At that moment, Dr. Atkins quickly turned around. "I'll give you two some privacy," he said walking away. He couldn't walk out the room fast enough.

Alyse grabbed Lance by the arm. "There must be a mix-up in the lab or somethin'. I swear to you, I ain't never cheated on you," she said, trying to prevent him from leaving. "Lance! Please wait! You know I would never do somethin' like 'dat to you."

"Bitch, get out of my way!" he yelled, as he shoved her to the side. He was in complete overdrive. Lance was so mad he threw the pitcher of water that was sitting on Brie's little rolling table against the wall and stormed out.

Both Alyse and Brie began to wail like two newborn babies.

# Chapter Sixteen

Even though it wasn't Omari's first time at Roslynn's house, he was always excited every time he came to visit. So excited, he'd been running around the house since arriving the day before. Roslynn knew Adrian was extremely irritated with Omari's hyper behavior, but she tried her best to ignore it. However, what she couldn't ignore was the fact that Vince had rung their doorbell several times throughout the night, and yelled Jazmine's name to the top of his lungs. This behavior went on until one of their neighbors eventually called the police, which turned into yet another circus. After accusing Jazmine of kidnapping Omari, Vince pleaded with the police to let him see his son, but once they informed him to handle his affairs in court, he eventually left.

Everyone hoped that he would at least get locked up for disturbing the peace, but since Vince was an officer himself, he'd obviously talked them out of jail time. In all the years Roslynn had lived in her neighborhood, she'd never even seen a squad car cruising around, so she had to admit it was embarrassing. Adrian didn't even speak to her before going to bed, and she knew it was only a matter of time before he blew his top. She and Jazmine had to hurry and come up with a plan before they both got put out.

Roslynn, Adrian and Jazmine were all sitting in the living room when the chef, Ramon came in and asked Roslynn what they would like for breakfast.

"I think we should let our guests decide," she replied.

"I think not," Adrian commented before turning the page of the Wallstreet Journal.

Roslynn was about to ask him if that was necessary, but with Omari staring at her she quickly changed her mind.

"Please. Whatever you fix Ramon is fine. Omari's not

choosy, and neither am I," Jazmine said. The last thing she wanted to do was be anymore of a burden to her friend after she'd graciously invited them to stay.

"Oh, yeah. Let's have Omari decide," Roslynn stated. When Adrian gave her another evil look, she tried to force a phony smile.

"It doesn't matter," Omari said softly.

Ramon smiled. "So you're telling me you wouldn't want to try one of my Belgium waffles with strawberries and whip cream?" Omari's eyes lit up. "That's what I thought. Do you want to come help me?" Ramon asked.

"Yes, sir," Omari said, following him into the kitchen.

Despite all of the problems Omari faced everyday, he was still a polite and well mannered little boy, which surprised Roslynn. He'd been through so much in his short seven years. It must've been hard living in a physically and mentally abusive household without having somewhat of an anger issue.

Once Omari was out of the room, Roslynn didn't waste anytime asking Jazmine what were her plans. She loved her friend, but having a child in the house along with all the drama definitely made things tense with Adrian.

"I appreciate you and Adrian letting us stay here, but I think we should look for another place," Jazmine said. She was well aware of Adrian's dislike for children and was not about to be somewhere her son wasn't welcomed. Hell, she wasn't even welcomed.

Roslynn had to at least play the part of a good host. "Girl, shut up! You know damn well I ain't lettin' you stay no where else when we have all this room here."

When Adrian immediately looked up from his paper and frowned, Roslynn actually cursed at herself. She'd completely forgotten to use her proper accent.

"So, when your friend comes around, you instantly turn into a hood chick?" Adrian asked. "What, you want her to know that you're *down*?" He threw his hands in the air like a rapper in a video.

Roslynn was embarrassed. "No, not at all."

"Then don't use that ghetto-ass language in this house." He looked at Jazmine. Actually, you don't need to wear out your welcome here. After putting up with your son running around here and that foolishness last night, I've had enough." Adrian stood up, adjusted his Polo robe, then headed to his office before shutting the door.

The room was silent for a few moments. "I'm so sorry for his behavior, Jazz. I can't believe he just said that," Roslynn admitted.

"It's cool. This is his house, so I have to respect that. Plus, I'm used to people talking shit to me. I'm kinda immune to it actually."

"Well, you shouldn't be." Roslynn looked around to see if Adrian was coming. "I know you married to a fuckin' fool, but don't get used to niggas talkin' to you like that. Girl, don't you know if I didn't need Adrian's money, I wouldn't let him talk shit to you like that. He woulda been cursed out."

"Is the money worth it, Ro?" Roslynn was caught off guard by her question. "I mean coming from someone who's had to use their husband's money, too. I would rather be broke in exchange for happiness. A piece of mind."

Roslynn looked around her house. "I don't know about that. All this shit seems pretty worth it to me." Both women started laughing. "By the way, what happened to your hair? I forgot to ask you that."

Jazmine rubbed her hand through her jagged short hair. "Vince cut it with a pocket knife."

"Are you serious? Girl, you really need to leave that crazy muthafucka alone. I'll call Ty to see if he can squeeze you in on Tuesday," Roslynn said. "You are gonna press charges about the rape aren't you?"

Jazmine disagreed. "No."

"Jazmine, are you trippin'? Why not? What the hell are you scared of?"

At that moment, Roslynn's cell phone rung, and almost sent Jazmine hiding under the couch. Her nerves were so fucked up. Roslynn told her that she could calm down because it wasn't

Vince. However, she also told Jazmine to be on the look out for Adrian while she took the call. Roslynn wasn't in the mood to talk to Kamilla, but she knew if she didn't answer, Kamilla may do something crazy.

"Well, hello, Mrs. Washington. How you doin' on dis beautiful spring day?" Kamilla asked sarcastically.

"Go to hell, bitch!"

"Now, is that anyway to talk to someone who holds yo' future in they hands?"

"What do you want?" Roslynn asked biting her tongue.

"I need that money."

"It ain't been no week since I talked to you," Roslynn responded.

"Yeah, I know, but I need my shit now. Got things to do wit' my loot."

"Why are you doing this? Why can't we just stick to the original plan, we have all this time."

"Because dat shit ain't workin' for me no more. I heard you came through the block wit' a BMW dat had thirty day tags and shit, so you obviously doin' the damn thang. Hell, I wanna be like you," Kamilla taunted.

Roslynn sat there for a few seconds, then reluctantly told Kamilla she would try and wire the money the next day.

"Don't fuck wit' me," Kamilla threatened just before Roslynn hung up.

"What was that all about?" Jazmine asked.

Roslynn knew she could only lie so much without raising any suspicion. "My irritatin'-ass cousing, Kamilla. She always callin' for money."

"Kamilla? I haven't seen her in years. Didn't she have a…"

Roslynn quickly interjected. "I ain't tryin' to talk about her ass. What we need to talk about is how we're gonna get some money."

Suddenly, Jazmine got serious. "I know you were joking bout us robbing a bank before, but do you think we would get away with it?" she whispered.

"Well, I think I might have something else we can do. Montee was tellin' me the other day that he was workin' on somethin' that was gonna get him paid. Maybe he'll let us in on it if we help him."

The mention of Montee's name made Jazmine instantly think of Vince and what she'd seen before leaving home. "I saw Montee's name come up on Vince's phone before I left, and at first I wondering what the hell they had to talk about, but then I found out."

Roslynn's eyes got big. "Don't tell me."

"Yep. Vince is on heroin. He was so drugged up before I left, he still had the syringe stuck in his damn arm. Hell, when Miles came to the door, Vince was completely naked." She made a mental note to call Miles and thank him for getting her out the house.

"Are you serious?" Roslynn yelled. "See, I knew that nigga had to be on somethin' actin' like that. Montee gettin' Vince his supply more than likely. Shit, he still the go to guy."

"Ssshhh.. Girl you better stop all that cursing before Adrian come back out here."

Roslynn looked around. "Oh, yeah you right."

"Call him," Jazmine said, handing Roslynn her cell phone.

"Call who?"

"Montee."

Roslynn could tell that Jazmine was serious. "Shoot, I gotta better idea. Let's go talk to him in person after we eat and get ourselves together. He not gonna want talk over the phone."

"What about Omari? I can't take him with us."

"Oh, Adrian will watch him," Roslynn said with a huge laugh.

Jazmine laughed, too. "I can't even take him to Ms. Gloria's cuz Vince might show up there."

"I gotta idea." Roslynn immediately yelled for Ramon. When he came running into the living room, she told him she needed him to watch Omari while her and Jazmine went shopping. Shopping was Roslynn's alibi for everything. "Actually, I'll make sure Mr. Washington pays you extra if you take him on a nice little boy's day out. Like the movies, or whatever else kids like to do."

Ramon happily agreed.

The girls looked outside first before they got into Roslynn's car three hours later. Knowing Vince's deranged-ass, he was probably staking out the house in full FBI style. As soon as they got into the car and pulled off, Jazmine looked out the side view mirror expecting to see him behind them at any moment, but there wasn't one car on the street.

Jazmine looked over at Roslynn. "Wow, I can't believe he's not following us or something?" However, before Roslynn could reply, Jazmine's cell phone began to ring. It was Vince. She showed Roslynn the caller ID.

"See, when you talk about the devil, his ass pops up," Roslynn said snatching the phone. She answered it and pretended that she had no idea where Jazmine was.

"How the fuck did you get her phone then, bitch?" Vince asked.

"Oh, it was a gift to me after she left town." Roslynn laughed while Vince cursed her out. "Yeah, I gave her ten G's so she could start a new life without you, Mr. Wife Beater."

"I'ma have her charged with kidnappin' for takin' my son without my permission. You better tell that bitch to bring her ass home!"

"It's her fuckin' son, too. So good luck with pressin' charges and while you at it…why don't you tell'em how you been beatin' her ass everyday? So they can lock yo' ass up or better yet, tell'em you been shootin' up heroin everyday as well. Picture that shit, a cop who supposed to be gettin' drugs off the street is usin' the shit himself!"

Vince was extremely quiet.

"That's right. We found out yo' lil' secret, nigga. Now, leave my friend the fuck alone!"

**∗∗∗**

Roslynn and Jazmine finally reached their old neighborhood, after being stuck in a bit of Sunday afternoon traffic. It had been a while since Jazmine had been there and she had to admit, it

wasn't exciting. Besides not wanting to be reminded of her childhood and broken home, Vince would never allow her to be seen
anywhere near that side of town anyway. She looked around and
was at a lost for words when she saw how the neighborhood had
changed from bad to worse. It wasn't the fun place she remembered growing up, and it certainly wasn't somewhere she wanted
to hang out on a regular.

"It ain't the same. Is it?" Roslynn asked.

"Not at all," Jazmine replied. "How did you know Montee
was still around here?"

Roslynn laughed. "I come around here all the time."

"Are you serious? You weren't scared that these young
thugs will car jack your ass. As a matter of fact, lock these damn
doors until we get to Montee's spot."

"Shit, I come around here all the time, but I ain't no damn
fool either. Trust me. I locked my damn doors, just so I can take
my fuckin' car back to Paramus."

Jazmine was sure Roslynn was loosing her mind. When
Roslynn slowed her car down for a white woman who was obviously an addict from the looks of her clothes and raggedy mouth,
she wondered what her friend was doing.

"Ro, what are you stopping for? She's probably looking for
drugs."

"And if she do, I'll tell her to go to yo' house," Roslynn
joked. "No, girl, she's cool," Roslynn said, pulling up next to the
woman. She rolled her window down.

"Montee said come up to the house. You can park here. I'll
watch yo' car," the woman said snifflin' and wipin' her nose.

Before Jazmine could protest, Roslynn had already stepped
out. Jazmine didn't move. "Get yo' ass out of the car."

Jazmine looked at Roslynn like she was terminally ill,
when she finally got out. "So, you gon' let a crack head watch your
shit?"

"Well, I ain't worried now. Montee will handle his
peeps…crack head or not. Plus, her ass should know how he rolls.
I personally wouldn't want to have to open the door for that fool
when he comes knockin'."

After setting her alarm, Roslynn handed the addict a twenty dollar bill she'd retrieved from her Gucci purse.

"Thanks, girlfriend," the addict said smiling. "I'll make sure don't nobody fuck wit' yo' ride."

Roslynn shook her head after seeing the woman only had four rotten teeth left in her mouth.

"Drug addiction is a terrible thing."

As Roslynn talked, Jazmine was preoccupied with what time it was. She'd become so accustomed to being home at a certain time that she couldn't seem to break the habit of looking at her watch.

"Jazz, will you stop checkin' the damn time," Roslynn said, grabbing her by the arm. "You don't have to go home to that maniac tonight."

After walking into one of the buildings in the Felix Court projects, the stairwell leading to Montee's apartment was buzzing with addicts. At one point, there was even a fight over a needle, which Roslynn and Jazmine were used to seeing. It instantly brought back old times as they approached Montee's door. However, before they even had a chance to knock, the door opened.

"Welcome to Montee's," he said grinning. Roslynn told him to shut up and move out of the way. "Who dis?" he asked.

"Muthafucka stop playin' so much. You know who the hell that is!"

Montee stared at Jazmine for a while, then laughed. "Oh, shit. What up, Jazzy?"

Jazmine smiled after hearing her childhood name even though no one called her that anymore. Vince would call her that sometimes when they first started dating and he was trying to win her over, but that quickly changed after they got married.

"Hey, Montee. How are you?" Jazmine asked.

"A lot better than you, I see. What bitch-ass nigga usin' you as a damn punchin' bag, Ma?"

Jazmine pushed her sunglasses up even though they didn't completely cover all the bruises. A blind man could see that she was fucked up.

"Oh, we just found out that you actually deal wit' this so

called bitch-ass nigga," Roslynn said.

Montee frowned. "Who you talkin' 'bout Ro 'cuz you know I do a lot of foul shit, but I don't get down wit' punk-ass women beaters. My faggot-ass step daddy used to do dat same shit to my moms for years until I got rid of his ass."

Roslynn wasn't shocked by Montee's confession. "Vince...Vince Anderson. You just called him yesterday."

Montee turned to Jazmine. "A yo' somebody told me you was married to 'dat punk-ass muthafucka, but you know I'm here...there so I ain't paid too much attention to dat shit. Yeah, I supply 'dat nigga and he spend mad money on dat shit." He rubbed his hands together. "Yo' Ma, you need to leave dat nigga cuz he out there wit' dat shit for real."

"Yeah well, I've already done that," Jazmine mentioned.

"Shit, Ma yo' husband almost came home in a body bag when I first found out his ass was a cop. I thought dat nigga was a undercover until he kept comin' round dis mufucka high all da time. I still have my boy record 'dat nigga every time he come 'round here just in case though."

Roslynn tried to change the subject by asking Montee for something to drink, but he refused. "You might be da Queen B in Paramus, but yo' ass just Ro 'round here. Get yo' own shit, Ma," he said, plopping down in a chair.

Jazmine sat back and admired Montee's apartment. She couldn't believe how nice it was inside with its color and grey color scheme.

Roslynn grabbed a bottle of Dasani water from the fridge. "Look, Montee we need to talk to you 'bout somethin'," Roslynn said, takin' a seat on his leather sofa.

However, before Montee even said a word, a tall light skinned guy walked out of Montee's bathroom, then made his way toward them. The closer he got, Roslynn began to smile because she knew exactly who it was.

"Cordell, what the fuck you doin' over here nigga?" Roslynn asked.

"What' up, Ro. I ain't seen you in a while." Cordell looked at Jazmine. "Damn, Jazzy at da spot, too. What's good Montee?

You ain't tell me 'dese fine ladies would be up in here."

"Nigga, did you blow my shit up?" Montee asked.

When Cordell began to laugh, the razor blade he always hid under his tongue fell out. "Hell yeah. I wouldn't go up in dat mufucka fo' a while."

For some reason, Cordell always reminded Roslynn of Fat Joe, but a slightly smaller version. Standing at 6'5, he was of Puerto Rican and Cuban descent, and had beautiful hazel colored eyes. Back in the day, his good looks got him tons of pussy, and probably still did.

"Oh shit, where my girl at? Where Alyse?" Cordell asked placing the blade in his hand.

"She's with her daughter," Jazmine mentioned.

"Oh, yeah. I heard she had a pretty lil' daughter. Damn, I messed up wit' 'dat girl," Cordell confessed. "Hey, call Alyse up so I can holla at 'er."

Suddenly Montee spoke up. "Look, y'all ain't come over here to make no fuckin' love connection. Let's get on to business. Shit, time is money."

"You right, nigga," Cordell agreed. He walked over to Montee and gave him a pound. "I'll be ready to do 'dat in 'bout a hour. Hit me up before you roll out." As Cordell made his way to the door, he looked back at Roslynn and Jazmine. "Tell Alyse fine-ass I said what up." After that, he walked out the door.

"Okay, now 'dat Cordell is gone, y'all need to let me know what's up. As you can see, I gotta busy schedule."

When Roslynn asked him about the big scheme he was planning, he cut his eye at her.

"Ro, come on man…don't be puttin' my fuckin' business out there like dat." He looked at Jazmine and said, "No offense Jazzy, but its not like we roll wit' da same crew. You been gone for a minute now, plus yo' man is 5-0."

Jazmine smiled and said, "None taken."

He was beginning to feel a little uncomfortable about them even being in his house. Roslynn told Montee to chill out because Jazmine was cool to talk around, and he had her word on that. He was still a little hesitant, but ended up telling them that he had a bank scam in the works, but it fell through.

"Da bitch who worked on the inside got smart out da mouth wit' her boss and got fired, so we ass out now. Da only way we can pull da shit off now is if we get someone inside a bank who can access da accounts," he said, lighting a blunt.

Jazmine glanced at Roslynn and saw the wheels in her head spinning.

"I think I know the perfect person," Roslynn stated.

"You're not talking about Adrian are you?" Jazmine asked.

Roslynn laughed at her naïve friend. Surely Adrian wouldn't be a part in anything illegal. He didn't even drive over the speed limit, so he would never go for something like that.

"No, I'm talking bout Jerry," she mentioned.

"Who da hell is Jerry? He from 'round the way?" Montee asked, choking on the smoke from the blunt.

Roslynn told him that Jerry was the V.P. at her husband's bank and that she'd caught him with another man at a hotel not long ago. Montee wondered what Jerry being gay had to do with anything, until Roslynn told him that Jerry's father-in-law was a top politician in New Jersey, so there was no way he would want that shit to get out.

"If his wife found out about his secret, that shit would be major. Not only that, Adrian would have to fire him because he would be a liability to the company after the scandal hit the papers," Roslynn said. "And trust me, I would go straight to the fuckin' Star Ledger, New York Times, everything."

Jazmine couldn't believe what she was hearing. "Ro, this is getting out of control. We can't go around tearing up people's families."

"As long as that dick sucker does what we tell him then I won't have to." She diverted her attention back to Montee. "Trust me. He can get the info we need."

She could tell Montee wasn't sure about her plan, so she told him that the payoff from her husband's bank would be three times bigger because most of his customers were wealthy.

"What about Adrian?" Jazmine asked sharply.

"What about him? No one's gonna get hurt, besides the

money is just sittin' there anyway. The accounts we're goin' after are called dormant accounts. That money is unclaimed. I can get the list of accounts with the names from Jerry."

"She right," Montee added. "I remember dat bitch we had on the inside say somethin' 'bout those accounts. All we gotta do is get some ID's made with da account holders name on it. If we need anythin' else, you gotta get dat info from yo' boy."

"That's right. So, what's it gonna be," Roslynn asked Montee.

He thought about it for about a half a minute before saying, "Fuck it. Let's roll wit' it!"

Roslynn looked over at Jazmine. "We all need this money so are you in or out? If you don't do this how the hell are you and Omari gonna start over. It ain't like you sittin' on some dough. Don't you need to hire some top notch lawyer to represent you when you divorce Vince's crazy-ass?"

Roslynn needed Jazmine to see the magnitude of what could happen if she didn't get some money and get it quick. Jazmine was quiet as she pondered her decision. After weighing all her options, she reluctantly said she was in.

"Now, all I have to do get at Jerry then let Alyse in on what were gonna do," Roslynn said.

After telling Roslynn to call him as soon as she had the list and the information they needed, Montee walked with them out the door. When they left, Roslynn thought about how she'd been out of the game for a while, but because her circumstances were out of control she'd been pulled back in. Not wanting to get Alyse's hopes up, the girls were going to wait until they were sure Jerry was going to be on board before they told her about the plan. As usual, Roslynn swung right in action. She called Jerry and told him to meet her for lunch at the Grand Lux Café off Route 1, on Monday. He was about to tell her no until she mentioned the incident at the hotel.

"Be there by one o'clock and don't fuck wit' me fruit cake. If you do, I'll be sure to tell yo' wife you gettin' it in the ass. Or are you givin' it?" she asked with a slight laugh.

# Chapter Seventeen

Alyse walked down the hall toward the elevators in a complete daze. Nothing about the last seventy-two hours seemed real, certainly not her daughter having Sickle Cell or Lance not being Brie's father. She'd been calling Lance almost every ten minutes since receiving the devastating news on Saturday, but he'd yet to pick up. Sometimes the phone would even go straight to voicemail. Now it was Monday, and he still wasn't answering. She could only imagine the pain he was going through, and didn't blame him for going off on her, but she just wanted to talk in order to try and work things out. Alyse especially wanted to talk to him now since she'd just been informed that the Board of Directors had decided to meet about Brie's case later on that afternoon. She didn't want to go through this all alone, and needed Lance now more than ever before.

Thinking that he may be home, and just not answering the phone, Alyse decided to finally leave the hospital and go look for Lance. She also wanted to take a real shower, and get more clothes, if the hospital would be her new place of residence for a while.

When Alyse walked out into the hospital parking lot, she wondered around for her car for at least ten minutes before realizing that she didn't drive.

"Shit!" she yelled, breaking down.

She was in a very fragile emotional state when she walked back into the hospital and asked the receptionist at the information desk if she could call her a cab. After receiving the news that cabs normally hung out near the emergency room entrance anyway, she walked toward that area, out the door and right up to one of the yellow cars. Exhausted, Alyse plopped down in the cab, before leaning her head back up against the seat and giving the driver her address. With so many things happening all at once, she really did-n't have to think about why she'd decided to deceive her husband four years ago, but it was a secret Alyse never thought would come out.

She knew all along that her old boyfriend, Cordell was Brie's father, but tried her to best to block it out of her mind. Hell, Brie even looked like Cordell when she smiled, and even had his hazel eyes. Knowing her body from two other miscarried pregnancies, Alyse knew she was already pregnant when she first met Lance, but never told him. She actually never told anyone, not even her friends. Luckily, she and Lance had sex without protection on their second date, which allowed her to ultimately choose Lance as the father. Besides, by Cordell being a high profile drug dealer, she knew Lance would be a better candidate anyway. It was messed up, but at the time Alyse thought she was making the best decision, now she wasn't so sure.

Once the cab driver dropped Alyse off in front of her building a few minutes later, she quickly walked up to her apartment, hoping that Lance was inside. She had a lot of making up to do with her husband, and couldn't wait to see if he would give her another chance. After placing the key in the door, she opened it with a wide swing, then immediately called Lance's name.

"Lance…honey," she said.

There was no answer. Looking around, Alyse noticed several hangers on the floor which started in the living room. Following the trail, which led all the way to the closet in the bedroom, Alyse was completely shocked to see that all of Lance's clothes were gone. She was both worried and angry that he would just leave her and Brie without saying a word. She went back into the living room and picked up the cordless phone sitting on the table only to find out there wasn't a dial tone. It had been cut off. She grabbed her cell phone and dialed Lance only to hear the annoying operator say, "The number that you dialed is no longer in service." Alyse dropped to her knees and cried.

\*\*\*

"Dr. Atkins," Alyse called, as she followed the doctor into the hallway. "I know you about to meet wit' the board."

"Yes, I am."

"I'm sure 'dis has to do wit' us not bein' able to pay for Brie's medical expenses."

"Actually, amongst other things it does."

"Dr. Atkins, I know you and Ms. Edwards have a job to do…I understand the hospital's policy, but is there any chance the board will make a different decision than they have in the past? I mean...do you have children?"

He nodded his head. "Yes, Mrs. Greffen, I do. I have three as a matter of fact, two boys and a girl."

"That's a true blessin' to be given three children. My husband and I were only blessed wit' one."

"Yes, I would consider myself blessed."

"You love yo' children, right?" Alyse asked. Her eyes were filled with tears.

"Mrs. Greffen, may I ask what you are trying to get at?"

"I'm not tryin' to get at anythin'. It's just crazy dat' the fate of my child rest in the hands of a Board of Directors."

She wondered if Dr. Atkins had the heart and courage to go into a board room filled with big shots and state the fact that a child is dying because her parents lack health insurance. She didn't have faith that he could make them understand that they should give her the adequate care that Brie needed.

"Mrs. Greffen, this is very unfortunate that you and your family are going through this, but you're not the first nor will you be the last case that I have to explain to the board," Dr. Atkins responded in a frustrated tone.

Sensing his frustration, Alyse caught a quick attitude herself and lapsed out momentarily. "Fuck you! Who the hell do you think you are? Don't compare my daughter to any other case you had to take to the board. As much money as 'dis damn hospital got it can't fund a few uninsured people. What the hell kinda shit is 'dat? You people can add additional wings just to make yo' damn fancy cafeteria and a goddamn Starbucks, but my fuckin' child can't get medical care because we don't have insurance."

Dr. Atkins turned red. "Mrs. Greffen, please lower your tone. Clearly a person without insurance can receive medical care, but just not at this hospital. It is neither my problem nor the hospital's problem that you have failed to adequately insure your family."

"My husband provides for us. Just because a man falls down on his luck don't make him like every other case. He's worked very hard to take care of us and now you think you gonna kick him while he's down. Dr. Atkins, you better tell the *board* my daughter ain't leavin' 'dis fuckin' hospital until she is well enough to go *home*," Alyse stated.

The doctor turned the corner down the hall. Alyse walked back into Brie's room. She whispered, "I'm not letting them send you nowhere baby."

Thinking about what she had just done, Alyse ran behind the doctor. "Dr. Atkins!" she yelled, grabbing him by the arm.

Dr. Atkins snapped. "Look, Mrs. Greffen. That's enough. I'll see what I can do to help you out, but you're directing your apparent frustration to the wrong person. I don't make the decisions. It's up to Jan Edwards and the board."

"Doctor, I'm sorry I lashed out at you. I'm just at a dead end. I apologize for my actions, but I don't apologize for my words. For one moment put yourself in my shoes, you would feel the same way. I just ask that you do all 'dat you can for Brie as you would do as a father for yo' children."

As Alyse walked away, Dr. Atkins thought to his own children and how enraged he would be if he were in that situation. He also thought of how so many families go without health insurance and expect miracles. He decided to go with his thoughts as he walked toward the conference room.

Inside the board meeting, silence filled the space. Members of the board deliberated and although Dr. Atkins pleaded his case with high emotions, and logical explanations, the board made its decision as it had done so many times in the past. Brie would have to be transported to University Hospital once a room was available.

An hour later, Alyse was awakened by the sounds of the

beeping machine after falling asleep. She arose to find the nurse in her room removing the medicine packs from the machine. Unsure of what was going on, Alyse wasted no time asking.

"What are you doin'?"

"I'm sorry Mrs. Greffen. Has the doctor been in to see you yet?

"No, he hasn't." She rose from her chair to face the woman.

"Mrs. Greffen, I received orders from Dr. Atkins to remove all the penicillin packs."

"Why?" Alyse inquired.

"Ma'am, I'm not sure. I'm just following the orders I received."

Alyse went off. "Well, since you don't know the reason, how 'bout you find me someone who does?"

"Ma'am, as soon as I..." the nurse tried to say.

"No, I don't think you understand." She started toward the nurse. "You ain't removin' shit 'til my questions are answered."

The nurse immediately left the room in search of Dr. Atkins.

Moments later, he entered the room to check on Brie and to explain the changes he'd ordered.

"Mrs. Greffen," Dr. Atkins spoke in a somber tone.

"Cut the shit doctor" Alyse scolded. "What's goin' on?"

"Mrs. Greffen, I need to tell you about the news from today's board meeting."

Alyse sat down and prepared herself for the bad news.

"First and foremost, I have to apologize to you for my words earlier today. I found myself responding to your rage that wasn't necessarily directed toward me, but at the situation. You had the right to respond as you did. I don't agree completely with your behavior or words, but I do understand where it came from."

"Thank you. I apologize for my actions as well. But Doc, I have to know what's goin' on," Alyse pleaded.

"Mrs. Greffen, I entered that board room today and fought for you. I fought as hard as I could for your daughter. I fought as if she were my own child needing the best care that only this hospital could provide. I suggested charities that could help you and even mentioned an anonymous charitable donor that I'm aware of."

Tears began to flow from Alyse's face as she knew where this conversation was headed.

Dr. Atkins continued. "The board decided that without medical insurance we would have to treat this case as we've treated every other case bought to them to avoid any lawsuits or discriminatory acts. So, with that said, the board denied the request to keep Brie here. She has to be given the minimum generic medications and be taken off others. We are only required at this point to maintain stability of her condition until a room is available at University Hospital. We anticipate an available room over there within the next week."

Alyse bellowed over in agony. She knew the road for her only child was nearing an end. University Hospital, as everyone knew would not be able to provide the necessary care for a person with a simple cold let alone a Sickle Cell patient.

"But what about the blood transfusion that she was scheduled to have 'dis week? Brie is startin' to complain much more about her pain, so I know her condition is gettin' worse, and she's always weak."

"I'm so sorry, but I'm not gonna be able to perform the transfusion now. I've been ordered to not only reduce Brie's medications but to also minimize my check ups throughout the remainder of her stay." The doctor felt an emptiness in his stomach because there was nothing he could do. "Mrs. Greffen, I'm deeply sorry for the outcome of all this."

Alyse walked out of the room and headed toward the stairwell. She wanted to be alone. She wanted to go somewhere and release her pain. Her child, her only child was knocking on deaths door, and there was nothing she could do about it. She felt helpless. If only Lance had told her about the insurance situation before, just maybe she could've sought help elsewhere

Unsure of her next move, she entered the stairwell and sat on the cold concrete steps, and silently began to pray.

# Chapter Eighteen

The fact that he was bisexual was something Jerry thought no one would ever find out about. He was very careful when it came to meeting places and only messed with other married bisexual men. That way he could never be threatened, but this time he'd obviously fucked up.

When he showed up fifteen minutes late, he found Roslynn sitting in a booth in the back of the café drinking her second Iced Tea like nothing was wrong.

"You're late," Roslynn stated.

He kept quiet for a minute studying her mood. "Sorry. I had some last minute things to do at the office," Jerry said, taking a seat across from her. "So, what's this all about?"

"Well, let's see. I have one friend who needs to get away from her abusive-ass husband and my other friend has a daughter who's sick. They're both in dire need of a large sum of money, and that's where you come in." She knew he would take great pleasure in knowing she had money problems so she intentionally left herself out of the equation.

Before he could ask Roslynn if she was on something, a waitress walked over and asked Jerry if he would like to order something. He told her no, but Roslynn told her to bring him an Iced Tea as well. "You're not gonna let me drink alone are you?" she asked smiling.

"Fine, I'll have a glass," he said gritting his teeth.

When the waitress went to get the drink, Roslynn went in for the kill. "So, how long have you been suckin' dicks?"

Jerry bit his bottom lip. "Lower your voice," he whispered across the table.

"Don't tell me what to do, faggot!"

"I'm just asking you to not announce my sexuality to everyone in here, that's all."

"Well, I won't announce your sexuality to everyone if you can get me the names of those dormant account holders you and Adrian were talkin' about in the office that day."

Jerry laughed. "Are you insane?"

Roslynn smirked. "No, I'm not insane. But you my friend are gay and married to a popular politician's daughter who will divorce yo' ass if she ever finds out. How am I doin' so far?" She waited for Jerry to answer, but he never did. "Oh, and you'll make the front page of every newspaper and lose yo' job at the bank. What about now?"

Jerry felt his temperature rising, so he clenched his fist. "What the fuck is wrong with you? Don't you have anything better to do then go around blackmailing people? Do you like going around destroying families? Is this shit fun to you?"

"Why do you say that? Aren't you havin' fun?"

"Yeah, a blast," Jerry sarcastically said.

Roslynn got very serious. "Look, my friends need this money and you're gonna help me get it for them."

"Roslynn, I can't get that information."

She pulled out her cell phone and went to her pictures. "See, I knew this would come in handy one day." She clicked on the one of Jerry and his lover and enlarged it so he could get a good look. "Jerry, don't fuck with me. All I have to do is email this sick shit over to yo' wife, and it's a wrap for yo' gay-ass. Now, in that case you have two choices. Either get me the fuckin' list by tomorrow or get ready for all hell to break loose."

Jerry ran his hand down his face. "Roslynn, you don't understand. Besides Adrian, I'm the only one who has access to those accounts. If one thing goes wrong we're gonna get caught."

"No, we won't because you're gonna tell us exactly what to do in order to get the money without causin' any suspicion. For example, if any of those accounts specialists call you for authorization, you're gonna sign your name and keep it movin'. Got it!"

Jerry finally nodded.

"So, what do we need to make this happen? An

ID…what?"

Jerry was extremely hesitant before answering. "Yes, you'll need an ID in the estate manager's name. All of our dormant account holders are deceased so their funds are now handled by an estate manager. They are the only ones at this point who can take out the money."

"Okay, what happens after that?"

"Roslynn are you sure about this? It has to be another way for your friends to get money. What about a loan? I can push a few buttons and approve a loan for them," Jerry said.

Roslynn threw up her hands. "Muthafucka, they don't need no shit they gotta pay back, dumb-ass."

Jerry paused when the waitress finally came back with his tea.

"Are you all ready to order?" she asked.

"Do y'all serve ass crack by any chance," Roslynn asked. "My friend here loves ass crack."

Jerry was completely embarrassed.

The waitress looked confused. "I don't understand what you're saying."

"No, please give us a few more minutes," Jerry said. He didn't say anything else until the young girl walked away.

"Now, tell me what the fuck happens from there," Roslynn threatened.

"Well, from there you'll need to open up an account in the estate manager's name. A dummy account…at another bank of course. Once the account is open, someone would need to come into Washington Savings and have the money from the dormant account transferred to the dummy account. A wire transfer is the easiest way."

"That don't sound too difficult."

"It'll only gets difficult once someone tries to get the money out of the dummy account. If you try and get cash, it can't exceed $10,000. Anything over that has to be reported to the IRS."

"Okay…so what do we do?" Roslynn asked. She wasn't sure if Montee knew how to do all this, but wanted to know for her own benefit.

"The only way to fly under the radar is to pull the money out a little bit at a time, and even then you can't get over $10,000 within a twelve month period. Otherwise, you would have to get an off shore bank account."

"Man, we ain't goin' through all that shit. The damn names and address are gonna be fake anyway so who cares what they report. We need all our money at one time. That's why when you give me that list, we goin' after the accounts with the most money."

"But some of those accounts have thousands of dollars. It'll send a red flag instantly."

"So fuckin' what? We ain't pullin' out no lil' bit of money at a time."

Jerry rubbed his bald head. "You've been saying we a lot. Are you in on it, too?"

"No, I aint' in on it, but you are." Roslynn went in her huge Chloe purse and pulled out an 8x10 picture of Jerry caught in the act, then slid it over to him. "I had the picture blown up just in case you wanted to put it up on yo' desk at work."

Jerry couldn't believe how Roslynn was acting. In all the years he'd known her, she was always kind, respectful and never said one curse word. Now, she was a completely different person.

Grabbing the picture, Jerry quickly ripped it up. "I never would've thought Adrian was married to such an evil and devious person," he boldly stated.

"And I never would'a thought Adrian would hire a punk-ass sissy such as yourself," Roslynn shot back.

Meanwhile, while Roslynn and Jerry went over the final details, Jazmine sat out in Roslynn's car and thought about where her and Omari were going to go. By Adrian making it very clear that he didn't want them at his house, she had to figure out something. However, with no money her options were limited.

Jazmine pulled out her phone to call Miles, but decided not to. She figured that he would only ask her a bunch of questions that she didn't feel like answering at the moment. She placed the phone on her lap, and stared out the window at two women who gave each other a high five, then laughed. The women didn't appear to be girlfriends because of the obvious age difference. The younger looking one wore booty shoots, while the older one with grey colored hair, had on out of style high waist Levi jeans. They both appeared to be having fun, and obviously shared a close bond. Like mother and daughter. Jazmine watched them until they got into a minivan and drove away.

Suddenly, an overwhelming amount of sadness came over her, and she knew exactly why. Seeing the two women instantly reminded Jazmine of the relationship she used to have with her own mother. It had been almost two years, since she'd seen or talked to her mom, and it hurt to know that their relationship was non-existent. Since Vince drove a wedge between them, Jazmine used to long that her mother would eventually reach out to her, but it never happened. Now, Jazmine felt as though it might be a good time to reconnect.

Picking up her phone again, Jazmine's hands began to shake as she dialed the ten digit number. It was amazing that she even remembered it. When the phone began to ring, she became even more nervous.

"Praise the Lord," her mother answered. When Jazmine didn't say anything, her mother repeated her greeting. "Praise the Lord."

She cleared her throat. "Ma."

This time her mother was quiet for a second. "Jazmine."

"Yeah, Ma. It's me." When her mother paused again, Jazmine knew she was probably surprised. "How've you been?"

"I've been hanging in there. My goodness. I just can't believe you called," her mom responded.

"Yeah, I know. It's been a while."

"How's Omari? I know he's getting big now."

"Indeed he is," Jazmine responded. After that it was more awkward silence. Like neither one of them knew what to say. At that point, Jazmine decided to go in for the kill. "Look, Ma I know things have been bad between us but…"

Her mother interrupted. "Well, things didn't have to be bad, but you allowed that husband of yours to come between us."

"I know, and I'm sorry for that."

"Believe me, I'm a Christian woman, so I know a wife is supposed to honor their husband, but how could you listen to someone who constantly called me out of my name and told me that it was a good thing your father left me."

Jazmine didn't reply.

"I raised you to be a strong woman, Jazmine. How could you allow someone to put evil things in your head? How could you stop bringing my grandson to see me? How could you stop taking my phone calls? I begged you to talk to me. I begged you to come to the hospital after I had a minor stroke, but you never came. You left me all alone. Why would you do that?" It seemed like her mother had tons of questions.

"I don't know, Ma."

"That husband of yours is just like your father…evil, and I don't want no parts of it," her mother stated. "Look, this is making my blood pressure go up. I need to go."

"Ma, wait. Can me and Omari come stay with you for a while?"

"And have that devil come to my house looking for you all, no way."

"No, I finally left Vince, so he's not gonna bother us. I promise."

"Jazmine, I've been hurt for the past two years over this, and honestly I'm just starting to let my wounds heal. I don't think I want to reopen those same wounds."

Jazmine began to cry. When she looked out the front window and saw Roslynn making her way over. "So, are you saying no?"

"Yes, for now I am. Please give my love to Omari. Good-bye."

Visibly upset, Jazmine threw her phone on the floor, just as Roslynn got in.

"Girl, it's on now. Wait 'til I tell you the plan." Roslynn looked at her friend. "What's wrong? Have you been talkin' to Vince?"

Jazmine lowered her head. "No, my mother."

"Your mother? You called her?"

Jazmine nodded. "Yeah, but it might've been a complete waste of time. I asked her if me and Omari could come and stay and she said no."

Roslynn knew the pain Jazmine was going through all too well. She also longed for a healthy relationship with her crack head mother up until the day she died.

"Aren't Christians supposed to forgive?" Jazmine asked.

"Well, maybe she forgave you, but just can't forget," Roslynn responded. "But hey, then again, what the fuck do I know? I'm far from being a Christian. All I know is that we about to get this paper, and after that you and Omari ain't gonna have to worry about nobody."

Jazmine wiped her face. "So, what happened?"

"Jerry's down wit' the shit, that's what happened. Well, not that he had much of a choice. Now all we gotta do is tell Alyse, and we straight."

Roslynn started up her car, and quickly pulled out of the parking lot headed toward the hospital. The two friends talked all the way there about how the money would change their lives and keep their lives from falling completely apart. For Jazmine, it meant a life free from abuse and fear. It wasn't going to be that simple for Roslynn. Sure she could finally get caught up on her bills but it wasn't going keep Kamilla off her back for long. She was definitely going to have to get rid of her cousin, once and for all.

✳✳✳

That same afternoon at the bank, Jerry went into his office and closed the door. He pulled out his laptop and logged on to the bank's computer network. He had forgotten that in order to get into that particular area of records you had to be logged in under your access ID and password. If he used his own access code that would leave him wide open to be linked to the scheme if they were caught. He needed to be on someone else's terminal, so he went out on the floor and searched for an empty computer that was already logged into. He found one in the customer service manager's

167

office. It wouldn't be unusual for him to be in her office because he worked directly with her all the time. He went in, closed the door, and went to the deceased records. He was amazed at how much money was sitting in the accounts. When he saw the total of all the accounts was a staggering two million dollars, he shut his eyes and opened them again to make sure he wasn't seeing things. He printed off the names and the account numbers and logged out and maximized the window she was previously on. He got up from behind her desk and walked over to the printer to retrieve the copies.

"Hey man, what you up to?" Adrian said, surprising Jerry.

"Umm...I just had to take care of that stuff for the dormant accounts. I called the estates and a couple of them will be withdrawing the money soon."

"Oh good. I'm quite sure they could use the money," Adrian replied.

"Hey, what's Roslynn been up to?" Jerry asked. He was trying to feel Adrian out.

Adrian let out a sigh. "Running a fucking hotel in my house that's what she's been up to."

"What do you mean?"

"A friend of hers along with her son, are staying with us. Don't get me wrong, I do feel for her friend's situation because she was abused by her husband, but I'm just afraid they are going to be there longer than expected." Adrian said.

"Wow. I didn't know Roslynn had friends like that."

"Not only that, I don't want her friend hanging around thinking we're going to be providing her with money because that's not going to happen."

Normally Adrian didn't vent to Jerry, but for some reason, this time it felt necessary.

"Don't worry. I'm sure her friend will come into her own money soon," Jerry replied. *Literally*, he thought to himself.

"I hope you're right." When Jerry finally turned around to leave, Adrian called out for him. "Hey, thanks for taking care of those accounts."

Jerry smiled, told him no problem, and got the hell out of there. He felt bad about what he was about to do to Adrian, but he had no choice. If his wife found out about him being bisexual he would have to give up everything he'd worked so hard for. Not to mention, his own family. His father would definitely disown him. Adrian wasn't worth him losing all that.

# Chapter Nineteen

Standing in the doorway of Brie's hospital room, Jazmine and Roslynn watched for a few moments as Alyse read a *Backyardigans* book to Brie. She hadn't been responding much over the past few hours, and looked helpless. She was even too weak to even say hello to the girls when they walked in. It was a frightening sight. Brie's weakness could've played a part of her not having much of an appetite lately, which was another thing for Alyse to be concerned about. The last thing Brie needed was to lose some weight. As Roslynn and Jazmine walked over, they could tell Alyse had barely slept because her eyes were red and she had the words sleep deprived written all over her face.

"Hey, girls," Alyse said barely able to get up from the chair. She looked as though she'd lost a few pounds herself.

Jazmine gave her a huge hug. "It seems like forever since I've seen you."

"I know," Alyse agreed. "What did you do to your hair?"

Jazmine was definitely self conscience about her short hair. "It's a long story, but let's just say this new style was compliments of Vince."

Roslynn walked over and kissed Brie on her forehead. "Auntie Ro loves you."

Brie forced a smile.

"Hey, where's Lance?" Jazmine questioned.

At that moment, Alyse wanted to cry, but felt as if she didn't have any tear ducts left. Instead, she just gave a blank stare.

"Alyse, what's wrong? Is Lance okay? Where is he?" Jazmine reiterated.

This time Alyse managed to hunch her shoulders.

"When's the last time you left this room? Let's go downstairs to Starbucks for a moment. We have to talk to you about somethin' important anyway," Roslynn suggested.

"No, not right now y'all," Alyse replied.

"Come on, Alyse. Let's get an Iced Mocha or something. You look like you could use the energy. We'll come right back up," Roslynn said with her own agenda in mind.

Alyse ended up agreeing to go with her friends, although she didn't want to leave her daughter's bedside. While kissing her daughter's forehead and rubbing her head, Alyse told her she would be right back. Brie didn't respond. She just laid there not wanting to move so the pain wouldn't kick in. The disease seemed to be taking over her little body in a rapid pace. As the three women walked down to the cafeteria, Alyse's thoughts were with Brie. She would give anything to be able to trade places with her. She didn't deserve this. No child did.

After getting to the popular coffee spot, the last thing on Alyse's mind was eating. So when Jazmine put a banana muffin and an Iced Vanilla Latte in front of her, she pushed it to the side.

"Thanks but I'm not hungry."

"You need to eat somethin'," Roslynn said, pushing the muffin and coffee back toward her. "You lost a lil' weight since I was here a few days ago."

"Did the hospital make a decision about letting Brie stay here?" Jazmine inquired.

Alyse sighed deeply, then told them that she had to be moved to University. "They might as well let her go home. I stand a better chance takin' care of her than 'dat place."

Roslynn hated to bring the subject up again, since Alyse didn't have any answers a while ago, but she had to ask. "Alyse, where Lance at?"

"Gone," she replied in a low tone.

Roslynn frowned. "Gone, where?"

Alyse sat quietly for a moment, before speaking up. "Lance found out 'dat Brie wasn't his daughter, so he left. I ain't seen 'em since."

Jazmine spit out the water she was drinking. "What?" She wiped her mouth with the back of her hand.

"What the hell are you talkin' about Alyse?" Roslynn asked.

Alyse became slightly irritated. "He's gone, I said. Brie is not his daughter, and he found out."

Both Jazmine and Roslynn looked at each other with a dumbfounded expression.

"I know y'all confused. I never told y'all or anybody else 'bout 'dis but Cordell is Brie's father, not Lance," Alyse admitted.

"Shut the hell up. Bitch, you lyin'," Roslynn said. She wanted to call Alyse a ho so bad, but felt it wasn't the right time.

Alyse moved her head left and right. "No, I'm not. I was already pregnant wit' Brie when me and Lance hooked up."

"Why didn't you tell us?" Jazmine was curious.

"I don't know. I guess I got so wrapped up in my own lies 'dat I started to believe the shit myself. Plus, I just knew 'dat Lance would be a better father 'cause everybody knew Cordell won't father material," Alyse replied.

"Well, at least Cordell would'a had more money," Roslynn laughed.

Jazmine sucked her teeth. "Ro, stop being so damn insensitive."

"I ain't thinkin' 'bout her ass," Alyse said.

"No, I'm serious. Plus, I always wondered what you saw in Lance anyway 'cause he's not the cutest thing," Roslynn admitted. "I also used to wonder why the hell Brie was so light. Now, the shit make sense. She looks a lot like Cordell."

"So, did Lance tell you he was leaving?" Jazmine questioned.

Alyse frowned. "Nope, by the time I got home he had packed all of his stuff and left."

"Don't worry. He'll come around. He's just in shock right now," Jazmine advised.

Roslynn fidgeted in her seat not sure if she should mention what they were planning. She was pretty sure Alyse would want to do whatever she needed to help her daughter, but she wasn't sure if she would do something illegal. She wanted to be there for her friend, but at the same time all she had was money on the brain.

# GOOD *Girl* GONE **BAD**

Roslynn gave Jazmine a look that said, 'Why don't you bring the bank scam up'.

"Why the hell y'all actin' so weird? Y'all keep lookin' at each other like y'all hidin' somethin' from me." She was so out of it, she hadn't even noticed the fresh bruises on Jazmine's face. "Vince still beatin' on you?"

Neither Jazmine nor Roslynn responded. Instead they just looked at one another again and tried to come up with a lie.

"Look, I know I got issues but I still wanna know what the hell is goin' on. Talk to me!"

Suddenly, Jazmine began to tell Alyse everything that went down between her and Vince, which ultimately helped Alyse forget about her own problems for a minute.

"Where you stayin'?" Alyse inquired.

"I've been staying with Ro. I'll probably be there one more night, and then me and Omari are gonna leave. We'll just go to a hotel or something."

Alyse seemed confused. "A hotel?"

"Yeah, Adrian is actin' like a bitch, so I'm gonna give her a few bucks so she can have her own space," Roslynn enlightened.

As much as Roslynn wanted to cry the blues all day with her friends, she needed to discuss the task at hand. She eased into the subject gently by first asking Alyse if she could get her hands on the money for Brie's hospital bill.

"No, and if you know a way for me to get the money short of killin' somebody then I'm prepared to do it. My daughter's heath depends on it."

"Well, you wouldn't have to kill nobody, but the shit would be illegal," Roslynn stated.

Alyse didn't even think twice. "So, what's the plan?" she said willing to make the ultimate sacrifice for her daughter.

"Montee came up with this scheme to get..." Roslynn tried to say.

"Wait Montee. What made y'all hook up wit' him?" Alyse interjected.

"Never mind the reason. Check this out. There are a lot of dead people who still have money in their bank accounts because

**174**

they didn't have wills and shit I guess. We gonna get this list of accounts from Jerry, then make fake ID's of the account's estate manager so we can go into another bank, open up a dummy account, then withdraw the money," Roslynn explained in a low tone. Even though there was quite a bit of noise in Starbucks, she hoped that Alyse understood the process, so she wouldn't have to repeat it.

"The gay guy Jerry is in on 'dis?" Alyse asked.

Roslynn smiled. "Hell yeah, that faggot is in on it. He don't have much of a choice."

"So, what do I have to do?" Alyse questioned.

Roslynn looked around before answering. "Well, we have to go into Adrian's bank in order to get the money transferred to the dummy account, so I can't be involved in that part. That's where you, Jazmine and Montee will come in. I just need a picture of you to put on one of the fake ID's. Y'all will be the ones to go in and withdraw the money out the dummy accounts, too. It's really simple."

Alyse couldn't believe how serious Roslynn was. "Oh my, God. What about Adrian?"

"What about 'em? Shit, if this thing works out, I just might leave his ass anyway. I need to be myself, and he won't allow it. I hate that about him. Besides, it's not like we stealin' directly outta Adrian's pocket. That fuckin' money don't belong to him."

Alyse wasn't sure about Roslynn's plan to get the money, but she had no choice but to go along with it. She couldn't have Brie going to another hospital and that was final.

Alyse still had questions like when they were going to pull the scheme off. Roslynn told her some time before the end of the week. All they had to do was be patient and all of their money problems would be a thing of the past.

"I got about three thousand left on one of my credit cards. I'll take out an advance and give the hospital that money, then tell 'em that my husband and I will be paying for Brie's expenses. That way it won't be so suspicious when you give them the money. Plus it might buy her some time here," Roslynn said.

"Oh, that's a good idea," Jazmine replied.

Alyse's face finally lit up. It was the best news she'd heard in a while. "Dat is a good idea."

Roslynn smiled. "Shit, we about to come across some major paper, so it's the least I can do," she pointed at Jazmine. "And you. Once we get this money, yo' ass will have enough money to start over. You need to be on the first plane outta this bitch after everything goes down."

"Actually, I have something even better planned for Vince. Something that will keep him away for good," Jazmine confessed.

"You sneaky lil' devil," Roslynn said, laughing. "I knew you weren't gonna let that muthafucka get away with all that shit. You try to act all sweet, but that shit is just a cover up."

Jazmine grinned. "No, I don't plan on letting Vince get away at all. Just know, no matter what, I love you guys more than life itself." She looked at her watch. "Oh, I have an appointment at Omari's school."

"It's crazy how you take small things for granted. I actually miss pickin' up Brie from school," Alyse said, then looked at Jazmine. "Is Omari in school today? Are you worried 'dat Vince will show up there?"

"No, I'm not worried 'cuz Omari is not there, and I don't plan on sending him back. I actually plan on finding a new school for him, so that's what this meeting is all about. I need to talk to his teachers."

"Where is he then?" Alyse asked.

"He's been hanging out at Ro's house with the chef Ramon and having a ball. He probably don't ever wanna go back to school anyway. Ro, I'll meet you back at your house later on," Jazmine stated.

"And how are you gonna do that. I drove remember," Roslynn responded.

Jazmine sighed. "Shit! I forgot."

"Here girl!" Roslynn said, throwing a set of keys.

Jazmine looked shocked. "Hold up. These are my keys."

"I know. I had Montee go get your car when Vince left for work today," Roslynn said. "Yo' ass better be glad you don't have a fuckin' garage."

Jazmine started jumping up and down then told Roslynn

how grateful she was.

"Oh, shit. I need to go too," Alyse said, jumping up. I told Brie I would be right back." Luckily, she had her wallet so she handed Roslynn her old hotel badge. "I don't have a picture, but maybe he can use 'dis."

"I'm sure his crooked-ass will be able to pull it off," Roslynn replied.

After saying their goodbyes, Roslynn was about to get up from the table when her cell phone rang. It was the number to Adrian's bank.

"Hey, baby."

"Not!" the male voice replied. "Meet me in an hour at the same place."

When Roslynn heard Jerry's voice, she got excited because she knew that meant he'd obtained the list. She finished up the sandwich and left right afterwards. Strolling out of the hospital's corridor sporting a pair of Versace sunshades that looked like they were designed especially for her, she got into her car and let the top down. She ran her fingers across the dashboard and turned the radio on. When she heard Junior Mafia's "Get Money" she laughed.

"Damn right. That's what we about to do baby!"

She wanted to make sure she was on time, so she sped down Garden State Parkway disregarding any type of speed limit.

\*\*\*

"Hello, Mrs. Greffen. I'm Dr. Thompson," the young black male doctor said, observing Jazmine's badly bruised face.

Jazmine returned the greeting. He immediately asked her what the reason was for her visit, not wanting to assume it had anything to do with her face. She thought carefully before she answered. She didn't need him to know the real reason. If she played him just right, her plan to get Vince out of her life permanently would work without any snags. Fearing that something would go wrong, Jazmine didn't even let Roslynn and Alyse in on her plan.

Like the fact that they both thought she was having a meeting at Omari's school when in reality she was sitting at the East Orange General Hospital emergency room. Unbeknownst to her friends, there was no meeting, at least not this particular day.

He looked in her file. "So, I see you've been here before with the same types of injuries."

Jazmine started acting nervous and scared. "Yes, I have. My husband beats me. This time he raped me, too." Even though what she said was true, Jazmine closed her eyes then opened them as fake tears ran down her cheeks.

"Where exactly are you in pain?"

"I'm actually in a lot of pain in my vaginal area, face and near my abdomen."

The doctor assured Jazmine that anything she said to him would be strictly confidential. "Have you talked to the police about any of this domestic violence?" Dr. Thompson asked.

"No!" Jazmine shouted. "I don't want the police involved. He said he would kill me and my son if I did."

"Ma'am, I see woman like you in this emergency room all the time. The only way to stop this is to go to the police." Every time the doctor would touch one of bruises, she would jump. "So, what exactly hurts on your body?"

Jazmine hesitated for a second. "Maybe you're right. I'll have my mother take me to the station once I get examined," she lied.

The doctor knew there was a good chance Jazmine wouldn't keep her word, but there was nothing he could do about it. He called in a nurse for assistance then prepared to start the rape kit. Jazmine had already taken off her clothes and changed into a hospital gown.

"You know, Mrs. Greffen, the hospital can provide you with a number to several rape crisis centers in the area. These centers help with advice, counseling, and support," the doctor informed her.

"Thanks," Jazmine said. "Doctor Thompson, do you think you could run some blood tests also. I think my husband has been sleeping around on me and just want to be sure he didn't give

**178**

me anything."

"Of course. Actually, blood and urine tests are standard procedures after a rape incident. After the exam, I can also prescribe you some medication to ward off or treat any potential STD's. I have to warn you though, HIV, syphilis, gonorrhea, Chlamydia and Hepatitis B can take time to appear, don't be surprised if you have to come back later for more testing."

Once Jazmine nodded her head, the doctor asked her to stand against the wall so he could take pictures of all her bruises. Next, he asked Jazmine to get on the table so he could swab her mouth and genital areas. The tears and bruises around her vaginal and rectum made his stomach turn. After pulling out the long Q-tip looking stick, he moved it around the affected vicinity then placed the stick inside a glass tube. Lastly, he took two hair samples, then whispered for the nurse to collect all the evidence.

Once the exam was complete, Dr. Thompson wrote down a few notes, then handed Alyse a prescription. "Mrs. Greffen, it's standard procedure to hold your rape kit here at the hospital while you decide whether or not you're going to report the crime to the police. Until you make that decision, we'll protect your privacy by not disclosing your name. Rape kits are just a case of insurance, but I highly advise you proceed with criminal charges. Your husband shouldn't get away with this," he advised.

Jazmine lowered her head like she was contemplating. "I understand."

"Well, the last part of the exam is the blood sample, but I don't need to be present for that. Nurse Vines here will assist you in that area." The doctor stood up, then shook Jazmine's hand. "Take care of yourself."

When he left the room, the nurse walked toward Jazmine holding a tray with a needle and several tubes. Jazmine was reminded of her husband doing the same thing when the nurse tied the rubber band around her arm.

*How the fuck did I not know he was using? All the signs were there,* Jazmine thought to herself.

She took a deep breath when she felt the needle prick her skin, then watched as each tube was filled. When the nurse finished, she placed a bandage over the injection spot. After placing a sticker with Jazmine's name over each tube, she put all the tubes in a plastic bag. From Vince beating on her like a punching bag, Jazmine had been to the hospital's emergency room several times before, so she knew their protocol. As always, the nurse walked over and placed the bag in a little box labeled *Lab Corp* then closed it. Normally the Lab Corp boxes located outside doctor's offices were locked, but in this case, the box was highly accessible.

The nurse turned around. "Okay, Mrs. Greffen, your test is complete. Please feel free to put back on your clothes."

"Thank you," Jazmine replied as the nurse left finally left the room.

Jumping up off the table, Jazmine opened the door slightly and peeped out to make sure no one was coming. When she didn't see anyone, she went directly to the box and grabbed the bag. After making sure she had the right blood, Jazmine quickly placed the bag inside her purse and then proceeded to change her clothes. She wanted to get out of the hospital as soon as possibly just in case the nurse or anyone else came back to retrieve the blood.

Minutes later, Jazmine was dressed and had begun walking down the hall when suddenly she heard Dr. Thompson calling her name. Part of her wanted to keep on going, but she didn't want to raise any suspicion. She stopped and turned around slowly.

"Mrs. Greffen, didn't you forget something?" the doctor asked.

Jazmine was scared when the doctor walked up to her with a disturbed look on his face. She wondered what explanation she could possibly give a judge for stealing her own blood. So she took her handbag off her shoulder and reached inside.

"Mrs. Greffen, your prescriptions and release papers. You left them inside the exam room," he said handing everything to her.

She let out a goofy laugh. "Oh yeah. I'm such a loser sometimes." She took the papers from him and slid them in her bag.

Just as she was leaving, her cell phone began to ring. Thinking it was Roslynn, she quickly grabbed the phone and looked at the screen. It was an unrecognizable number, but she answered anyway. Hell, even if it was Vince she couldn't hide forever.

"Hello."

"Hey, how are you?" a man asked.

"Fine. Who's this?"

"Oh, so you don't know my voice now?"

Jazmine was already annoyed. "Hell no, I don't know your voice, and I'm about to hang up if you don't stop playing games."

"Calm down. It's Miles."

For some reason, hearing his voice, made Jazmine's face light up. "Oh, Miles, I'm sorry. I didn't recognize your voice. Hey by the way, thank you so much for what you did for me the other day. I realize you didn't have to get involved."

"I was happy to help, but you know Vince is not going to let you stay away for too long. Those drugs have him acting extremely erratic."

"You knew he was using?" Jazmine asked.

"There's been rumors floating around the station for a while, but after the way he acted the other day, I'm sure of it."

"Yeah, well, as crazy as it sounds I didn't know he was using either, but I'm glad I know now," Jazmine replied. "Miles, I know I'm being a pain, but can you do me another favor?"

"Sure."

"Are you at work right now?" she asked. "Is Vince there too?"

"Yes, I'm at work, and I believe Vince is here as well."

"Good. Can you keep Vince occupied for about an hour? I need to go and get something from the house."

Miles tried to think of a way to do what she asked. Then it hit him. "I can handle that. I'll just call Vince into a mandatory meeting with the Chief about a case."

"Sounds good to me. Please Miles. If you see him leave the station for anything, please call me."

Jazmine knew she was taking a big chance on what she was about to do, but hopefully it would be well worth it.

✳✳✳

Jerry didn't even bother going inside the cafe to wait for Roslynn. All he wanted to do was give her the list and get out of there. When she pulled up, he suddenly imagined her car blowing up, which caused a wide smile across his lips. Stepping out of his car, Jerry straightened the coat on his black Hart, Shaffner and Marx suit and walked over to Roslynn's window. He looked so powerful and his swagger was definitely on ten.

"What a waste," she said, rolling down her window.

He strolled over to her car after canvassing the area to make sure no one saw him. "Here don't ask me for anything else," he said throwing the list and copies of the account holder's signature cards.

"Muthafucka, I'll ask you for whatever I want, so don't get cute fruit cake, especially if you wanna live to see another day," Roslynn replied before quickly pulling off. She loved saying gangsta shit.

She also loved the fact that the scam was about to go down, which made her panties wet. Pulling out her Blackberry, she called up Montee and told him she would bring him the list and the pictures for the ID's. Everything so far was good to go.

# Chapter Twenty

Jazmine looked down the hall to make sure nobody was following them before inserting the key card into the hotel door. Once she and Omari were safely inside, she locked the door then threw their bags on the floor. Looking around the small crammed room that had a slight mildew scent, she wasn't excited about being there, especially after sleeping in the plush bed at Roslynn's house. She also hated dragging her son from one place to the next, but at this point, they didn't have too many choices. Adrian's nasty attitude was a strong indication that her and Omari weren't welcomed, so Jazmine thought it was only right to leave. Besides, her and Vince's marriage was already fucked up, she didn't want Roslynn to follow in her footsteps.

"Ma, why we gotta stay here? I wanna go back to Auntie Ro's house," Omari said, jumping up on the bed. He'd been pouting since they left Paramus.

"I bet you do. Sweetie, we need our own space, so it's best that we stay here for a while."

"Well, can Ramon come and get me? He's gonna take me to the movies again."

Jazmine hated disappointing him. "No, baby. Ramon has to stay at Auntie Ro's house."

She could tell from Omari's attitude that he was still mad about being cooped up in a hotel room, so she suggested they go get some snacks from the store. Snacks probably couldn't compete with him missing the perks from Roslynn's house and her chef, but hopefully her bribe would at least get him to smile.

His eyes widened. "Yes. Can we get some ice cream and some cookies? Oh, and some fruit cups?"

Jazmine quickly calculated in her mind how much money

Roslynn had given her to see if they could afford everything Omari wanted. "I don't know about everything on your list because we gotta keep some money for regular food, but we'll see."

"Okay. Can we go now?" Omari begged with a huge smile.

Jazmine was glad to see him smiling again. "Sure. I'll even race you to the elevator."

After grabbing her purse and the card key, Jazmine ran out the door with Omari close behind. After she purposely let him pass her, Omari was having fun taunting his mother for not being able to keep up with his fast pace strides.

"Oh, so you think I'm old…huh!" she said jogging behind him. When she caught up, she threw her arms around him and gave him a huge kiss on the cheek.

"Ma! Don't do that!"

"Whatever…you're my baby."

Once they got outside, Jazmine decided to walk to the Rite Aid drug store, which was only a few blocks away as opposed to driving. She figured spending quality time with her son would not only make him happy, but make her happy as well. It also took her mind off her problems for a minute, which was desperately needed.

When they entered the store a few minutes later, Omari grabbed a small hand held basket like he always did when they went shopping, then followed Jazmine to the right aisle. After reaching the small food section, Omari immediately started pointing to everything he wanted. Jazmine threw in several bags of chips and even some animal crackers before stopping at the cookies. While trying to decide whether to get the Oreo's or Chips Ahoy, she heard Omari start to scream.

"Grandma Diane!" Omari yelled as he ran up to her.

Jazmine froze as she watched her son jump right into his grandmother's arms. It was hard to believe that she was standing there.

"Oh my goodness Omari look at you…you're a big boy now," her mother responded. She kissed him on the cheek several times before hugging him tightly.

"I missed you," Omari said.

"I missed you, too," her mother responded. She then looked at Jazmine. "Hello."

Jazmine's throat was so tight she could barely speak. "Hi." At age fifty-two, her mother's smooth skin and shoulder length hair made her look ten years younger. She looked good even though she still dressed conservative. Her long black skirt, basic pumps and white oxford shirt reminded Jazmine of a politician.

Diane put Omari down. "So, how have you and my grandson been?"

Jazmine told her she and Omari were doing well, but her mother could tell from the bruises on her face that statement was a lie.

"Sweetie, go to the front of the store and pick out the gum you want then bring it back here. Me and Grandma need to talk." When Omari turned around, Jazmine stopped him. "Oh, but what do we do if a stranger says anything to you, especially if they want to take you somewhere?"

"Run away," Omari stated.

"Exactly," Jazmine agreed.

As soon as Omari cut the corner, Jamine looked at her mother. "Ma, what are you doing in East Orange? You hardly ever leave Newark."

"My new dentist is not too far from here, so that's why," Diane said, placing her hands on hips. "I told you that man was no good for you, but you wouldn't listen. Instead you let him pull you away from me. The only family you got. Now look at you! That man done broke your heart and your spirit."

Jazmine couldn't even argue with her mother. Everything she was saying was true. She stood in front of her mother and embraced her with tears in her eyes. "I'm sorry. I should've listened to you and everyone else. I feel so ashamed. I mean I didn't even come and see you after your stroke." She wiped her tears. "I wanted to, but Vince told me if I left the house I would regret it. Can you ever forgive me?"

Her mother looked in her eyes and saw her apology was so sincere that she couldn't help but embrace Jazmine and tell her she did. Jazmine wept in her mother's arms and told her how much she had missed her. As they held hands, Jazmine spoke of how Vince had been abusing her physically and mentally for years. Her mother stood in silence before telling her she needed to come home.

"We're family and family should always stick together."

"I know, but I'm gonna stay in a hotel for a few days just to get my head together."

"Are you sure?" her mother asked.

Jazmine nodded.

"Well, why don't you let Omari stay with me? I've missed him," Diane said squeezing Jazmine's hand.

Jazmine didn't even think about it before she told her yes. "I'll bring him by tomorrow."

"Oh no. I'm taking my baby home with me right now. "

Jazmine smiled. "Okay."

Her mother was so happy. She was finally going get to spend some time with the grandson who'd been taken away from her. Her mother looked at her watch. "Oh Lord, I need to get back to the house. The sister's of the church are coming by. It's my night to host Bible study."

Walking up with his hands full, Omari threw all kinds of gum in Jazmine's basket and asked his mother if she was ready. Jazmine explained that there was a change in plans and instead of him going back to the hotel with her he would be going to stay with his grandmother. He was excited but wanted to know if he could take his snacks with him. She told him yes and assured him she would be by first thing in the morning with a change of clothes.

As Jazmine was leaving the store, she waved at her mother and Omari with a big smile and blew them a kiss before quickly strolling back to the hotel. She was glad Omari would be spending time with her mother because that would give her some time to talk to Miles. She ended up calling him and asked if he would meet her at the hotel, he gladly accepted the last minute invitation.

Jazmine wandered around the room nervously awaiting Miles' arrival for about fifteen minutes. When she finally heard a knock at the door, she went over to the mirror to check her makeup. The reflection in the mirror made her feel sick. Her once beautiful face was so bruised and battered that even her foundation wasn't covering it up anymore.

As soon as Jazmine opened the door and saw Miles' standing there in a nicely fitted black suit, her body temperature went sky high. He was extremely attractive and just for a second she thought about what it would feel like to be with him.

"Jazmine, you alright?" Miles asked.

"Oh…yeah. I'm sorry I was just thinking about something. Come in."

Miles walked inside and took a seat in the chair next to the bed. "So this is your new home…huh?"

"For now. At least I'm safe here."

He was so happy to see her. Miles asked Jazmine to come stand next to him. When she complied, he grabbed her hand and kissed it. "I've always had a crush on you, but out of respect for your husband, I never acted on my feelings," Miles said. "I never thought Vince was good enough for you."

Jazmine blushed.

"Sorry, I just had to get that off my chest. Now, what did you want to talk about?" he asked.

Jazmine slid into the conversation with Miles cautiously. She knew being a Detective was in his blood. She needed him to go to the chief and let him know that Vince had been beating her and doing drugs. Jazmine knew that Miles hated Vince and wouldn't give up a chance to throw him under the bus. She was actually banking on it. Miles had no idea he was a vital part of her elaborate scheme to get her husband out of her life once and for all. Once Miles got the wheels started she could execute the rest of her plan.

Miles jumped at the opportunity to help her out. Little did she know, not only did he care for her, but his decision was also based on the fact that he himself had grown up in a home where his father abused his mother daily. It was the reason he wanted to go into law enforcement. All that mattered to him was that Jazmine had taken the first step and left Vince. "I'll do anything for you Jazmine," Miles said. "I hate to see you like this."

**187**

"Hopefully, I won't have to live like this anymore, especially if you help me."

"You need to get yourself a lawyer," Miles said, handing her a card with a number on it. When Jazmine looked at card, Miles noticed her uneasiness. "It's okay. I know this guy and he's good."

"Miles, you know before Vince goes to jail he'll leave town. I'll have to watch my back everyday. Hell, I won't have a moment's peace."

When Miles told Jazmine he would stand behind her a hundred percent it immediately made her feel better, but she still had a long way to go before she would be completely healed.

"That's why I have to make sure he's out of my life forever," Jazmine said.

"Yeah, I understand."

"I'm gonna need you to help me do something else to keep him away."

Miles looked at Jazmine with a suspicious stare. "And what did you have in mind?"

"First of all can I trust you?" Jazmine asked.

"Do you really have to ask that?"

"Well, this is serious so I just need to make sure I can trust you first."

"Wait a minute. You're not trying to have him killed are you?" Miles questioned.

"No, not at all. I would never do anything like that." Jazmine could sense the uneasiness from Miles. "You know what, never mind."

"No, Jazmine go ahead. I didn't mean to make you uncomfortable."

"Thanks, but maybe this is not the time. If I still need your help, I'll make sure to talk to you about it later on."

Miles sighed. "Are you sure?"

"Yes," Jazmine confirmed.

Once they finished up their conversation a few minutes later, Miles stood up to leave. However, he didn't leave quietly. He gently grabbed Jazmine's body and pulled her close to him and slowly slid his tongue in her mouth. Her body trembled from the feel of his strong yet gentle hands, and she tried to think back to the last time she felt so safe, but she couldn't.

Not thinking of any repercussions, he ripped his jacket and tie off with one pull. Miles then picked Jazmine up and carried her over to the bed and luckily she didn't resist. He laid her down and slipped his hand underneath her shirt caressing her breasts with gentle strokes. Holding on to him with a tight grip, Jazmine moaned as he planted wet kisses on her neck and shoulders while unbuttoning her shirt.

She knew what was about to happen and she was eager yet nervous about it at the same time. She'd never been intimate with anyone since she married Vince and even though they weren't living together she still felt a little guilty. As much as she wanted to give into her temptations, she couldn't. Tearing her mouth away from his, she sat up and told Miles she couldn't. She was expecting him to get angry and storm out, but was surprised when he didn't.

"I'm not like Vince. I would never hurt you so if you say you're not ready, I'll respect that. Let's just lay here together," he said cuddling her into his arms.

Those words meant the world to Jazmine as she snuggled up against him. She was so used to Vince taking sex whenever she told him no, that she was really taken aback with Miles' response. He was the perfect gentleman, and Jazmine hoped he would stay that way. Who knew, maybe once all the drama with her husband was over, they could have something special.

Within thirty minutes Miles was sound asleep, but Jazmine was nowhere near tired, especially not with the plan to get Vince away from her, running through her mind all the time. She slipped from under Miles' arm and slowly got up. Not trying to wake him, she grabbed Omari's backpack from under the bed and opened it.

When she pulled the blood covered shirt out of a plastic bag, it immediately jolted her memory of all the beatings she'd suffered at the hand of her own better half. She wondered what the world was coming to when a respected police officer would have the audacity to beat his wife the way Vince had done. Domestic violence to her was real on all levels. She had trusted this man to love and take care of her and instead he treated her like a possession. For years, she was treated like a prisoner who was serving a life sentence. However, he had no idea he was about to get a glimpse of what that feeling was like.

Placing the shirt back, Jazmine then retrieved the tubes of blood she'd taken from the hospital, but when Miles made a sudden move, she quickly placed the items back into the backpack and slid it back under the bed. Jazmine hoped that she could eventually tell Miles what was going on so he could help, otherwise the plan might not be as successful.

After climbing back onto the bed, Jazmine thought about how patient Miles had been with her. He was the kind of man she should've been with all along. Instead, she'd allowed herself to fall in love with a lunatic who made her life miserable. *Never again,* she thought. *I'm taking back control of my life starting today.*

# Chapter Twenty One

Timothy White had been chief of police for fifteen years now, and by the way he looked, he didn't appear to be a day over forty. With his clean cut appearance, salt and pepper hair, and charming smile, he had a strong resemblance to actor, George Clooney. Dressed in his stiff police uniform with razor sharp creases, he arrived at the precinct shortly after roll call started. Normally, on Tuesdays he met with the Capitan and several officers to go over briefings, and to hear the complaints from the K-9 unit, but today the Chief had to deal with one officer in particular. He knew in advance that this meeting wouldn't go well for him or the officer, but it had to be done.

Good morning ladies and gentlemen," the chief said, addressing everyone in the room."

"Good morning, Chief," they all replied in unison.

"Officer Anderson," the chief called out.

"Yeah, Chief," Vince said.

"Follow me to my office, please."

Vince didn't hesitate springing right into action. "Yes sir."

As the two men walked out of the room, Vince wondered why he'd been singled out, and what this was all about, but didn't bother to ask. Instead, he did exactly as he was told.

Moments later, Chief White opened the door to this office, and welcomed Vince inside.

"Have a seat, Anderson," White demanded, as he closed the blinds to give them some privacy from the bright morning sun.

Positioned in his leather winged-back chair, the chief spoke directly to Vince in a firm tone. "Anderson, how long have you been on the force?"

"Sir, it'll be nine years in May."

Looking through Vince's personal records that he'd asked his secretary to pull, the chief asked, "Have you ever been in any trouble, or had any complaints?"

Vince shook his head. "No sir…not at all."

*Oh yes, this must be about my evaluation and promotion. I didn't expect to have it this early though, but hey the quicker the better,* Vince thought to himself.

When Chief White twirled his thumbs and stared at him for a few seconds, Vince grew nervous. Chief White had never glared at him that way before, and it made him feel a bit uneasy. He began to wipe the sweat from the palm of his hands.

"How's your son. Omari is it?" Chief White asked.

"Yes sir, he's doin' quite fine actually. Growin' up faster than I want, but doin' well. Thank you for askin'." Vince squirmed in his seat.

"And the wife? How is she these days?"

"My wife is excellent as well. Stayin' busy raising our son and spendin' my money." He managed to chuckle, while the Chief's face was stone.

"Vince, I agree you do have a lovely family. Your wife is gorgeous and that son of yours is a very polite and smart young man."

"Thank you, chief." Vince wanted to know where all this was going.

Chief White told Vince that he and his wife had been married for thirty years. He then went on to tell him how she'd been through a lot including his transition from precinct to precinct, the scandals of the job and not to mention the stress he constantly took home.

*Okay, he's really taking up my time with this shit. I wish he would get to the damn point so I can get the hell out of here.*

"I know what you mean, sir."

Chief White smirked. "Do you really?"

"Sir, I do."

"Anderson, you're a smart person and an even smarter officer. Wouldn't you agree?"

Vince didn't want to toot his own horn, but he had to agree with him. "Sir, I understand the importance of my career and I wouldn't jeopardize it for anythin'."

Raising from his chair, Chief White leaned toward Vince. "You're such a fucking liar!"

The look on Vince's face read complete shock.

"I received a call about a case of spousal abuse. Care to know who the victim is Anderson?"

Vince tapped his foot rapidly as he responded. "Sir, I'm not sure if I would want to be apart of someone else's personal business."

"Oh, but I think you would. Matter of fact it is personal, so personal that the last name matches yours."

"Chief, I don't understand what you're implyin'. I would never hit my wife." He tried his best to play it off.

"Anderson, I've seen scum bags like you come and go during my years in law enforcement. But I never would've thought you would turn out to be one of those people. However, I've been wrong once or twice in my lifetime."

It didn't take a rocket scientist to realize that this meeting wasn't about a promotion.

Pointing directly in Vince's face, the chief's face grew red. "Anderson, it appears that you not only have a problem physically abusing your wife, but you're a substance abuser as well."

Vince's mouth fell open slightly.

"Yes, that's right. The caller also informed me that you've been indulging in heroin."

Vince jumped up. "What the hell are you talkin' about? This shit is crazy!"

"No, what's crazy is that you're a damn officer of the law. You're supposed to be getting the drugs off the street, not use them."

Vince sat back down while beads of sweat ran down his face.

"Officer Anderson, you need to hand in your badge and your gun," Chief White demanded.

"What?" Vince asked in total shock.

"You will no longer be an officer of this or any other precinct. Now, hand over your fucking badge and your gun!"

"I can't believe this bullshit!"

As if it was planned, four officers entered Chief White's office and stood directly beside Vince.

"This isn't an open debate Anderson. It's time for you to go. Please clean out your locker."

Vince's whole attitude changed. "You know what, fuck y'all then." He grabbed his badge and threw it across the desk. When he went to grab his gun, the officers stood even closer, waiting for something to jump off.

"Don't even think about throwing that fucking gun or anything else." Chief White stated. "As a matter of fact, Officer Grier please remove Anderson's weapon for him please.

When the officer went to grab the gun, Vince pulled back his fist and attempted to land the punch, but unfortunately never got the chance. At that moment, the three other officers in the room quickly sprung into action. Jumping on him from every angle, the officers pinned Vince to the floor, then carefully removed his firearm.

"Get the fuck off me!" Vince yelled like the maniac he was. When one of the officer's hands came close to his mouth, Vince didn't hesitate biting as hard as he could.

"Shit!" the Hispanic officer yelled out. He struggled to free his hand until one officer was able to assist. "That sick bastard just bit me!"

"Get his ass on his feet!" Chief White belted.

After wrestling with Vince for a few short moments, the officers were finally able to stand him up. By this time, Chief White's face was entirely pink.

Vince stood there breathing hard.

"Officer Lopez, do you want to file assault charges against this man?" the chief asked.

Officer Lopez looked down at his hand. "That's alright, Chief. I'll live. The skin doesn't seem to be broken."

"Anderson, if I find any truth to these domestic violence allegations, I'll be sure to have your ass prosecuted to the fullest extent of the law. The people up in Riker's Island will love you."

"Fuck you!" Vince yelled.

"Get this piece of shit out of my office," the chief stated. "Also, figure out how you all are gonna get him back in regular street gear."

Even though Vince was pissed, he knew he'd fucked up. All his bullshit had finally caught up with him, and it wasn't a good feeling. With two officers on each of his arms, they escorted Vince out of the office, and toward the locker room. When they entered the smelly room moments later, Miles was standing by his opened locker with a huge grin.

"What up Anderson? How's the wife and kid?" Miles sarcastically asked.

From the look Miles gave him, Vince knew that he had something to do with the mysterious phone call to the chief.

He gave Miles a long evil stare. His contempt for him was coming to a boiling point, but he wasn't going to play that game with Miles because he knew that's exactly what he wanted.

"This shit ain't over," Vince said stepping back.

Miles shook his head and said, "No, actually it is."

***

Jazmine dialed Vince from her cell phone. As soon as she heard the call go through, she hung up. However, he called right back as she'd hoped.

"Yes," Jazmine answered.

"Bitch, I can't believe you did this to me," Vince barked. "You wait until I find your ass!"

"What are you talking about?"

"Don't fuckin' lie to me. You and that red Al B. Sure lookin' nigga got me fired. Which one of y'all called my superior and told him all those lies?"

Jazmine smiled, even though he couldn't see her. "I have no idea what you're talking about."

"Go ahead. Keep on actin' like you don't know what the fuck I'm talkin' about."

195

"I don't know what you're talking about. Look, I just wanted to tell you that Omari is fine, especially since you talkin' about somebody kidnappin' him," Jazmine said.

"Where's my son?"

"He's here safe with me."

"Bitch, I know that much! Where are you?"

"We're at the Ramada," Jazmine replied.

"Which one?" Vince asked.

The plan was going exactly as planned, but Jazmine had to play it off a little bit so he wouldn't be suspicious. "I don't think it's a good idea to tell you that. Omari doesn't need to see us fight, Vince."

"I'm not gonna touch you, bitch. I just wanna see my son."

She knew Vince was lying, but played right along with him. "Are you sure? I thought you were mad about your job even though I didn't have anything to do with it."

"Didn't I fuckin' say so? I just want to see my son!" Vince repeated.

Jazmine hesitated for a moment, then responded. "We're at the Ramada on Evergreen Place. Room 323, but don't' come here starting no shit or I'ma call the police. You know the police you don't work for anymore," she said, then hung up abruptly.

Hoping she was doing the right thing, Jazmine roamed around the small but clean room and waited for Vince's arrival. When an hour had passed and there was still no sign of him, she wondered if her plan would even work. Hopping up off the bed, Jazmine looked at her watch and saw that it was getting late.

"Shit, maybe he's not coming," she said to herself.

It wasn't like Vince not to jump at an opportunity to whoop her ass, so she was surprised that he hadn't shown up. Wondering what could've changed his mind, Jazmine looked at her watch again, when suddenly there was a loud knock at the door.

Completely high, Vince pounded on the door in a blind rage as he glanced up and down the hotel hallway.

Jazmine stood close enough to the door to be heard. "Who is it?" She knew exactly who it was.

"Bitch, open the damn door," he ordered. "It's Vince."

At that moment, Jazmine ran over to the hotel phone and immediately called security. "Yes, this is Jazmine Anderson in room 323. My husband is at my door yelling and trying to get in my room. Can you please come up here? Please hurry," she said, just before hanging up. Her voice made it seem like she was scared for her life.

She went back over to the door to taunt Vince until security got there. "Vince, go away. I don't want to talk to you."

"I ain't come here to talk to you. I came to see my son, so you might as well open up the damn door 'cause I'm not leavin' until you do."

"You're not going to see your son tonight or any other night for that matter. We're leaving and we're not coming back."

"What? I can't believe this. You told me on the phone that I could come. Oh, so you wanna play games? Bitch, I'll see you dead first before I let you take my muthfuckin' son. Open this damn door!" he continued to yell, as he pounded even harder.

By this time, the other guests were starting to come out of their rooms.

"Hey, yo' son we ain't tryin' to hear 'dat shit all night!" a fat man yelled.

"Nigga, shut the fuck up and get your fat-ass back in the room. Mind your business!" Vince yelled.

As Vince and the guest went back and forth with one another, a security guard ran down the hall at top speed.

"Sir! Sir!" he yelled. He was trying to get Vince's attention, who was still arguing with the obese man. "Sir, what's the problem here?" the guard questioned.

Vince told the guard to get out of his face, then turned around and continued to pound on Jazmine's door.

"Sir, I'm not going anywhere until I find out what's going on. Besides, the police have already been called so I would advise you to try and settle this before they arrive."

Vince still wouldn't settle down. He looked at the security officer and laughed. "Fuck you, toy cop." He then turned to the man he'd been arguing with. "And fuck you too, Heavy D. Ain't no Snickers out here, so carry your ass back in the room."

The two men started going at in again, this time getting in each other's face. Even though the guard got in between the two men several times, it wasn't until the police arrived a few minutes later before the men simmered down.

When the two officers saw Vince, they were completely surprised.

"Anderson, what's going on man?" one of the officers asked.

"That bitch won't let me see my son, Pierce!" Vince yelled.

"Who are you talking about?" the same officer asked.

"My wife. She won't open the door." Vince pointed. "Room 323. She's in there with my son, and won't let me see'em."

After glancing at the door, the officer lifted his hand and knocked before telling Jazmine to open up.

"You're not gonna let my husband hurt me, right? He's trying to kill me," she said.

After getting some reassurance that Vince would not assult her, Jazmine finally opened the door. When the two officers walked in, she had mascara running down her face.

"Are you okay Mrs. Anderson?" Officer Pierce asked.

"I think so. I'm just so scared. He said he was going to kill me," Jazmine sobbed. "He's gonna kill me, I just know it."

"I don't think your husband would do that. He's just upset. I promise you we won't let him hurt you," Pierce stated. He looked around the room. "But he just said you wouldn't let him see his son. Is this true?"

"I don't even know what Vince is talking about. My son isn't even here. He's just using that as an excuse to get to me." Jazmine sat on the bed. "He's been beating me, so I left him. If you don't believe me, you can call Detective Miles Gardner or Chief White." She wiped her face.

Pierce looked back and forth between Jazmine and Vince like he was trying to see who was telling the truth. "Can you give me a minute to talk to him? I'm quite sure we can handle this without getting Chief White or anybody else involved."

Jazmine told him okay, but just make sure they kept Vince away from here. More importantly, she wanted a police report written up.

The cop went back out and tried to talk some sense into Vince. After several minutes of going back and forth with him, he finally convinced Vince to leave. They wrote up a report and handed it to Jazmine after assuring her Vince would no longer be a threat. She tearfully thanked them.

As they were leading Vince away from her room, he turned around and gave her the finger. When the officers weren't looking Jazmine gave him a big smile and whispered the words "Fuck you."

# Chapter Twenty Two

Despite Adrian being against the entire idea, Roslynn decided to have a dinner party at the house the following evening. To him, it was just going to be another annoying get together with his wife's friends, but to Roslynn it was a pre-celebration bash for what was about to go down. It was going to be a day or two before Montee would be ready so Roslynn decided to take advantage of the free time. She invited Jazmine and Omari along with Jazmine's mother, Diane and even Miles. She'd also invited Alyse, but with Brie's health not improving, she decided it was best to stay at the hospital.

Miles and Adrian drank beers and checked out Adrian's restored 1967 Corvette Roadster outside while Jazmine and Roslynn drank expensive wine in the family room. Diane opted for a Sprite. As they all held wide smiles and watched Omari run around as usual, Roslynn made a mental note to buy him a Wii to keep at her house whenever they got the money.

"Look how happy he is. He loves it over here, huh?" Diane mentioned.

"Yeah, he really does. I know Adrian is not really feeling this, so thanks for inviting us over," Jazmine added.

"Girl, it's no problem! Omari is a kid and should be doin' stuff like this," Roslynn replied. "I can't wait until Brie can come back over and run around with him."

"I feel so bad for Alyse," Jazmine stated. She turned to her mother. "Ma, maybe you can go up to the hospital and pray with her."

Dianed nodded her head. "I sure will. God knows that child needs all the prayer she can get."

"She sure does 'cause Lance served her wit' divorce papers

yesterday," Roslynn stated.

Jazmine's mouth flew open. "What?"

"Yep. He strolled his behind right in the hospital yesterday, told Brie he loved her, handed Alyse an envelope and then walked back out. I don't know how his broke…" Roslynn wanted to say ass so bad, but stopped when she saw Diane hanging on to her every word. She knew Diane was a church-going woman. "His broke behind got divorce papers that fast."

"I can't believe she didn't call and tell me," Jazmine said.

"Oh, don't feel bad. I called her right before you all came over and had to force the information out. Trust me, I don't think she wanted to tell anybody right now. I guess the wounds are just too fresh," Roslynn responded.

"I'm gonna call her after we eat," Jazmine mentioned.

"Well enough about all the sad news. What's goin' on wit' you and Miles?" Roslynn asked her friend. "He hasn't been able to keep his eyes off you since y'all got here. Adrian had to almost pull him by his ears to do a lil' male bondin'.""

Jazmine displayed a little grin. "What do you mean? It's nothing. He's just a friend."

"Well, he better be. You're not even out of your marriage yet, so don't be bringing no other men into Omari's life. It's too soon," Diane felt the need to say.

Jazmine sighed. "Ma, don't worry. I know"

"Jazmine, I've been meaning to ask you anyway, have you noticed any changes in Omari's behavior since he's obviously encountered Vince's outbursts among other things?" Diane inquired.

"Well, he's a little more isolated at school and his grades slipped about a year ago. He also got into a couple of fights at the beginning of his school year, but hopefully he's just acting out. I hope he doesn't grow up thinking its okay to hit women because his father did it," Jazmine replied.

Diane looked at her grandson again. "I heard that happens, but I think he's gonna be fine. You just have to sit down and talk to him. You should get him some counseling just to be on the safe side. You could benefit from some yourself. I'm also gonna register him in a school in Newark first thing tomorrow because he's been out long enough."

Jazmine nodded her head. She was grateful to have her mother back in her life. Now, she didn't feel so alone.

When Omari saw Ramon coming with a special meal of pizza and fresh cut french fries just for him, he instantly stopped running, but started jumping up and down.

"Where's our food, Ramon. Our guests are hungry?" Roslynn asked.

"It's coming, Ma'am. We're having such a huge meal tonight, that it's taking a little longer than usual. The crab-stuffed Portobello mushrooms should be out soon as an appetizer."

"Mushrooms?" Diane said looking confused.

Jazmine laughed. "Don't worry, Ma. Roslynn likes booshie food now, but it's normally good."

Roslynn hit her friend. "Thanks, Ramon."

"Yeah, thanks Ramon. This is great!" Omari yelled.

"I haven't seen him this happy in a long time. I shoulda' left sooner," Jazmine admitted.

"Jazmine, what's done is done, so please stop beatin' yourself up about Vince's dumb…," Roslynn was about to curse again.

Roslynn was just about to continue, when Adrian walked into the family room. She was sure he was about to lay down the law about Omari running around the house or even worse, eating on the floor, but he told her she had a visitor instead.

"A visitor! Who the hell is it?" She quickly threw her hand over her mouth. "Oh, sorry Diane."

Adrian gave his wife a very judgmental look. "Diane…what about me? Don't I get some respect?"

Jazmine shook her head. Even though Adrian was a good provider, he was also a major asshole. She was done with men who had less than flattering personalities.

"Sorry, babe," Roslynn said, then patted her husband on his shoulder. "I didn't even hear the doorbell."

"Well, you wouldn't. I was outside showing my car to Miles, remember?" Adrian asked.

Over the past few days he'd been noticing how pre-occupied Roslynn seem to be. Adrian threw up his hands. "I just don't know about you lately," he said before walking back out of the room.

Jazmine slapped Roslynn on the arm. "Adrian is gonna kick you out if you don't watch yourself. You know he's no nonsense."

"Honey, that'll be the day. I suck that di…" Roslynn had to stop herself from cursing again. *Diane need to take her ass in the movie room or somethin' cause I can't be myself,* she thought.

At that moment, Miles walked into the room and sat beside Jazmine. He then looked at her mother. "Ms. Diane, are you okay? You need anything?"

Diane smiled. "No, honey I don't, but thanks for asking. By the way, don't try to butter me up in order to get to my daughter because it's not happening. She's not ready for that yet. She just left her crazy husband."

Roslynn burst out laughing.

Jazmine almost choked. Her mother had always been very blunt. "Ma!"

"No, it's okay Jazmine. I appreciate and respect your mother's opinion," Miles replied. He then turned to Diane. "Don't worry. I don't have any underhanded tricks up my sleeve."

Diane never backed away from her watch-dog mentality. "You better not."

As the three continued to talk, Roslynn went to the door to see who could've been coming to see her unannounced. She tossed the wine she'd been sipping on then walked at a fast pace toward the door. However, she stopped dead in her tracks when she saw her cousin, Kamilla, standing boldly in her living room talking to Adrian. Roslynn stood there for a minute desperately trying to get her thoughts together. Her heart almost stopped beating, when a little girl with two long pigtails, a pink glittery top and jeans emerged from the downstairs bathroom.

*Oh my God, what the hell is Kamilla doing in my house and why did she bring her here? I'm gonna fuck 'dis bitch up,* Roslynn thought to herself as she stood in complete awe.

When Kamilla spotted Roslynn in the hallway she yelled, "Hey Cuz!"

Kamilla still looked and acted the same. She was loud, bold

and extremely overweight for her 5'1 frame. She also wore a ridiculous honey blond wig that wasn't very flattering.

Roslynn didn't respond, but looked at Adrian in order to get his reaction. He was obviously studying her body language because of the perplexed look on her face.

"Why did you have these young ladies waiting for you, Roslynn? I told you someone was at the door," Adrian said.

"Yeah Roslynn, how rude," Kamilla said with a sneaky smile.

Roslynn strolled over to Kamilla "Hi."

"Girl, come here. I ain't seen't you in forever!" Kamilla said, grabbing Roslynn and giving her a big hug.

"What you doing here?" Roslynn asked, gritting her teeth.

Kamilla grabbed the little girl by the shoulders and introduced her as Aisha.

"Aisha, say hello to yo cuzins Roslynn and Adrian." The girl waved. Kamilla adjusted the purse on her shoulder. "Oh no Aisha, you give yo' big cuzin Ro a hug." The little girl did what she was told.

"You know, its funny how Ro and Aisha look just alike ain't it Adrian?" Kamilla asked.

Unsure where the comment came from, Adrian looked at both of them and had to admit that they did have a resemblance to one another. "Well, actually your daughter and Roslynn do look a lot alike, but you all are family so it's not surprising that some family resemblance is there." He turned to his wife. "How come you've never mentioned Kamilla to me? It's obvious she's a pretty close family member if she knows where we live."

Roslynn was a bit speechless. "Well...I mean I've sent Kamilla birthday cards before and I always include a return address, so it wouldn't be hard for her to find the house. I just didn't know she was coming today." She gave her cousin a look of death.

"Well, I wanted my visit to be a surprise," Kamilla replied. She looked back at Adrian. "Now, back to 'dis resemblance thing. You know, it's crazy Adrian cuz Aisha is not even my blood daughter. I adopted her when she was an infant. Yes sir, an infant not many hours out of her momma's womb." Kamilla smirked, then gave Roslynn a quick wink.

Roslynn's eyes popped out of her head. She couldn't believe the words coming from Kamilla's mouth. "I don't think
Adrian even cares about all that Kamilla. So, what are you doin'
here anyway?"

"I came to see you, cuz," Kamilla responded.

"Well, I'll let you ladies catch up. Roslynn, let me know if
your company is staying so I can inform Ramon," Adrian said before exiting the room.

As soon as Roslynn heard the door to Adrian's office
closed, she looked at the little girl. "Aisha, how would you like
some pizza?" Roslynn asked with a fake smile. When Aisha nodded her head, Roslynn kneeled down and pointed. "Well, if you
walk straight down that hall, and make a left, you'll see another little boy in there eating a big pepperoni pizza. Tell him Auntie Ro
says to give you some."

"Okay," Aisha said before skipping off.

"Wow, who you got callin' yo' ass Auntie Ro?" Kamilla
asked.

Without a moment to think, Roslynn grabbed Kamilla by
the throat and whispered. "What the fuck are you doin' at my
house?"

"Bitch, don't get cocky. You betta get the fuck off me before I let our lil' secret about yo' daughter get out to Adrian."
Kamilla warned.

As Roslynn slowly released her grip, Kamilla rubbed her
neck then sashayed around her cousin's home. "Nice spot you have
here. I knew yo' ass was caked up."

"Never judge a book by its cover," Roslynn rebutted.

"I beg to differ cuz. From what I see 'round here, you have
quite a fabulous lifestyle. Got you a fine-ass husband, big ole'
house wit' marble floors, probably a big pool in the backyard, and
some sweet-ass cars in the driveway. Was 'dat a brand new Beamer
I saw sittin' out front?"

"Look, everything is not what it seems. You came all the
way out here for what? I already sent you all the money I had for
now."

"I want everything you got, bitch. I been raisin' yo' fuckin' daughter ever since she was born while you livin' it up. You never even called and checked up on her, not one time. Dats fucked up." Pointing her finger in Roslynn's face, Kamilla asked her, "Do you have any idea what I go through on a daily basis? I didn't want no kids, but since you fucked around and got knocked up by the owner of 'dat strip club, I didn't have much of a choice. Why didn't you just have a fuckin' abortion? "

Roslynn was quiet. Thinking back to almost eight years ago, she had no idea why she didn't have an abortion. It wasn't like the married strip club owner wanted the baby to begin with. Right before giving birth, she was able to convince Kamilla to keep Aisha for just a few weeks until she got herself together. Of course, Roslynn told her cousin that she would give her all the money she wanted just for taking on the responsibility.

Not allowing anybody in the hospital but Kamilla, Roslynn told all her friends that the baby was sick and had to stay for awhile to buy her some time. Roslynn really didn't understand why she didn't want Aisha in the beginning and had every intention on going back to get the baby as planned. However, once she started dancin' at the strip club again and met Adrian, it was a wrap. She eventually told everyone the baby had a rare disease and died.

"You never came back to get yo' own child. What kind of shit is 'dat?" Kamilla yelled.

Roslynn looked around, then told Kamilla to lower her voice because she didn't want Adrian to hear her.

"Fuck 'dat. I want everything you got. You the one livin' like Diddy up in 'dis muthafucka. I deserve the same lifestyle you got. I put my life on hold to help yo' ass out and now I want mine. I'm tired of gettin' 'dat lil' bit of money here and there," she said, throwing her purse on the foyer table. "You see 'dat? I gotta rock Baby Phat while you rockin' Gucci, Prada and Louie. Fuck 'dis...enough is enough."

"What more do you want? I don't have a damn job," Roslynn said. She reminded Kamilla that she was the one who'd settled for a certain amount each month and that she had kept her end of the deal.

"I ain't gotta keep no type of fuckin' deal. Don't you see, I'm the one runnin' 'dis show? You should be willin' to give me anythin' I ask for, considerin' the information you done kept from yo' husband. How do you think Adrian will feel if he knew you had a child by a married man? You got 'bout two minutes to make yo' mind up or all hell gonna break loose in 'dis mothafucka!"

Hesitantly, Roslynn responded. "Okay…okay this is the deal. I got somethin' I been workin' on that will place a lot of money in my hands. With that money, you can live very comfortably for a while. You just have to be willin' to stay low and keep yo' damn mouth closed. Once everything is set, I'll call you and let you know where to meet me. Then I want you to stay the fuck out of my life for good!"

"Umm, sounds interestin', but fuck 'dat. Whatever you got planned I want in on it 'cuz you love to play games. You ain't gonna keep givin' me the run around," Kamilla said.

"I don't know about that."

"Well, you better figure the shit out 'cuz I'm not leavin' here until you tell me what's up."

At that moment, Ramon finally came into the foyer and told Roslynn that dinner was ready.

"You wanna think about it while we eat?" Kamilla asked.

"We? Bitch, you ain't invited," Roslynn shot back after Ramon left the area.

"Damn, 'dats fucked up. You ain't seen yo' daughter in years, and 'dis is how you treat her? You can't even let her eat at yo' fuckin' table?"

Roslynn sighed. "It's not that, Kamilla. It's just that I don't want Adrian askin' a whole bunch of questions."

"Right…so what you gonna do?" Kamilla inquired. She placed her hands on her wide hips.

"Alright, fine. You're gonna need a small picture of yourself. Almost like a passport photo but smaller. Go to one of those dumb photo booths inside the mall or somethin'. I can't tell you what's goin' down right now, but you got my word that you'll know what's goin' down in about two days."

Kamilla smiled indicating that the small amount of information was good enough for now. "Bet, but if you try and fuck me, it's on." She called Aisha back into the room.

Running in a few seconds later, Aisha asked, "We leavin'? But me and the boy, Omari, are havin' fun."

Roslynn couldn't help but stare at Aisha. She'd done a good job and created a beautiful little girl. She then began to wonder what her and Adrian's child would've looked like.

"Yeah, we out," Kamilla said, walking toward the door. "Oh, one more thang before I go. Why don't you give me 'dat Beamer out front to drive for a few days? I know the shit is paid for. You can take my raggedy-ass Honda Civic."

Rage covered Roslynn's face. "Kamilla, get the hell out. You not takin' my car."

"Fine, but just remember. I'ma definitely be drivin' 'dat muthafucka if you try and fuck me." She turned to Aisha. "Say goodbye to yo' moth…I mean cuzin Ro."

Aisha waved her small hand. "Bye."

Roslynn waved back but didn't say a word. As she closed the door behind them she told herself she couldn't wait to get the two of them out of her life forever.

# Chapter Twenty Three

When Roslynn got up and pulled her silk curtains back the next day, the sun immediately hit her right in the face. Just by the little bit of heat that seemed to bounce off the window, she could tell it was going to be a hot-ass day. She'd planned to lounge around the house all day and catch up on all the shows she'd recorded on her TiVo, but those plans were interrupted when Montee called and told her everything was ready and for her and the girls to meet him at his house. She told him she would be there in an hour. The first part of the plan was finally going down and Roslynn was pumped and ready to go. She immediately called Jazmine then Alyse.

"Hello," Alyse answered. Her voice sounded like she had the weight of the world on her shoulders.

"Hey. How's Brie?"

Alyse started crying. "She's not getting any better. They won't start her meds back up, and now they're saying she's really gonna have to be transferred."

"Listen to me. No, she isn't because Montee just called me. He wants us all to meet him at his house. It's going down Friday, so you'll have the rest of the money to give to the hospital." Alyse didn't say anything. "Did you hear me?"

"Yeah." Her response didn't sound too convincing.

"Okay, I'll probably go get Jazmine first, then swing by to get you. Be ready to go in about an hour."

As promised, Roslynn also called Kamilla and told her to get ready as well. She knew her friends were going to be surprised that Kamilla was in on the scheme too, and she really didn't feel like explaining, but for Roslynn it was a do or die situation. She had no other choice.

Exactly sixty minutes later, all four women were inside Roslynn's car and on their way to Montee's house. For some strange reason, so far everyone had been extremely quiet, which was odd for Kamilla's loud mouth. However, the silence finally came to an end when Jazmine spoke up.

She turned around and looked at Kamilla and Alyse who were sitting in the backseat. "So, Kamilla I haven't seen you since our days at Baxter Terrace. Where you been hiding?"

"Yeah, somebody told me you had a daughter," Alyse added.

Jazmine jumped in. "She does, her name is Aisha. She was over Ro's house yesterday playing with Omari. She's such a sweet lil' girl. Where were you, Kamilla? I didn't see you yesterday."

"Me and Ro had to take care of some business, so I stayed in the foyer the whole time," Kamilla glanced at Roslynn, who kept her eyes on the road. "Hold up, so you ain't tell yo' girls either? You mean you kept 'dis shit from them, too?"

"Kept what from us?" Alyse questioned.

Roslynn acted as though she didn't hear the question until Alyse reminded her that she was the one who insisted that they never keep secrets from each other.

"Exactly. What's up, Ro? I was scared to tell you guys about Vince, but I did."

"This is different!" Roslynn finally yelled. She was pissed that Kamilla had even mentioned anything.

"How is it different?" Alyse asked. "What the hell is goin' on?"

Concentrating on the road, tears fell from Roslynn's eyes. The burden of carrying this dirty little secret for over ten years was finally beginning to get to her.

"Ro, talk to me," Jazmine said, holding her hand.

"Speak up, bitch. They waitin'," Kamilla chimed in.

"Shut the fuck up, Kamilla. That's what's wrong wit' you now. You talk too damn much!" Roslynn boasted.

Kamilla didn't hesitate to fire back. "Who the fuck you talkin' to? Don't get mad at me 'cuz yo' ass been hidin' a fuckin' daughter for almost eight years."

The whole car fell silent. Both Jazmine and Alyse had their mouths opened so wide, a whole family of flies could've made their way inside.

Kamilla continued to rant. "Yeah, y'all didn't know yo' girl was capable of doin' some fucked up shit like 'dat, huh. Y'all probably think she ain't have no problems…that shit was all good, but in reality, Ms. Booshie is just as fucked up as the rest of us. She ain't perfect, even though she wanna be."

Jazmine couldn't believe what she was hearing. "Is this true, Ro?"

It was hard for Roslynn to talk about it, but it was time to get it off her chest. "Yes."

After hearing her two friends gasp, Roslynn went on and told the whole disgusting story. Not only that but she also told them how much debt she was in with all her credit cards, so she needed money just as bad as they did. It killed Roslynn to tell her friends about all the problems she had because she knew they looked up to her. However, now the façade of having her shit together had to come down.

"I can't fuckin' believe you lied to us about yo' baby dyin'," Alyse commented. "I mean, here I am worried to death about my sick daughter, and you didn't even want yo' child."

"Don't judge me, Alyse," Roslynn replied.

"Why not? Kamilla is right. You walk around talkin' about everybody else like you the shit. Now come to find out, you ain't shit," Alyse retorted.

Roslynn wanted to turn around and slap Alyse and Kamilla, but didn't want them to crash in the process.

"Come on, Alyse. That's not necessary. Everybody makes mistakes," Jazmine said, trying to come to her friend's defense.

Alyse frowned. "How the fuck is givin' up yo' child a mistake?"

"You know a mistake, Alyse. The same mistake you made by lyin' to Lance about bein' Brie's father," Roslynn countered.

Jazmine threw her hands in the air. "Whao…can ya'll stop with the cheap shots?"

"No, don't stop 'em. I'm enjoyin' 'dis," Kamilla said with a big smile.

Both Roslynn and Alyse took Jazmine's advice over Kamilla's and were quiet until they reached Montee's. As usual Felix Court was off the hook. As soon as Roslynn reached the front of Montee's building she double parked and called a crack head over and gave him instructions.

"You're not gonna park right here, are you?" Alyse asked.

Roslynn was still annoyed with her friend. "No, Alyse. Just sit back and let me handle this. I just told him to go get Montee so he could make someone move."

The crack head emerged within minutes with a set of keys in his hand. He jumped into a Crown Victoria that was parked in front of Roslynn's car and quickly moved it. After making sure her car was perfectly parked, Roslynn looked at Jazmine, and only glanced at the others.

"Let's go," she ordered.

As they were walking into Montee's building, a guy pulled out several dresses and tried to sell them. All of the women shooed him away except Roslynn of course. She immediately knew one of the dresses came from Saks. "I'll take this one," she said, handing him a twenty dollar bill from her purse.

"Hey, that dress cost thirty five hundred. You could at least give me a ball fifty for it," the guy said.

"You right I could, but I ain't. Now get the hell out of here," Roslynn replied, then walked away.

The guy wanted to say something to her, but he was well aware of who she was. If word got back to Montee of how he treated Ro, he would definitely have a problem on his hands.

They continued up to the apartment, carefully stepping over all the drunks in the hallway. After knocking on the door, Montee opened it and they all marched inside.

"Hold up ain't 'dis yo' cousin, Kamilla, Ro?" Montee asked.

"Yeah. I need her to be in on it wit' us," Roslynn replied. She knew Montee wasn't going to like the change of plans. He hated that.

Montee scratched his head. "You vouchin' for her?"

"Oh, of course," Roslynn responded.

"Good. Well, I guess da shit work out anyway since it was supposed to be three people goin' in. I had a bitch on my side, but she started cuttin' up so I let her ass go." Montee extended his hand. "Do you have a picture so I can make yo' ID?"

"No, I didn't have time to get one," Kamilla admitted.

Roslynn sighed. "Yo' dumb-ass fuckin' up already."

"You vouchin' for her." Montee laughed. "Well, you need to give me yo' real license or somethin'. My people are good. They got a way to duplicate yo' picture and shit. I can have da ID by the time we make 'dat move tomorrow." He then looked at Alyse. "Oh, shit I ain't seen you in a minute either."

"What up, Montee?" Alyse asked.

"Nuthin' much, baby. Just doin' my thing, you know? Ever since Cordell seen yo' girls 'dat day, he been askin' about you like I know where da fuck you be at," Montee revealed.

Alyse wasn't impressed. "Oh, really. Well, you still ain't seen me."

"Shit, you might need to get wit' that nigga to see if he got any kids. If he do, maybe they can be a bone marrow donor for Brie," Roslynn added.

Alyse sucked her teeth. "You talk too fuckin' much, Ro."

Roslynn threw her hands on her hips. "The hell wit' you then, bitch. I was just tryin' to help."

"Help, what? By puttin' my business out there. You love to do 'dat shit," Alyse shot back.

"Yeah, I can agree, but hold up, Cordell yo' baby father?" Montee questioned.

"Absolutely not. Brie has a father," Alyse replied in a stern tone.

"Well, that nigga don't wanna be. He gave you divorce papers!" Roslynn shouted.

As the two friends starting arguing about Roslynn always running her mouth, Montee quickly intervened. "Chill...chill. Act like I didn't even bring Cordell name up, for real. We ain't got time for no fuckin' cat fights." After taking Kamilla's license, he handed

Jazmine and Alyse their cards. "Okay, here are da ID's and da estate manager's signature cards. Y'all need to make sure y'all got 'dem thangs down pack."

Roslynn then began to explain. "Look, this is simple, and Kamilla you really need to pay attention, since you comin' in at the last minute. All ya'll gotta do is go in and tell the account specialist that you're an estate manager over the account and want to withdraw the funds, then have them deposited into another account. Ask for a wire transfer."

Montee stepped back in. "Y'all each have an account set up for you at First National Bank in Manhattan. The account is in da name you pretendin' to be. We gonna wait 'til Monday before y'all go in and withdraw the money."

"Why wait so long? Why ain't we goin' on the same day?" Kamilla inquired.

"Because da shit don't look so hot 'dat way. It looks more legit to at least wait a minute," Montee responded. "So, don't go before Monday, got it?"

He looked at each woman with the exception of Roslynn and asked if they understood what they were supposed to do. He told Roslynn that since she couldn't go in the bank, she needed to make sure Adrian wasn't there. That way he wouldn't see Jazmine, Kamilla or Alyse.

Roslynn smiled. "I know my role, boo."

"We don't need no damn mistakes," Montee responded.

"I know that," Roslynn shot back. "Kamilla, you got it?" .

Kamilla looked a bit confusd. "Yeah, but what bank we hittin'?"

Montee spoke first. "Washington Savings."

Kamilla looked at her cousin and laughed. "What? So, you 'bout to rip off yo' own husband's shit? Wow…you a real cruddy bitch."

Roslynn began to make her way over to Kamilla, but Jazmine jumped up and blocked her.

"Ro, later for 'dat bullshit. We need to make sure y'all got those signatures," Montee explained.

The three women began practicing each of their signatures

for at least twenty minutes before Montee finally approved them. After making sure everybody was on the same page, he relayed even more instructions. "A'ight, cool. Y'all meet me in da parkin' lot of the shoppin' center in front of the bank at nine."

"You're gonna go in, too," Jazmine asked Montee.

He laughed. "Hell, yeah. I need to be there just in case anything goes wrong. Make sure you dress professionally. No hooker dresses. Oh, and take separate cars."

"Are we all goin' in at the same time?" Kamilla asked. "Wouldn't 'dat shit make the account specialist a lil' suspicious?"

"It'll be a few minutes in between, but don't worry. We got people on the inside who will approve the transactions," Roslynn notified. "Oh, and I can go to the mall today to get y'all some dressy stuff if you want 'cause I know y'all don't have anything to wear."

"Is the mall all you fuckin' think about?" Kamilla replied.

"Fuck you. Yo' fat-ass need to go there and get a new wardrobe!" Roslynn barked.

To make sure they knew what to do, they role played for about an hour until Montee was sure they were confident about what they had to do before he let them go. They all left with smiles on their faces knowing that after that day they wouldn't have to worry about money anymore.

After getting back in the car, Roslynn took Kamilla back home and Alyse back to the hospital. Jazmine, however, wanted Roslynn to take her by her old house first before going back to her mothers. A request that Roslynn couldn't wrap her head around. On the way to East Orange, Jazmine grabbed her faithful backpack.

"What the hell is in that bag? Every time I turn around you got it in yo damn hand?" Roslynn asked.

"My future," Jazmine said rubbing the bag.

"I don't even want to know."

Roslynn parked around the corner from Jazmine's house and let her out. Jazmine knew from Miles, who finally knew her plan and decided to help, had four plain clothes officers keeping tabs on Vince. She knew that her husband was at a bar in Jersey

City, which left her more than enough time to sneak inside and do what she needed to do. It was the perfect time and opportunity. After going into the house, Jazmine emerged about fifteen minutes later without the bag. As soon as she got in the car, she took one last look at the place she used to call home then asked Roslynn to drive off.

***

"Baby, I'm really starting to feel neglected," Roslynn said with a sad look on her face. "Stay home with me today."

It was the morning of the bank scheme, and Roslynn had to work quickly in order to keep Adrian from going to work. She'd tried to convince him the night before with sex, but Adrian was so tired, he couldn't even get aroused.

Adrian sat down on her side of the bed. "Honey, what are you talking about? It's Friday and I'm already running late. I can't take off today. Besides, what are you doing up so early. The malls aren't open yet." He cracked himself up at his own joke.

Roslynn got up and pouted. She had her work cut out for her if she was going to get him not to go to work. Adrian was a complete workaholic and only took off if their anniversary date fell on a weekday.

"I'm serious, and you're trying to be funny." She threw on her Victoria Secret robe like she had an attitude and went downstairs.

"Ro…Ro!" Adrian yelled.

She ignored him, hoping he would follow her. When he did she pretended to cry. The pressure to get him out of the bank at least until later in the afternoon was rattling her nerves. She walked around her gourmet kitchen throwing dishes around and pretending to be angry as he poured himself a cup of coffee and tried to explain why he needed to be at work.

"You know what? Go to work!" she said pissed. She hated the fact that he wasn't cooperating. "I'll just find someone else to spend time with me."

"What the hell is that supposed to mean?" Adrian asked,

sitting his cup down on the counter.

She put her hands on her hips and pulled her weave to the side. "Is it to much to ask to have my husband spend just one day with me? Hell, I'll even take half a day. I mean you go to work Monday through Friday, then on Saturday you're hanging with your golf buddies. By Sunday you're too tired to do anything," she said, sounding sincere.

There was a long period of silence between them. Adrian was a little surprised because he thought she liked having her freedom to go and do as she pleased. As much as he loved his company he did love his wife even more. Adrian walked over to the counter and picked up the cordless phone.

"Sabrina, patch me through to Jerry."

The few moments passed before he picked up. When Jerry finally got on the phone, Adrian told him he would be taking the day off. Jerry was surprised. Adrian never took off work, not even when he was sick. Roslynn had managed to pull off the impossible.

After giving Jerry a few more instructions, Adrian hung up. "I'm all yours."

Roslynn was so relieved. Now all she had to do was get him out of Paramus until she was sure the girls were out of the bank. "I love you," she sang as she ran upstairs. "Let's go to the country club today. You can show me how to play golf."

Adrian smiled. Next to the bank, golf was what made him happy.

While Adrian ran upstairs and got in the shower, Roslynn picked up her cell phone to make sure Jazmine was ready to go. Alyse had already called and said she was on her way. So was Montee. The two talked for a while until Roslynn heard Adrian call her name.

"Okay, I gotta go. Good luck and be safe," she said, rushing off the phone. "Call me when you guys leave."

Running back up to her room, she took off her robe and stood in the bathroom doorway naked.

"Are you trying to give me a heart attack?" Adrian asked, imitating Fred Sanford. The sight of her luscious breasts and firm sexy body made him horny, so he dropped his towel and led her to the bed.

Thirty-five minutes later, Alyse, Kamilla, and Jazmine were in the parking lot of the shopping center and nervously waiting on Montee. He pulled up a minute or two later in a silver SLK Mercedes Benz. When he stepped out wearing a navy blue Roberto Cavalli suit with a powder blue shirt and polka dot tie, each of their mouths dropped. He didn't even look like the same person.

"Damn, he look good!" Kamilla said.

Montee greeted them and handed them each a manila folder with the Washington Savings account number along with other information about the account holder, the dummy account number in Manhattan and a copy of the signature card, just in case they forgot how to sign the name. "Now remember ladies, act professional, be precise, and most of all stay cool and collected no matter what. Got it?"

"Got it," they said in unison.

Montee instructed Alyse to go first, then told Jazmine to go in fifteen minutes later. "Kamilla, you walk inside another twenty minutes after Jazmine. I'll go in and act like I need some information about a home loan in a few minutes." He looked at the women, who'd tried their best to look professional. "It's show time."

After walking into the bank and putting her name on the list, Alyse fished through her cheesy suit pockets and pulled out a piece of gum as she sat waiting to be called. She felt a tingling sensation in the pit of her stomach. She'd done a lot of crazy shit back in the day, but nothing on this scale. She took several deep breaths to try and calm her nerves. As Alyse was being called to the back by an account specialist, Jazmine walked in and signed the waiting list. They made sure not to make any eye contact.

The associate was polite and comical which made Alyse relax a little after sitting down at her desk. "So, what can I do for you today?"

"Yes, I'm here to close an account."

"Oh, I'm so sorry to hear that. Your business is very much appreciated." The woman typed a few things into her computer.

"Now, what's the account number?"

Alyse went into the folder and pulled out the correct piece of paper then read off the numbers to the woman. After she typed in the last number, the woman looked up at Alyse with a strange expression.

"So, you're here to close a dormant account?"

Alyse smiled and tried to put on her best voice. "Yes, I am. My name is Elizabeth Rubin, and I'm the estate manager for the account." She'd memorized the name so it could roll off her tongue with ease.

"May I ask why you're closing it, Ms. Rubin?"

Alyse shifted in the chair. She couldn't remember Montee or Roslynn going over this question. "Well, the family of the de-ceased has decided to give a portion of the money to charity as well as other private matters which I can't discuss."

The women stared at Alyse for a few uncomfortable sec-onds. "Well, if I can just see some identification, we'll start the process."

Once Alyse gave the woman her license, she typed even more things into her computer. "Okay Ms. Rubin, I have to get the Vice President to sign off on this paper work, so if you'll just wait here, I'll be right back. Oh, how are we disbursing the money?"

"I would like a wire transfer, please. I have the account number."

"Certainly. I'll make sure I inform the Vice President of that as well."

While Alyse waited for the woman to come back, Jazmine was with another specialist. Her specialist however wasn't as nice. She asked Jazmine a thousand questions and wanted her to open an account with their bank. She told Jazmine it would be easier to transfer the funds from the dormant account to another account within the same bank. Jazmine needed to get this lady off her back.

Her heart almost lost a beat, but she just kept remembering Montee saying keep cool. "Can I speak with your manager or someone even higher than that, actually? I don't appreciate your harassment."

The woman looked around to make sure no one heard

Jazmine. "I'm so sorry, Ms. Gibson. I didn't mean to sound so aggressive. Of course, you don't have to open an account here. I was just making a suggestion."

"Thanks for the suggestion, but I'm afraid I won't need another account at Washington Savings today."

Following the same procedure, Jazmine's specialist asked for her ID as well, and typed in several things into her computer. She also told Jazmine that she had to get the Vice President's approval then quickly walked upstairs.

Even though it might've looked suspicious, Jazmine couldn't help but to look around. By that time, both Montee and Kamilla had made their way inside. Kamilla had just sat down with a male bank employee and Montee had put his name on the list. So far, everything was going according to plan.

Five minutes later, Alyse could see Jerry walking downstairs and toward her with the specialist trailing a few feet behind. At that moment, she wasn't sure if he'd changed his mind about authorizing the transaction, so she began to get nervous all over again, especially from the expression he carried. His face was cold as stone. She quickly looked over at Montee, to see his reaction and could see him going into the inside pocket of his suit jacket.

Little did everyone know, Montee wasn't reaching for a handkerchief but more so taking his gun off of the safety. He also wasn't feeling Jerry's expression, and even worse he didn't even know who Jerry was. He'd been doing this for a long time and he could always sense when there was trouble. He looked at Jerry, hoping to get some type of eye contact in order to get a better reading of the situation, but Jerry never once looked his way. Montee was a thug, and in his mind, he knew that he would blast Jerry's ass if shit was about to pop off.

"Ms. Rubin," Jerry said extending his hand. "I'm the Vice President of Washington Savings and Loans and wanted to come down and speak with you personally."

Alyse cleared her throat then put her hand out as well. "Hello."

"I see that you're closing a huge dormant account with us, so I just wanted to say how sorry we are to be losing the account holder's business. However, I'm sure there's a suitable reason, which I won't inquire about."

*Enough wit' all the fuckin' talkin' Jerry. Just get on wit' the shit,* Alyse thought.

"I'll just need you to sign in all the areas where I've placed an X," Jerry instructed.

With the real Elizabeth Rubin's signature in mind, Alyse signed in all the appropriate places then slid the paper back across the desk.

"Well, that pretty much does it, Ms. Rubin. I'll let Ms. Hawkins here take back over, so she can wire the $150,000."

Alyse almost fell out of her chair. She couldn't believe that her account had that much money. This entire time she was thinking that the accounts didn't hold anymore than $10,000, and she was glad to be wrong.

Ms. Hawkins sat back down. "You know, I thought we had to have Mr. Washington's signature too when we closed these big accounts," Ms. Hawkins said.

*Bitch just sit yo' ass down and wire 'dat money. I wanna get out of here,* Alyse thought to herself again.

"No, my signature if enough verification. Besides, Mr. Washington is not here anyway." Jerry looked at Alyse. "Thanks again, Ms. Rubin." After that he made his way over to the desk where Jazmine sat.

Ms. Hawkins once again typed some things into her computer then smiled. "Okay Ms. Rubin, the transfer has been made. Please check with that particular bank to find out when the funds will be available." She stood up and shook Alyse's hand then watched as Alyse left out the bank.

Montee watched as well, and after seeing Jerry visit with Jazmine and Kamilla, he figured it was time to go.

"Mr. Irving. Mr. Coby Irving," a customer service rep called out.

Standing up, Montee straightened his suit then walked over. "I'm Coby Irving, but I have a business meeting to attend so I need to go. I wanted to inquire about a home loan, but I will just come back tomorrow."

"Oh, okay. No problem, but please come back. With the way the market is now, we have great interest rates."

Montee gave the male rep a hand shake. "Thank you."

As he was leaving, Montee noticed a police car parked in front of the bank's door. He then looked back and saw the associate watching him like something was wrong.

*Shit, 'dat Jerry muthafucka must'a set my girls up. Think! Think!* Montee said to himself.

He walked back over to the small waiting area and grabbed a newspaper. Kneeling down and pretending to tie his shoe, he grabbed his gun without being seen and wrapped it up the newspaper. Walking toward the door everything seemed to be moving in slow motion. His ride or die mentality had Montee ready for battle. When he got to the door, he took a deep breath and waited for them to come inside. However, when the two cops walked by him laughing and talking about how they were broke, he quickly released a sigh of relief. Wiping the sweat from his forehead, Montee got in the Mercedes and left. On his way back to Newark, he grabbed his cell phone and called Roslynn.

"Mrs. Washington speaking," she answered.

Montee wasn't used to her proper act. "Look, I just called to let you know everybody good. Shit, everythin' went so fuckin' smooth we should try and pull off the shit again."

She couldn't really talk because Adrian was sitting next to her, so she gave Montee her infamous laugh and said, "I'm so glad to here that. Be sure to tell Lance I said congratulations on his new job."

"Dat nigga you wit' ain't got no idea what da fuck he got on his hands."

She laughed even more. "Honey, you are so right about that. Talk to you later."

# Chapter Twenty Four

It was an unseasonably warm eighty-four degrees outside and this particular Monday morning hadn't started off good for Vince. He'd just finished pumping weights, and now was in need of a fix. He grabbed his supply and placed everything neatly on the coffee table then tied his arm with an old tie he had. After slipping the needle into his vein, he looked straight ahead and waited for the dope to take effect. When it did, he dropped the needle and slumped down like he was paralyzed. He was so high, he didn't even look up when several cops busted in.

"What the fuck are ya'll doin'?" he said when four officers threw him down on the floor and handcuffed him. Vince began kicking wildly.

Most of the officers knew Vince, and couldn't believe how low he'd stooped. They stood Vince up and sat him down on the couch. The chief investigator told two of the officers to start in Vince's bedroom. He instructed two others to go down into the basement while one searched Vince's truck.

"Is somebody gonna tell me what the hell is goin' on?" Vince asked, looking around the room. "What the fuck y'all doin' in my crib?"

The detective grabbed a chair from the kitchen and sat it in front of Vince.

"Why don't you tell us what's going on, Mr. Anderson?" the detective said, holding up the needle.

"It's Officer...Officer Anderson."

"Not anymore, it's not. Now, explain to me what's going on?"

Vince held his head down. "Okay, so I got a lil' fuckin' drug problem, so what? I got the shit under control. I been gettin' high for over a year now and none of y'all muthafuckas noticed anything." He laughed. "All ya'll call yourself the police."

When he lifted his head, the detective was staring at him with pity. "What a waste of a fuckin' officer," he said, taking notice of the track marks on Vince's arm. "Mr. Anderson, we received an anonymous tip that there was a disturbance here last night, but then things cooled down. The caller didn't think anything of it until they saw you put what appeared to be a body in your truck and drive off. Do you know anything about that?"

Vince started slurring his words slightly. "Hell…no…what are you talkin' about?"

"Where is your wife, sir?"

"How the hell…am I supposed to know that? I haven't seen her in months."

One of the officers grabbed the back of Vince's head. He knew for a fact that Vince had indeed seen Jazmine because he was the one who was called to the hotel the night Vince threatened Jamzmine, and it wasn't months ago.

"Detective, can you come here for a moment?" a rookie officer asked. He took the detective to the basement. The detective took out his pen and picked up the shirt that was behind the door. Seconds later, he was called away again…this time to Vince's truck.

"There's a lot of blood back here," the officer said, pointing but not touching anything.

"My God! What has he done?" one of Vince's old colleagues said when he saw the back of the truck.

"Yeah, there's blood in the basement, and some leading up the stairs. He must've cleaned up the rest because there would be blood everywhere if he was dragging something," the detective said.

They all looked around the car a few more seconds, then walked into the house, but before they could began their questioning again, Jazmine's mother burst through the door like she was on a mission. She was completely frantic. "Did you find her? Did you find my baby?"

When no one in the entire room said anything, she ran over

to Vince and screamed, "What did you do to my daughter? Tell me!"

"Old lady, you better get yo' ass outta my damn face. I don't know what the hell you talkin' about," Vince said defensively.

Jazmine's mother continued to scream and told anyone who would listen that she hadn't seen Jazmine in three days and that Vince had threatened her daughter's life on more than one occasion. "I have a missing person's report already filed!"

"Miss, we will certainly look into it," the detective stated. "Hey, Turner please escort her out here. Have her wait in my car, if she wants to tell me anymore information," the detective stated.

"The Lord don't like ugly boy!" Diane yelled before they took her outside.

"Now, Mr. Anderson, whose body did you place in your car?" the detective asked.

"Man you need to leave me the fuck alone!" Vince shouted.

"Where's your wife's body?"

"What body? What the hell are you sayin'?" Vince asked.

"I'm saying, with a missing report out for your wife along with the incident report last night, all the blood stained clothes, and the large amount of blood found downstairs and in your truck, there's enough probable cause to charge you with murder."

✳✳✳

Jerry sat at work wondering if Roslynn was going to double cross him. It had been hard for him to concentrate at work since giving her the information to rob the bank of hundreds of thousands of dollars. $400,000 to be exact, but after they'd pulled it off and no one suspected anything, he got back into his normal routine. Right after lunch, he was finishing up some paperwork when Adrian's secretary called and told him to go into Adrian's office.

Not thinking anything was wrong at this point, Jerry rushed into his bosses office, and closed the door. Jerry could tell the conversation Adrian was about to have was important from the displeased look on his face, so he sat quietly, enjoying his cup of coffee.

"Jerry, what is this?" Adrian handed him the report and waited for an answer.

"Umm…it look's like a couple of the dormant accounts were closed on Friday."

"I know that. Don't you think it's a little odd that they were withdrawn on the same day, at almost the same time, and transferred to the same bank?"

Jerry had to choose his words carefully. If he said yes then Adrian would want to look into it. If he said no, it could look suspicious. "Well, of course I had to sign off on everything, but I didn't suspect anything. If it would've been the same account specialist handling each transaction then I probably would be a little leery. One of the specialist was Jared, for goodness sake. If anything funny was going on, that inspector would've caught it even if the others didn't."

Jerry began to laugh, but Adrian didn't join in. Instead, he examined the report again and didn't necessarily agree with his V.P. He'd been in the financial business long enough to know that transactions like that were always suspect.

"Well to be on the safe side, I'm going to look further into this. Maybe even get the IRS involved so this way it covers our backs."

Jerry sat back in his chair and loosened his tie. It felt as if his airway had tightened up. "You want me to take care of it?"

"No, I'll be taking care of this. Something's up with these transactions and I'm going to find out what it is." He started to clear off his desk. "I can't do it today, though. Roslynn just called and said she has a surprise for me and wants me to meet her at some restaurant. As much as I don't want to, I gotta do it because she's been complaining about me spending time with her lately."

He grabbed his suit jacket and told Jerry he was leaving early and would see him tomorrow. Jerry smiled and told him to have fun, but his mood quickly changed when he reached his office.

"Fuck!" he said, throwing a pile of files across the room. He was so scared he dropped in his chair and sobbed. It wasn't going to take Adrian long to put the pieces together, and when he did Jerry would be looking at serious time in jail. He had two options. Wait and let the whole thing play out or get the hell out of dodge. He chose the latter.

He went to the storage room, grabbed some boxes and started packing up his shit. He ran around his office scooping up only the things he absolutely needed. On his way out, he wrote a very sizable check and had one of the teller's cash it. Without a word to anyone, he left. But he didn't even make it to his car before a man walked up behind him and said in a heavy baritone voice, "Going somewhere?"

✳✳✳

While waiting for Adrian at an exclusive restaurant, Roslynn called Jazmine to see how things turned out when they went to withdraw the money earlier that morning. When Jazmine didn't answer, Roslynn just assumed she was running some errands. She then called Alyse, but her phone went straight to voicemail, which wasn't unusual since she spent most of her time at the hospital and wasn't really supposed to have it on in Brie's room anyway. She started to worry though when she called Montee's phone and a mysterious man answered and starting asking her a lot of questions. She didn't have time to get the person's name because she hung up just as Adrian walked in.

"Hey, sweetie. You're looking especially beautiful tonight." He kissed her cheek. "Wow it's crowded in here tonight," he said, looking around at all the people who were dining there as well.

Roslynn agreed. "It sure is."

When Adrian took a seat across from her and saw how much she was glowing, it dawned on him that maybe she was about to tell him something he didn't want to hear. "Am I going to need a drink first?"

Roslynn pulled his hands close to her. "No, I just wanted to spend a magical night with my handsome husband. That's all."

Their waiter walked over and poured them a glass of champagne then told them he would be back to take their order.

229

"Let's make a toast," Roslynn suggested.

Adrian took the glass and asked what they were toasting to.

She thought about it for a second and said, "How about to our future and a lifetime of love."

"I'll toast to that," he said clinging his glass against hers.

Just as they were about to order dinner, three gentlemen walked in with black suits on and stood in front of their table. Not knowing what was going on, Roslynn was calm until they showed her their badges.

One of them identified himself as Federal Agent Hamilton with the FBI. He told Roslynn he needed to have a word with her in a harsh tone. Adrian introduced himself to the agent and asked him what this was all about. Roslynn was so ashamed when people started staring, that she tried to leave, but Hamilton insisted she take a seat.

Hamilton sat down while the other two agents stood guard at the door. He pulled out an envelope that contained pictures. The first picture was of Montee.

"Do you know this man, Mr. Washington?" he said, sliding the photo to Adrian.

"No, not at all," Adrian quickly replied.

"What about you, Mrs. Washington?" he asked, showing her the photo.

Roslynn acted insulted. "Do I look like the type of woman who would know someone like that?" She handed the photo back to him.

Hamilton was well of aware of Roslynn's type. She had money, but she also had game so he cut right to the chase. "Don't play dumb, Mrs. Washington. You know Montell Steward very well. I was told by another agent that you just called his phone. You know he told us all about your bank plans."

Roslynn was speechless. Montee was known for a lot of things, but never a snitch.

"What bank plans?" Adrian questioned.

"Mr. Washington, there were a string of fraudulent transactions done involving some dormant accounts from your bank on Friday," Hamilton continued.

Adrian interrupted him. "I was just asking my Vice President about those accounts today. He didn't think anything was suspicious."

Roslynn's heart began to beat so fast it felt like she was about to hyperventilate. Obviously things hadn't worked out as planned.

"Oh, well you should've asked your wife about the accounts because she knows all about it," the agent informed. "Your Vice President Jerry lied to you as well, Mr. Washington. He was well aware of the accounts being tampered with."

Wanting to make a run for the door, Roslynn got up and tried to leave again. "I have no idea what you're talking about! Honey, let's go," she said trying to get Adrian to get up.

"The only place you're going is to jail!" Hamilton shouted.

The other diners looked on in shock. Most of them were acquaintances of Adrian who'd known him for years.

"By the way, you'll want to hear this," Hamilton said pressing play on a small tape recorder.

Montee had no idea, but the FBI had been following him because of several drug deals he'd conducted several months prior. When they caught him walking out of his apartment and in route to the Manhattan bank earlier that morning, surprisingly he sang like a bird. He was a three time offender and looking at thirty years unless he cooperated by giving the Feds something they could use. He didn't hesitate to throw Roslynn and the others under the bus. He told the FBI all about the scheme and said that Roslynn was the ring leader. He even told them when and where they would be withdrawing the money.

She tried to explain to Adrian that it was all a mistake, but after listening to Montee's confession on tape saying Roslynn was the mastermind behind the whole thing and how she got Jerry to get them the list of account holders, there was nothing she could say. The Feds even showed Adrian the surveillance pictures of the girls from the cameras inside the bank. Adrian recognized Jazmine and Alyse right away. That's when he knew it had to be true.

Adrian felt extremely betrayed. The look on his face was one Roslynn would never forget. "How could you do this to me

Roslynn? After all I've done for you. I treated you like a queen. Wasn't that enough?" When Roslynn didn't answer, he continued to look at her for answers. "I hope you didn't do this because of the child you've been hiding all these years."

Roslynn's eyes increased three times their normal size. "You knew?"

"I was a little suspicious the other day when your cousin came over, so when I went into my office, I acted as if I'd closed the door when I didn't. Your cousin was right. The little girl had too much of a striking resemblance to you for me to let it go."

"I'm so sorry."

"Whatever the problem was, you could've talked to me, Roslynn," Adrian replied. He was making his wife feel even worse.

"Please…don't do this. I'm sorry!" she yelled as Hamilton began to cuff her. "I don't even have any of the money."

"You had everything to do with it, and your friends, too. Oh, and let's not forget about your cousin, Kamilla. We caught her going into the bank this morning as planned. Now, all we have to do is get Alyse, and we know exactly where to find her," Hamilton replied, then looked at Adrian. "Mr. Washington, we'll do our part, but you need to try and recover the money from the Manhattan bank as soon as possible. According to our nice informant, Mr. Montee, there were three wire transfers in all and everyone in-volved was supposed to withdraw the cash today, but we don't be-lieve that's the case, especially for Jazmine. I guess she got off in her own little way."

Roslynn frowned. "What do you mean by that?"

"Your friend, Jazmine. She's missing…or unfortunately could be dead. Several East Orange police officers arrested her husband this morning because they believe he might've killed her," Hamilton explained.

Roslynn let out an awful shriek. "What?"

"I'm sorry that you had to find out this way." Hamilton gave the other agents a nod, then started to walk Roslynn out.

"Was it worth it?" Adrian yelled out.

All Roslynn could do was lower her head. After everything she'd done to keep her marriage, she never thought she'd end up losing it anyway.

*　*　*

Alyse looked up at the clock on the wall and saw it was almost six o'clock in the evening. She knew Montee and the rest of the crew were going to be mad at her for not going to the bank in Manhattan as planned, but after Brie developed a serious kidney infection the night before, Alyse knew she couldn't leave until her daughter was at least stable again.

Alyse looked down at Brie, who looked as if she was suffering. Although Dr. Atkins had given the orders for Brie to obtain some penicillin, it didn't seem to give the little girl much relief.

"Don't worry, baby. Mommy finally got the money to get you well. They're gonna have to let you stay here now. So, it's only a matter of time before you'll be back to your old self again." Even though Brie couldn't respond, Alyse knew she could hear her. "Shoot, with all the money we got now, I'm gonna take you to Disneyworld when all this mess is over with."

The Federal agent at the door displayed a wicked smile before knocking. When Alyse turned around, he quickly flashed his badge then motioned for her to come into the hallway. As bad as he wanted Alyse, he didn't believe in arresting anybody in front of their kids.

Alyse began to panic. She looked back at Brie, then gave her a quick kiss on the cheek. "Umm...Mommy will be back in a minute, princess." She then walked out of Brie's room biting on her nails that were already numbs.

"Are you Alyse Greffen?"

"Yes."

"Well, you probably know why we're here, right?" the agent asked, as he pointed to two other men.

Alyse knew it had something to do with the bank fraud. She faintly answered yes before the alarms in Brie's room suddenly started to sound. When she turned around, she saw her daughter's body going into convulsions.

"Oh my, God!" Alyse yelled, before running back into the room. "Somebody get a doctor!"

Seconds later, she was pushed aside by the nurse on the floor and by a doctor who was on call.

"She's going into cardiac arrest!" the doctor yelled. "Get the paddles!"

"Please, leave the room," the nurse strongly suggested.

"No!" Alyse shouted.

With no time to debate, they worked tirelessly on Brie for a few minutes, and when she finally opened her eyes, Alyse was relieved. The doctor, however, had a heartbreaking look on his face. That's when Alyse looked at the heart monitor and saw it was flat. The doctor didn't even know where to start when he saw the distant look on Alyse's face.

Alyse ran over to the bed again. "No...no…no!" she said over and over. "God…please no. I have the money. I have the money to get her better treatment." She looked at the doctor. "Did you hear me? I have the money. Please do something!"

All the doctor could do was tell Alyse how sorry he was and that he'd done all he could. His words were little comfort to Alyse after she'd just watched her daughter die right before her eyes.

\*\*\*

"Attention passengers. Flight 1855 will be making its final descent," the flight attendant announced. "Please, put your seats and tray tables in the upright position."

"Ma, I can't believe we're going to live in…in… Ma where are we going again?" Omari asked.

"Italy, honey. I'm excited, too," Jazmine said with a huge smile. "We couldn't have done it without you," she said looking over at Miles.

"Trust me. It was my pleasure."

"Thank you for talking my mother into placing the missing person's report and for placing the blood in his car."

Miles gave off the same smile. "He deserved it."

"Are you gonna miss your job?" Alyse asked.

"Not at all," Miles replied. "Especially not with you and Omari by my side."

Jazmine snuggled up to the man who she knew was good for her and her child. Not to mention, the $200,000 in cash she had would be good for them as well. Unbeknownst to anyone who was involved in the scam, Miles waited for Jazmine outside of Washington Savings and drove her straight to the bank in Manhattan. Despite Montee's strict rules, she withdrew the stolen money right away. Jazmine felt guilty, knowing that her friends probably thought she was dead. It was going to be hard for her to stay away from her mother and start a brand new life in a different country, but in the end Jazmine knew she'd made the right decision. It was a hard choice, but a choice she could definitely live with.

# Also By Danette Majette

*Essence Magazine Bestseller*

# IN STORES JULY '09

Dominique Lewis spent most of her days as a high maintenance wanna-be. Although she had the perfect physique and facial features, she studied the charming behaviors of women who successfully landed pro-athletes, and mimicked the money-hungry ladies who were able to get into the pockets of hustlers. Her life-long dream was to become wealthy, and a house-hold name. By any means necessary, she vowed to get what she wanted.

As Dominique's mission unfolds, she manages to only rub elbows with the elite, and those who could get her to the top. Soon, after the tragic murder of her sister, all hell breaks loose, and Dominique's cover is blown.

Armed with revenge on the brain, and a status goal in mind, she lands a position as Rapheal's woman, the most sought after millionaire Atlanta has to offer. Raphael's lavish status in town puts her on a new level, right where she always dreamed. It was allabout money, sex, and power. There was only one problem; Rapheal had always been faithful to his former girlfriend, and had especially been off limits to Dominique. Unfortunately for, Dominique all rules remained the same. In an effort, to hold on to Rapheal, and all the elaborate material possessions, Dominique sets out on a deadly mission to remove anything that stands in her way.

# PICK UP YOUR COPY TODAY

Ghetto born, Demi Rodriquez, a beautiful half-black, half-Puerto Rican bombshell enjoys her lavish lifestyle. Unfortunately, she gets a taste of the broke life when her drug-dealing boyfriend gets sent to prison. In an instant, Demi is forced right back into her mother's cramped housing project in Harlem. Soon, everyday becomes a struggle and an emotional battleground until she meets a handsome movie producer from Los Angeles who thinks she has the sex appeal needed to make it to the top. In a quest for fame and fortune, Demi takes a chance and sets out for Hollywood where everybody and everything has a dream. Her chances of becoming an A-list actress get slim when she befriends a slick talking woman who dabbles in everything from drugs and prostitution to a life where some actresses don't wake up the next morning. Follow Demi as she finds herself on the wrong end of the film business which is destined to destroy her mind, body, and spirit.

# IN STORES NOW

The saying, I Love New York, brings chills to Chantel Ramsey's heart. For her, New York is a place of hatred, brutality, and self destruction. With her life on the line, she takes her new gritty environment in Brooklyn by storm. New tensions surface when she enters a new brothel where every conniving tenant is for herself. Conflict heats up when Chantel figures out she has to become just as ruthless and treacherous as her co-workers. Determined to end up on top, she uses her luscious body, and undeniable street skills to rake in the cash, and turn her life around. However, there s one problem that lurks in the darkness; pimps don t lay down easily. Chantel ends up running for her life with the possibility of being put six feet under.

**MAIL TO:**
PO Box 423
Brandywine, MD 20613
301-362-6508

**FAX TO:**
301-579-9913

# ORDER FORM

| Ship to: | |
|---|---|
| Address: | |
| City & State: | Zip: |
| Attention: | |

| Date: | |
|---|---|
| Phone: | |
| E-mail: | |

Make all money orders and cashiers checks payable to: Life Changing Books

| Qty. | ISBN | Title | Release Date | Price |
|---|---|---|---|---|
| | 0-9741394-0-8 | A Life To Remember by Azarel | Aug-03 | $ 15.00 |
| | 0-9741394-1-6 | Double Life by Tyrone Wallace | Nov-04 | $ 15.00 |
| | 0-9741394-5-9 | Nothin Personal by Tyrone Wallace | Jul-06 | $ 15.00 |
| | 0-9741394-2-4 | Bruised by Azarel | Jul-05 | $ 15.00 |
| | 0-9741394-7-5 | Bruised 2: The Ultimate Revenge by Azarel | Oct-06 | $ 15.00 |
| | 0-9741394-3-2 | Secrets of a Housewife by J. Tremble | Feb-06 | $ 15.00 |
| | 0-9724003-5-4 | I Shoulda Seen It Comin by Danette Majette | Jan-06 | $ 15.00 |
| | 0-9741394-4-0 | The Take Over by Tonya Ridley | Apr-06 | $ 15.00 |
| | 0-9741394-6-7 | The Millionaire Mistress by Tiphani | Nov-06 | $ 15.00 |
| | 1-934230-99-5 | More Secrets More Lies by J. Tremble | Feb-07 | $ 15.00 |
| | 1-934230-98-7 | Young Assassin by Mike G. | Mar-07 | $ 15.00 |
| | 1-934230-95-2 | A Private Affair by Mike Warren | May-07 | $ 15.00 |
| | 1-934230-94-4 | All That Glitters by Ericka M. Williams | Jul-07 | $ 15.00 |
| | 1-934230-93-6 | Deep by Danette Majette | Jul-07 | $ 15.00 |
| | 1-934230-96-0 | Flexin & Sexin by K'wan, Anna J. & Others | Jun-07 | $ 15.00 |
| | 1-934230-92-8 | Talk of the Town by Tonya Ridley | Jul-07 | $ 15.00 |
| | 1-934230-89-8 | Still a Mistress by Tiphani | Nov-07 | $ 15.00 |
| | 1-934230-91-X | Daddy's House by Azarel | Nov-07 | $ 15.00 |
| | 1-934230-87-1- | Reign of a Hustler by Nissa A. Showell | Jan-08 | $ 15.00 |
| | 1-934230-86-3 | Something He Can Feel by Marissa Montelih | Feb-08 | $ 15.00 |
| | 1-934230-88-X | Naughty Little Angel by J. Tremble | Feb-08 | $ 15.00 |
| | 1-934230847 | In Those Jeans by Chantel Jolie | Jun-08 | $ 15.00 |
| | 1-934230855 | Marked by Capone | Jul-08 | $ 15.00 |
| | 1-934230820 | Rich Girls by Kendall Banks | Oct-08 | $ 15.00 |
| | 1-934230839 | Expensive Taste by Tiphani | Nov-08 | $ 15.00 |
| | 1-934230782 | Brooklyn Brothel by C. Stecko | Dec-08 | $ 15.00 |
| | | | Total for Books | $ |

\* Prison Orders- Please allow up to three (3) weeks for delivery.

Shipping Charges (add $4.25 for 1-4 books\*) $

Total Enclosed (add lines) $

For credit card orders and orders over 30 books, please contact us at orders@lifechaningbooks.net (Cheaper rates for COD orders)

\*Shipping and Handling of 5-10 books is $6.25, please contact us if your order is more than 10 books. (301)362-6508